Gone Wild

I slip out of my shorts and stand naked in the tropical Cuban rain. I lift my arms up to the downpour. The boys just stand and look at me, understanding. I rub my hands over my body and openly caress myself – my tits, my tummy, my bush – and I laugh. My body feels great, my breasts are full and my nipples, as you'd expect, rock hard. I look the boys in the eyes, grinning. I'm as horny as hell. I'm a fucking she-devil, whore, seductress – a rutting wild cat. I don't know what happened at that *bembe* but I could eat men alive tonight. I need them, now. Good job there are two fine specimens to hand. I'm losing control of myself. Completely. I'm gone. I'm wild. I don't know or care about the boys. It's my pussy that's queen tonight.

Gone Wild
Maria Eppie

BLACK LACE

Black Lace books contain sexual fantasies.
In real life, always practise safe sex.

This edition published in 2005 by
Black Lace
Thames Wharf Studios
Rainville Road
London W6 9HA

Originally published 2002

Design by Smith & Gilmour, London
Printed and bound by Mackays of Chatham PLC

ISBN 0 352 33670 6

1

Alison was a shouter: y'know, the 'Aah, aah, aah, fuck me, *fuck me*, you big bastard!' kinda shouter. A big, loud, titian-haired Glaswegian with a penchant for dated music and a history of dodgy relationships that always ended in disaster, Alison was also a romantic. Her whole life she played at falling in love. Big surprise: one day, she really fell.

Don't worry, this is *not* a love story (I don't do love), but there is a point to this preamble, so trust me.

Alison was 36 and *still* living in multi-occupied squalor in Shepherd's Bush with the rest of us rampant twentysomething media freelancers. She was considered almost geriatric (natch) but everyone was kinda fond of her. She didn't become the designated house nutter till Damien. Damien? The preamble. The last and greatest love. When Alison met Damien it was the real thing. She wanted to shout it from the rooftops – and shout she did.

Like ... me and the other guys would be flopped round someone's room, cabbaged at three in the morning, when it would start: the creak of mattress springs; the rhythmic knocking of the headboard. The 'Aah, aah, *aaaaghs!*' There was no escaping it. The guys would smirk very cool and knowing but within five minutes they'd be surreptitiously rearranging their underwear and slyly giving me the look. You know, the demented, boggly-eyed, tongue-lolling look dogs get when they sniff a bitch on heat. *That* kinda look.

I'm not even saying I wasn't completely unaffected.

Sitting round alone with a roomful of horny young men, knowing that they've all got raging hard-ons and thinking about that pounding, sweating, clawing, biting stuff going on upstairs and knowing that they know that you're thinking about it too, and them knowing that you know that they know, and so on. Look, I'm a normal healthy gal, with regular appetites, et cetera, et cetera, and sometimes the atmosphere got a little charged. But come on, I was never actually going to fuck any of them. OK, there was that one time when things got slightly out of hand but nobody technically screwed or anything, and it never happened again because we all *knew* it shouldn't really have happened in the first place, right? Shit, things might have got around. As Paul puts it: bottom line is, word-of-mouth's big in film and TV. And no, I didn't want a bottom line like Big A's.

I know, I know. I'm not supposed to give a shit and I don't really. But I was new to the industry and I was determined to be taken seriously. No one took Alison seriously, not after Aaaghlison, please! (Of course, when I say no one, you may take it as read that I mean no man, the industry being what it is.) Like, some guy would say 'Alison? Duh, you mean Aagh-aagh Aaaghlision' and do that dopey *When Harry Met Sally* orgasm scene. So, the work dried up and people started laughing behind her back.

Don't get me wrong. I liked Alison. She was a laugh. When I first knew her, she was up for anything. Even though she was ten years older than me, we sometimes hung out together. Plus, Ali had loads of contacts and helped me get my first few jobs.

We were both freelance assistant directors; me a third, occasionally acting up, she an established second. Sounds exciting, doesn't it? Really glamorous? Well, it ain't. It's fucking hard work. ADs are the people who do the donkey work to hold shoots together, getting paperwork out, making sure everyone is in the right place, the schedule is kept to, and so on. The worst bit is chasing after the next job while you're desperately trying not to screw up the current one. But you *are* part of the industry. Alison had been doing it for ever, so really she should have been a first, maybe a production manager, by her thirties. That's my minimum. Actually, I intend to be a fully fledged producer by then. If I was still a second at 36, I'd be looking for a way out. I guess Alison was beginning to feel that way too. So, when Damien moved into the house, she saw him as the Last Great Chance.

Damien was five years younger than her – a soft-spoken sound recordist who'd just been kicked out by his girlfriend and needed a room. Cute, in a pseudo-Celtic, playboyish way. And completely wrong for Alison. Not that she could see it. She immediately expressed her intentions in code, through the voice of another almost-Irishman. 'I Want You.' 'Pump It Up.' Over and over and over again. Damien had no chance. One minute, full-volume Elvis bloody Costello. Next, Alison sashaying around naked under her kimono, which somehow just happened to fall open every time she had to squeeze past him. She wasn't bad (for her age). Everything she had (and she had a lot!) went in and out in all the right places, etc. But puh-lease!

It took her all of four days to get Damien into bed. Once she got him there, it seemed like she wasn't ever gonna let him out again. She was gonna give him her everything and time was of the essence. So, she went after a guy. So what? you're probably thinking. So, she could have shown some restraint, that's what. By screwing Damien she completely destroyed the fragile ecosystem that was the house and made the Alison Incident an inevitability. How? By breaking the rules, that's how. And no, I'm not the moral majority, I just happen to know there are rules. As Paul says, it's a mad fucking world and we need them to survive. I'm not talking KEEP OFF THE GRASS-type rules, or unspoken rules like never telling your best friend what you really think of her boyfriend. Or even universally acknowledged ones, like 'I'm not being funny but . . .' being the correct way to open a conversation when you mean 'I'm gonna pick a fight with you.' No, simple, basic rules. For instance, all the time I shared the house in Shepherd's Bush with Ali and the other guys, it was an unspoken thing that, everybody in the house being in the industry, we could all be friends but none of us would actually fuck each other. There's a basic rule: never shag someone you work with. Paul, my boyfriend, agrees. Ironic, considering how we got together.

Paul is a camera operator and a highly sought-after one, too. He specialises in docs but he shot this little Channel 4 drama I'd AD'd on as a favour for a mate. We were at the private screening (again, sounds glam but ain't) and I don't think he knew many people there. It was an in-yer-face screaming queen drama so a lot of the cast were in-yer-face screaming queens (natch) and I think without a camera to hide behind Paul was actually frightened. With my work head on, I was being quiet and efficient. I seemed normal, I guess, so Paul kinda latched on to me.

He came across as straight but cute – 33 and simultaneously solvent, handsome and attractively nonchalant. OK, he had a rep for being a tad anally retentive in the organisation department, but then he's a perfectionist. I kinda warmed to him and at the end of the evening, when he asked me if I needed a lift home, I said, 'Yeah.' The guy's a gent. He didn't even try it on at the doorstep, so I reckoned he was safe to invite into the house. I made him coffee in my room. Come on, the communal rooms are disgusting.

It was all very civilised, him asking about my career and making observations like, 'Filmmaking's about teamwork: you've got to fit in,' when there was a womanly groan from above. A first telltale squeak of the springs. Immediately Paul stiffened slightly. I knew from experience that this was merely the start of the matter, because a first groan from Alison was never the last. It was an overture, heralding a whole symphony of moaning and hollering. I, naturally, took all this for granted, but it was Paul's first experience, of course. When Alison let out one of her speciality wails, Paul jumped, tipping boiling-hot coffee into my lap.

Immediately, I whipped off my pants. No, not what you think, gimme a break. They were from Chloé. I got them in a sample sale and I didn't want them destroyed. I turned my back and gave a little shimmy as they fell over my hips. OK, that wasn't entirely necessary but I couldn't resist a little tease. Paul was so buttoned up it was like flashing at the vicar or something. I carried on the small talk, lounging on my futon in my red leatherette halter-neck top and not much else while Alison and Damien were fucking like there was no tomorrow up above. Paul didn't bat an eyelid. I assumed he just wasn't interested. Until Alison cut in with an '*Aaagghhhhhwoooh!!!*'

Paul looked startled, glanced at me, then grinned boyishly. I giggled. Then he bent over and kissed me. A sweet kiss, not the kind I was expecting. But when Alison gave it the Harder-Harder-Damien-Nows, everything sorta developed. Fast. One second, I'm nine years old practising kisses with the boy next door, the next, my top is over my shoulders and Paul is kissing my naked breasts. Then, Paul stops kissing and peels down my thong. He studies me admiringly. My body is one of my best features and I can hack being admired. I'm exposed and naked on the futon, except I'm still half trussed by the halter (which is tangled round my upper arms). Then Paul starts to slowly undress himself, all the while watching me, and it's my turn to return the admiration. This is getting interesting. See, camerawork is a physical job, so his shoulders are broad and muscular and his belly flat. I don't know if it exercises his cock as well, but that looks pretty well built, too, and neatly circumcised. Alison groans and Paul's dick gives a little spasm as it swells perceptibly. I lift my knees to let the dog see the rabbit. Paul, as the saying goes, is In Like Flynn.

Soon, he is ploughing me very energetically. Alison's volume has increased by several decibels to reach what I believe is technically known as Screaming Pitch. The harder she screams, the harder Paul drives in. Soon, I'm half off the futon and taking our combined weight on my shoulders on the floor. As Alison builds to her crescendo, so Paul gets all animalistic. I like this. I twist and turn till I free myself from the restrictions of my top and grab Paul by his hair. I kiss him hard and wrestle him off the futon till I'm astride him on the floor.

Within seconds, Paul switches me back underneath him. He grabs my wrists with one hand, pinning them down above my head, and rotates my arse ceiling-wards with the other, splitting my thighs even wider in the process so I'm completely restrained. Then he slides in up to the hilt. I moan involuntarily but my attempts at vocalisation are, naturally, restrained compared with Alison's (I have no intention of supplying wank fantasies to a houseload of assorted film and TV technicians). Anyway, my own contribution is hardly needed. As Big A finally lets rip with the Noisy O, so

Paul totally loses it himself. He plunges and thrashes against me till his cock is pumping into my pulsing cunt.

There was a sort of embarrassed silence afterwards and Paul made his excuses and left. I assumed that was that, till he turned up three days later with a present: a frock to replace the wrecked Chloé pants. Oh, kinda sweet, I thought. We went for a drink, we came back to the house, Alison provided a little night music from above and, of course, we fucked. I wasn't sure what the rules were here. It seemed a tad like he was shagging me while having phone sex with another girl. Paul commented wryly that he really liked the combination of Madonna underneath him and whore up above. I took this as a compliment, natch: Madonna's good for her age. Whatever, I was on the receiving end of his enthusiasm, not Alison, and she didn't get the frock. Paul kept pestering me for dates and, within a month, we were practically an item. C'mon, simultaneously solvent, handsome *and* cute – you think I'm mad? And, if there were any weird fantasies whirling round Paul's head, he never said. And he would have, 'cos I insisted on a rule about always being truthful, especially about other people. The honesty-about-infidelity clause.

I didn't have to think about it for long because, as a consequence of the Alison Incident, the good council tax payers of our street complained about the house being structurally unsound. It ended up being condemned as unfit for human habitation, giving the landlord the opportunity to evict us all and sell the house to a property developer. My previous life as an only occasionally employed Media Dogsbody meant that I was pitched into the metropolitan housing market somewhat financially unprepared. I mean, my lifestyle and my profession require a fair amount of

high-profile social networking and this did not necessarily marry with a regular savings regime. After sur-
veying my options, I volunteered to move in with Paul
till I found somewhere appropriate (cheap but vermin-
free). Well, it makes sense. We're in the same business,
we understand the pressures, we know the rules. And
Paul's really helped me with my career. He got me out
of the rut I was into at Shepherd's Bush. He got me
my first major break. Two months stand-in as floor
manager for Big World Media on *The Zone*. (Floor
managers are telly ADs and the contracts tend to run
for longer.) I think I did well, and apparently, so do
some other people. Paul has heard that Clare Dodderidge said that I did a good job. That's *the* (legendary)
Clare Dodderidge, exec producer at BWM, herself. How
cool does it get?

Probably about as cool as Paul's rather stylish flat
in Camberwell (natch, any boyfriend of mine will have
excellent taste). It's very minimalist: all laminate
wood flooring and modernist furniture. There's a very
butch hi-tech kitchen that's perennially gleaming.
Paul's Mr Spotless. He washes up immediately after
he's eaten. Now this is going to sound really strange
but, even though he has a dishwasher, he washes the
dishes *before* he puts them into it. Eccentric, I guess,
but that's part of his cuteness. So, no post-prandial
cigs with Paul. (Speaking metaphorically, there's a no-
smoking-in-the-flat rule. And Paul doesn't smoke, of
course.) If I want a fag, I have to go out on to the
balcony. No way, Jose. I've developed a little problem
there, since the Alison Incident. OK, it's a pain but you
have to make adjustments when you live with somebody, don't you?

Six months on, and we seem to have settled into a
routine. We lead pretty hectic working lives so we
don't even have time to fuck as much as we did at the

start. (The never-fuck-someone-you-work-with number? Simple. We don't work together.) But, hey, that's
healthy. I'm not one of those clingy let's-get-married-
and-reproduce kind of girls. I'm 26 and I've got a career
of my own to be getting on with. Paul made me see
how much energy I was wasting, running around, one
job after the next, and going out all the time as well.
'Zita, rule's quite simple. Get a goal, get organised and
go for it.' Now, Paul has heard that Big World are
looking for new floor managers. They have a new kids'
show starting soon, *Massive*. 'It will be,' he says. 'Send
your CV to Clare Dodderidge. Direct.' That's typical of
Paul: don't mess around, go straight to the top. He's a
go-getter, which is why he's so much in demand as a
camera op.

Which is why he's flying out to Cuba on a ten-week
documentary shoot first thing tomorrow morning.

Which is why I've ended up gaffer-taped, naked
and yelling, to his kitchen table.

2

It all started at Me'Met's. This is an extremely exclusive members-only club-bar in Soho, rumoured to have once refused admission to Madonna. So all the sad wannabes in the industry would *kill* for membership. Paul, of course, is a member. First time he brought me here, I was impressed, just a tad. It's a good place to hang on the grapevine. And hanging on the grapevine, in our chosen career, means hanging on to *work*.

Tonight, however, I am certainly not overwhelmed at being here. Like I said, Paul is leaving for Cuba on the 6.30 a.m. flight *mañana* and, as we've hardly seen each other recently, I had assumed we would spend our last evening together for ten weeks doing something radical like spending time *alone*. I mean, isn't that what couples *do*? Apparently not, 'cos Paul wants to spend it getting pissed and talking bollocks with his crew. I just don't get it. I mean he's going to be shacked up in the bush for nearly three whole months with these dudes. Isn't he gonna see enough of them then? But I don't want to spend our last night together arguing so I bite my lip and get myself frocked up, thinking I'd make the effort. Just a simple jersey dress from Joseph, but it clings to my figure nicely and makes my bottom look particularly pert and applecheeked. At least I can show him what he'll be missing.

So, we are in Me'Met's. We are drinking celebratory *mojitos* and the boys are giving a full-blooded rendition of 'Guantanamera', which is also something like the name of the flyblown town where they're gonna be shooting. I'm slightly happier 'cos of the cocktails, which are like Pimms but Cuban, and then some. I've decided that this is all a guy thing (male bonding or whatever hetero guys call it when they want to be sweet to each other), when this really posh female voice joins in. The beautifully modulated tones are somewhat tempered by her modification of the chorus: 'Cunt in the mirror, I saw her cunt in the mirror.' Everyone starts whooping and laughing and I assume it's some overanimated rugger-loving Sloane trying to get in on the act. I adopt my tolerant but fundamentally unimpressed look when Paul turns round and shouts, 'Sassy, you made it!' and it's hugs and air kisses all round.

Sassy is a thirtysomething tousled blonde with a big wide slash of a mouth and a very I-don't-give-a-fuck, bohemian-cookie style. *My* normal style, which she's robbed. I immediately feel overdressed in my stupid little frock and heels and skulk in a corner while she throws the lips on all and sundry. Then she sees me and it's 'You must be Zita.' Big hug, then 'God you are *so-o* understanding. I wouldn't let him out if it was my last night of nookie for ten weeks!' And she pokes Paul in the ribs in a way that I find frankly overfamiliar. 'Never mind, you'll be making up for lost time later, I suppose!' she leers, and everybody laughs heartily (including me, 'cos I know the form in these situations).

As the laughter finally subsides, I say, between hearty hahhahhahs of course, 'I'm not being funny, but who the fuck are you?'

She rolls her eyes (green and kinda buggy – I suppose some people might find them attractive) and says, 'God! Paul is such an ignorant bastard, I don't know how you put up with him. Sorry dahling, I *assumed* he told you. He's told me *so* much about you.' She holds out a well-manicured hand, 'Saskia St John-Smythe. Location manager and, ah, well … associate producer, I suppose, on this little Expedition up the Orinoco.' Then she gives me a big shit-eating grin. During this speech she has also managed to order more drinks, unilaterally deciding that we will switch to champagne, and simultaneously procured a corner of the little alcove with all the oriental divans in it (the area that is normally unavailable to the plebs, being roped off for superhip people with social clout). Quite spontaneously, I begin to despise her.

Paul has *not* told me about Saskia St John-Smythe, but I don't let her know that. Instead, I stretch out luxuriously on the cushions, light up a fag, swig back a mouthful of champagne and say, 'So what's Paul told you about me, then?' She slaps the carved Moroccan table between us so she has everyone's attention, and says 'Oh, that you're the one that lived with Aagh-Aaagh-Aaaghlison.' Hoh hoh hoh.

Something flares inside me and I say, kinda sniffily, 'She was a friend of mine, actually.' I'm about to say some more, too, when, shit, I remember everyone here's in the industry and I close my mouth.

Saskia just rolls those big bug eyes and says, 'It was a dreadful shame, but *wasn't* the poor cow a slapper? Mind you, can I talk. I'm the proverbial shithouse door. Bray like a fucking donkey when I come!' All the boys roar like mad at that. Including Paul. What?

Next thing, she's conducting a survey about the relationship between orgasmic decibel level (female) and sexual satisfaction (male), somehow combined with a philosophical debate about its feminist significance. Paul is laughing so hard that I think he'll piss his pants until she puts him on the spot and asks him what his preference is. He tries to smarm out of answering by saying, in a lounge-lizard voice, 'Depends on the lady.' But she obviously can't take a hint, 'cos she slams the table again and roars, 'You won't find out by fucking ladies!' and turns to me and adds, 'Will he, Zita?'

I've just taken another swill of my champagne and she doesn't wait for my answer anyway, so I keep quiet and concentrate on not letting my lips get too pursed. Don't you just hate totty that can't hold its ale? I help myself to some more fizz and think sourly no wonder the budget doesn't stretch to R+R visits from loved ones, they've spent most of it on boozing it up in Me'Met's. I decide that I want to go home now so I lie back among the plumped-up cushions and shift so my frock rides up my thighs a little. I tilt my head at what I hope is a provocative angle and catch Paul's eye. He smiles a happy, drunken smile at me, so I beckon him towards me and whisper kittenishly, 'I'm tired. Wanna take me home and put me to bed?'

Paul's eyes are attempting to focus on the shadowy area between my thighs and my crotch. He shakes his head and whispers back, 'Why? What are you planning to do, you prick tease?'

I pout and part my legs a little. Paul squeezes my thigh and I'm beginning to think at last that we can go home, when Saskia intervenes with a rather pointed, 'We seem to have run out of Bolly, Paul.' Is she doing this on purpose?

Paul orders another couple of bottles of fizz but, before it arrives, I take affirmative action and drag him on to the dance floor. It's a mark of how pissed he is that I've got him to his feet, because Paul doesn't do dancing, ever. He stands in front of me looking kind of amused as I go into my pole-dancing routine, with him as the pole. I can do this because:

1. Even in my heels, I'm still shorter than Paul
2. I'm quite fit, and
3. I'm pissed too.

The performance goes rather well on the whole. For a finale, I jump up and wrap my thighs round Paul's waist. My dress rides high up to reveal the tops of my hold-ups and a deal of upper leg. Paul staggers slightly under the weight but steadies himself and automatically fumbles for my arse. I feel his hands clasp on my naked cheeks. The dress has obviously risen rather higher than I first thought. Not quite what I intended but I'm gratified by the spontaneous public appreciation. The Guatanamera crew are all cheering and whistling now. Paul pulls a weird face, like his sodden brain is digesting the fact he's fondling my bare buttocks in public. I slowly unwrap my legs and let my body slide down his, ending with a twirl and a 'Da-dah!' My dress is more or less round my waist. If you've got it, flaunt it, I say. The Saskia bird brays over, 'Well done, dahling. You're as big a tart as I am!' I teeter a bit on my stillies, readjusting myself while I dredge for a witty retort. I'm beaten to it by one of Paul's cronies cutting across with, 'Not quite, dahling. Bit more practice needed yet, I think!' Everyone laughs hilariously and I smile sweetly. Hah! That's told her.

I manage quite easily to steer Paul to the exit. All this baring of flesh has reminded me about those nice, crisp Egyptian cotton sheets waiting for us back home. In the cab, I snuggle into Paul but he's gone sniffy on me. 'Wassup?' I ask, letting my hand rest along the crotch of his 501s.

He lifts my hand away. 'Did you have to show your arse to the entire crew?' he mutters.

Hey, I thought we were supposed to be having a laugh, cunt-in-the-mirror and all that? What's eating him? I accidentally on purpose let my arm jiggle about with the bumps and turns of the taxi till it's back in his lap. There's a definite ridge to his fly. He has that snotty expression on his face again. OK, Mr Cool, I think I'm gonna teach you a lesson for keeping me out so long when I need my bed.

After undoing a couple of buttons, I slip my fingers into the fly. Paul stiffens, everywhere, but stares straight ahead, pretending to ignore me. I whisper hoarsely in his ear, just loud enough for the driver to hear, 'A hundred quid and you can go bareback!' The taxi driver clears his throat and I see him glance at Paul in the rear-view mirror. I've managed to work my fingers inside Paul's pants and I can feel a distinctly moist patch on his Calvins. Paul swallows and gives the driver some directions. I like this game. After a bit of fumbling around, I manage to close my grip over his cock. The end is slippy, an unmistakable sign he's endured an erection for some time. I run my finger round the moist, plump tip and Paul immediately shifts his weight and slumps in the seat. I say, in a stage whisper, 'Two hundred and you can do *anything* you want.'

Paul coughs and I glance at the driver to see if he heard. He has. He stares straight back at me in his mirror. Paul's clocked it, too. I squirm a bit and snuggle up to him but he's gone sulky and tense again. Wassamatter, doesn't he wanna play any more? I notice smugly that his cock is still rigid, though.

We arrive back at Camberwell and, as we get out of the cab, the driver gives me his card and says 'Call me when you need a ride home.' I just nod and trot along after Paul, who has stridden on ahead without saying a word. I want to have a giggle about our little game but Paul seems to have gone into megasulk mode. He's getting tiresome. Once we get into the flat, I start kicking off my shoes and Paul finally speaks: 'Leave them on.' I ignore him, natch, 'cos they're fucking killing me, and continue unbuckling the ankle straps. Paul grabs hold of my wrist and puts his face very close to mine. 'I said, leave them *on*.' My heart is pounding. Paul has the same expression as the taxi driver had. I'm contemplating kicking him in the balls when he lets go of me and starts rummaging around in the hand luggage he's packed for Cuba. I stay still and watch. When he straightens up, he's holding his money belt. He looks at me and says, 'I assume you take dollars?' Hey, it's just the game, he's still playing the game.

I go into character and take the opportunity to light up in Paul's flat. I blow a plume of smoke into his face and demand cash up front. The corner of Paul's mouth twitches as he silently counts the bills into a pile on the floor. I'm not sure what to do now but Paul saves me from indecision by taking my cigarette from me and having a pull, which stuns me even more than his dumping me on the floor and telling me to pick my money up. I scrabble around sweeping the green-backs into a pile, while Paul lounges in the big chrome and leather reclining chair that's supposed to be Le Corbusier but isn't and watches me.

When I'm done, Paul says, 'Three hundred dollars, that's about two hundred quid. You said anything?'

I go to speak but Paul tells me to shut up and take my dress off. I wiggle out of it and stand in front of him in bra, thong, hold-ups and heels. I want to speed the action up so I slide my thong down over my silly spikey shoes and slink over to him, saying, 'Paul? Let's go to bed.'

Paul stands up and says coldly, 'Don't talk.' He takes me by the hand and leads me into the kitchen. He opens a cupboard and pulls out a reel of silver gaffer tape, the sticky stuff the camera department uses. It'll stick anything to just about anything else, and it's strong. Whole shoots are held together by it. It'll hold a girl to a kitchen table, no problem.

Which is where I am now. The table's some fancy stainless-steel contraption, like those hospital trolleys they keep instruments on, and I'm spreadeagled across it with my arms and legs gaffered firmly to the sides. My buttocks are perched on the edge and my thighs are stretched wide to expose my cunt, like I'm ready for an examination. I didn't have the chance to object. I was being taped down before I realised what was going on. Paul is quite fit (all that hand-held camerawork) and able to manhandle my girly body pretty much how he wants. OK, it's style-concept sex time. Fine by me, except this is not very comfy and I'm not *exactly* sure what he has in mind. I'm about to tell Paul this when he disappears between my splayed legs. Next thing, I feel a firm wet lick start at my pussy hole and then travel the full length of my slit till it reaches the top. My turn to stiffen. I tense, holding my breath, as a warm moist tongue starts to flick leisurely over my clit. My breath escapes in a sudden involuntarily gasp.

The licking immediately stops. From this position, I've got a perfect view of the industrial lighting on the ceiling, and very little else. I can hear a rustling noise but I can't tell what's going on. I'm anxious that Paul returns to the licking. I lift my head up as much as I can and glimpse Paul standing between my splayed thighs with his right hand moving backwards and forwards, while his eyes are glued to my crotch. Then I feel something spongy but firm pushing against the entrance, and working this way and that. I'm getting quite anxious for a bit of this way and that myself, so I wriggle and squirm against the gaffer tape as best I can to assist. The firm spongy thing slowly eases its way between my plumped-out pussy lips, gradually working towards my, by now, well-lubed hole. Then, with a strong, firm shove, the cock slips halfway into my gratefully receptive fanny and Paul is lying across my torso and heaving himself against my crotch. I groan in gratitude. Before I know it, Paul withdraws.

He brings his face close enough for me to smell myself on his mouth and whispers in my ear, 'D'you like that, you little prick tease?' He's starting to piss me off. I'm about to tell him so when he disappears between my legs again and his tongue slowly circles my clit. I bite back a moan. God, if word got out that I enjoyed this ... I decide to stay perfectly still. Paul's tongue continues to lap my pussy. I feel stranded in space, floating, all cunt and nothing else. Then Paul stops again and I remember that I am taped to a very uncomfortable glorified tea trolley. I hold my breath and wait for him to start the licking again. He doesn't. I risk permanent neck injury once more and strain to look at him. All I can see is his head silhouetted against that stupid fucking industrial lighting. He looks at me. 'Did you like it?'

A little ball of anger forms in the pit of my stomach. I know this game. I don't answer. Paul reaches down between my legs and inserts a finger into my hole. Immediately it contracts around it. Paul puts his mouth over mine. He tastes salty and sweet at the same time. His tongue flicks in and out of my mouth as he fingers my aching clit. Then he whispers, 'I'll do it again if you ask me.' I swallow and say, very patiently, 'Lick me.'

Paul stops flicking my clit completely and whispers, 'Can't hear you.' This is fucking stupid. I know what he's doing.

I sigh to let him know that I am not impressed and

say sarcastically, 'Lick me.' Paul licks the end of my nose and I swear if I could reach his Sabatiers, I'd stab him. Paul's head disappears between my legs again and I jump so much that the trolley moves. Then everything stops and all I can hear is the blood pumping in my ears. 'Paul,' I say in an ironic I-don't-really-get-off-on-this-kind-of-thing voice, 'lick me.'

No response. Paul says, 'That's no good. You've got to mean it.'

'Oh, you want me to *bray*, do you?' I snarl. 'If you want,' he says matter-of-factly. That's it. That's fucking it. I scream at the top of my voice. '*Paul, lick me, will you? Now! Lick me now!*'

There's a thump from upstairs. Paul's head's just a silhouette again but I can imagine his expression. 'Zita!' He hisses 'This isn't Shepherd's Bush.' Then he slaps a piece of gaffer tape over my mouth. I struggle but succeed only in making the table roll slowly towards the sink. I'm mad as hell but, like I said, that stuff is strong. But I can see Paul now. He looks at me and puts his hand round his cock again and wanks it very deliberately, very slowly for me to see. It's gone huge. He moves between my legs again and then he shoves. Brutally. My eyeballs feel like they're popping out of their sockets as his cock penetrates deep into me. Next moment, his pelvis is arching vigorously against mine. His mouth is suckling forcefully on my nip, his head just a bobbing shock of dark hair. I'm surging with confusing feelings: panicky from the restraint, hungry from the sensations in my cunt, angry 'cos his sucking's made my nip really hard and tense. I want to yell at him and I want to open my glistening hole and wrap my ankles round his back. But I can't do either: I'm fixed tight to the table. I can feel his cock as it ploughs me right to the hilt, pounding me with increasing power. Paul is panting fierce and animal-like. I feel a thrill of fear zigzag through my belly to my cunt. I'm gonna lose it any second. Then Paul's body tenses and he freezes and I realise that he has come. He lies, his weight on top of me, and looks into my eyes. 'Whores aren't supposed to come,' he sniggers, before pulling the gaffer off my mouth.

'Guess I'm not a whore, then, because I didn't!' I spit back. Paul looks at me, surprised. 'Oh, I thought you were enjoying it.' I am livid but I'm not going to let him know it.

As he ungaffers me, I sit up and shrug. 'I don't really get off on all this stuff. I just went along 'cos I assumed you wanted it.'

Paul looks at me quizzically and I hold his stare. Then he says, frostily, 'Yeah, I guess that's about the Zita style.' I stop rubbing my wrists and go, 'Excuse me?' but Paul just shrugs and says, 'Forget it.'

Yeah, right. I jump off the trolley and stomp around so that I'm standing in front of him and put my face in his. 'What d'ya mean, Paul?'

He does this big drama-queenie thing of running his hands exhaustedly through his hair and looking at his watch but I'm not letting this one go. Each time he turns away from me I step back into his field of vision. Eventually he throws his hands up in the air and says, 'I mean, as your idea of fucking is lying motionless on your back with your legs open, I *assumed* you were enjoying it.'

We both freeze. The sentence hangs between us like a speech bubble in a Lichtenstein painting. Paul turns away and starts repacking for Cuba. As he bends over his bag I decide to call a truce, even though inside I am seething. I tweak his balls from behind and say, 'C'mon big boy, let's go to bed'.

He mutters, 'You go ahead. I've got some stuff to sort through.'

I'm barely keeping a lid on it now. 'I'm not being funny, Paul, but if you hadn't insisted on going out tonight then this *stuff* would be *sorted* by now.'

This comes out with slightly more venom than I intended and Paul gets sniffy too and says, 'For fuck's sake, Zita, cut me some slack, will you?' and then we have the full-on row. He says that this is what his job's like and I should have known that when I moved in on him and I say, 'So you want me to go?' and he gets all exasperated and tells me, really condescendingly, that I'm drunk and should go to sleep and of course I can stay as long as I need to and we'll talk about it in the morning. I storm off to bed (making sure I'm on the very edge of my side of it), but I must have fallen asleep, because when I wake up he's gone. There's a note: 'Didn't want to wake you. Speak to you soon. Paul. X.'

I sit around that first day, nursing a hangover and turning over everything that was said. One phrase keeps going round and round: 'Stay as long as you need.' Not, 'Of course, I want you to stay.' Not that I ever planned to stay any longer than I needed to, mind, but it was fucking rude of him. I decide that, when he rings, I won't be in. That'll teach him. I settle down in front of the telly and don't bother to clean the sticky marks from the kitchen table.

Two days later and Paul still hasn't called. Not that I care about that. He just had better not be talking about me to his cronies, that's all. Especially that Saskia Dahling-Dahling. I can't concentrate on *Tricia* on the TV 'cos all these thoughts keep going round my head. What if Paul starts blabbing about our farewell session? Shit, they'll start calling me 'the Gaffer' or something. Fuck, I thought of that in ten minutes. Those bastards have got ten weeks to come up with a nickname for me. And that lying-on-your-back crack. I don't get it. I mean I thought Paul *liked* it that way. Whenever I've got on top, he's wrestled me off again. He's always pinning me down. Shit. I dunno if it's worse for Paul to tell everyone that I just lie back and think of England or that I like being tied to his fucking tea trolley. Great. They're gonna call me 'the Trolley Dolly', aren't they? I really don't get this. Am I supposed to like it or not? I mean, Alison had a rep for being a whore in bed and where did it get her? Is that what he wants, an Alison? Let's get this straight: I am not, and never will be, a fucking Alison.

Fucking Alison. Ah, yes, I was telling you about the Alison Incident. With Alison, love was always a high-octane kind of thing, but Damien resented becoming an industry joke in his own right. He wanted his life back. He jacked her in. Retreated to the privacy of his own bedroom. Alison responded by playing 'Love Don't Live Here Anymore'. Full-pelt. On a loop. Eventually, of course, she committed the ultimate faux pas: told Damien she couldn't live without him. She *told* him that she loved him. In fact, she told *everyone* that she loved him. Poor Damien was mortified. He started refusing even to talk to her. Wouldn't even answer his mobile. Seemed like Damien didn't want her ringing his bell no more and Alison could not bear it. Finally, she lost the plot. After an unsuccessful attempt to kick his door in, she opted for the surprise attack.

Alison's and Damien's bedrooms were on the same floor, the top. So, all she had to do was shin out of her window on to a ledge, shuffle along and in through his. Bingo, 'cept Damien, suspecting such a ploy, kept his window locked. Easy, thought Alison, I'll kick it in, my aim is true. Only it wasn't. She missed and lost her balance. Alison grabbed at the stucco balustrade round the roof but, after a century of neglect, it couldn't match the passion of her grip. It crumbled, dumping Alison and a pile of masonry into the street below. It was a lesson for us all. Taught me some. As Paul says, 'If you want to win the game, learn the rules.' Point being: Alison never did. Poor Ali didn't even realise it was just a game.

Which is why I don't care that Paul hasn't rung me and I have no intention of ringing him, either. I know that all he'll be doing is working, anyway. He's so hung up about the never-shag-people-you-work-with rule, he ain't gonna be playing away from home. Besides, I've got too much to do to think about him. I've got to get my CV to Ms Dodderidge and sort the formality of claiming my sensational new job. I'm gonna take my time, though. I mean, like with every-thing, it doesn't do to look too keen, does it?

Anyway, I so don't care that Paul hasn't contacted me that I don't read the text message he eventually does send me until an hour after I have received it. Like I said, I don't have a problem with his being away half a week and not bothering to contact me. But I do have a problem with, and I quote, 'Arrived safe. Mad busy. Connection difficulties. Paul XXX. PS: Remember, don't leave the blinds open. No loud music after twelve. No smoking and Nadine is NOT allowed in my flat. PPS: Get that CV in!!! Paul X.'

Now, I'm not being funny but I'm starting to won-der about how little interest Paul takes in my life. Nadine? I haven't seen Nadine for ages. Not 'cos Paul doesn't approve of her, which he doesn't. (He thinks she's a bad influence on me, which she may be, but that's beside the point.) No, I haven't seen her 'cos we drifted apart after I started seeing Paul. It's normal:

she's single, I'm in a couple. You start doing couple-y things. Whatever. I didn't stop seeing Nad 'cos of Paul: it just happened. It did! I'd barely thought of her actually, till Paul's 'Nadine is NOT allowed in my flat.' Fine.

I call her immediately, of course. Who said anything about letting her into the flat?

3

She's hot. I look up at her face and neck, slick with sweat. Beads of it are streaming down into the shallow rift between her tiny tits. Her hard nips push firmly against the net top she's wearing. The muscles in her skinny arms are trembling, radiating tension. A shoulder-length lock has fallen from her bandana and hangs damply along the curve of her cheek to the corner of her mouth. I wanna reach up and shove it away. Instead I push my own dripping fringe out of my eyes and I stare up at her, blinking the sweat out my lashes.

We've got that mirroring thing going. She bites her lip, I bite my lip. Mine are already chewed to a pulp, mind you. I'm just no good with suspense. It makes me angry. I know what she's up to, so I just go with it, let her take me there. I could sense her struggling to keep control, trying to hold that wave back. I feel for the rhythm, moving with her tempo. She seems to hold her breath, hovering on the edge. Then she closes her eyes. Concentrating, taking control, forcing the rhythm to slow, she drags the tempo down and down, dirtier and deeper, till the whole world seems to be one hot, humid, slowly pulsing mass. 'Are you there yet?' she mocks. I can't bare it. I'm pleading with her, begging her, screaming at her to crank it up. She begins counting out loud, flexing her body on each beat, then . . .

Wham! She doesn't just crank it, she slams it and my head explodes. I'm yelling and screaming, it feels so good. I'd forgotten it could be this great. The dance floor's gone crazy. I catch Nadine's eye. She pushes her 'phones back off her head and laughs at me and I laugh back. She's just so good at feeling the vibe, feeding off the crowd, taking them where they wanna go. That's a real quality club DJ. That's Nadine, four or five gigs a week, every week and she loves it. The crowd love it. I love it. I love everybody. Nadine always has that kind of an effect on me. I've done a pill and I'm dancing in the middle of a throng of half-naked boys and I love everybody. Hah, if Paul could see me now. Well, he'd disapprove. He thinks clubbing's like drinking alcopops. Kiddy stuff. Well, Mr Sophisticated, you ain't here, but I am. Me, the wild, wet, sweating, dripping, bikini-topped babe in the pit with the moshers flinging their hard, skinny, sexy bodies against mine. It's tribal. It's sexual. You can taste the testosterone. I whistle my appreciation long and loud.

Hunched behind her twin Technics, Nad drops some really funky breakbeats. A very fit, very strong black guy grabs me and we start dirty-dancing, his thigh between mine. I go with the flow and pick up on the baseline right away, his strong, sweaty hands supporting my bare waist as I lean backwards. My crotch is gripping his leg like I'm trying to *squeeeeeze* the blood out of those big, hard muscles. I'm getting some definite vibes from down below, riding his combat-covered thigh like the Lone Ranger on speed. Hey, *Que-no-sabe*, wait for me! My right leg's up against his crotch. I can feel his hard-on. I'm well on my way to a realisation. Not one of those Road-to-Damascus realisations, just a regular, practical, everyday one. Here it is now: it isn't the pills that get people horny, it's all those sweaty out-of-it strangers inhaling each other's sex odours. Oh, shit, when my talking-bollocks level's this high, it means only one thing. I'm getting rushy and outta control. Don't wanna do an Aaaargli-son. I've got this little rule of thumb: when I start thinking in gibberish, it's time to go someplace and chill.

I smile thank you at the nice man who gave me such a lovely dance and do a couple of laps of the club till I find myself back in the main room. It's thinned out considerably. A new DJ is starting to build his set. My addled brain is just about together enough to figure out that Nadine's must be finished. If I know Nadine, she'll be wanting to have some fun herself, now she's finished work. I make my way to one of the chill-out rooms and lean against a wall running with condensation while I check out the assortment of beautiful things stretching out on the few available comfy seats and the casualties piling up under the air-con ducts. Some community-spirited soul is juggling glow sticks but there's no fucking place to sit down.

I'm about to give up and go and check out when the main act's on, when I notice an older dude reclin-ing on a couch like a roman emperor at an orgy. He looks about forty, sort of long-haired and raddled but, in a way, distinguished. His flower-pattern shirt is unbuttoned so I wonder if he's done a pill too and it's all turned out too much for him. It's cool for older people to be going clubbing, but I'm not really sure about the leather trousers. And it's definitely not OK to be reclining over four spaces when I badly need to crash. I decide to give him the benefit of the doubt and saunter across with a friendly scowl on my face. The Emperor leers at me and raises his bottle like in a toast. Stolichnaya Cristall. Jesus, he could have made an effort and decanted it into a water bottle. He obviously does not know the rules. If Security see him with that, he'll be bouncing his way across London Bridge in no time. On his arse.

It's then that I notice he appears to be reclining over Nadine. Assuredly, he must be cool, because Nadine would never let somebody who wasn't recline on her. Whatever, I don't care. All I know is that she has someplace to sit, so I bounce over and wriggle myself in between her and the flower-power shirt. 'Hi,' says Nadine. I notice that her skin is all glowing and damp like my own. We do some whooping and squeezing and admire each other's breasts. Mine are just about to tumble out of my tiny leopardskin top. What she's wearing amounts to little more than a string vest, her nipples poking rather saucily against the crisscross mesh, but Nadine's got such neat tits, she can get away with it. She tells me I seem to be nicely loosened up and makes a big deal of stroking and hugging me before she turns to the Emperor-dude.

'Hey, meet Ivan, you'll like him. He's a famous Russian film director,' she says by way of an intro, adding, 'This is my friend Zita. She's gonna be a famous English film producer.' I wince but it doesn't matter. She might as well have said, 'Meet Ivan, you'll like him. He's a fornicating lying bastard on the skank.' I know so, because I'm having one of those inspired 3 a.m. insights. We all have them. Like when you realise that you really, really, honestly think your best mate is truly wonderful. Usually after you've just shared a couple of bottles of tequila with them. Anyway, it's clear to me this man has more than a passing acquaintanceship with decadence. There's something mad and sad in his face. I look into it hard to see if I can spot anything of the crazy axe murderer in there but it's a gentle face, though there's something manic about his eyes and mouth. And, I notice, a definite hard-on underneath all that leather.

Anyway, me and Nadine continue petting each

other. This used to be our regular act when we found ourselves in horny male company, partly because (I mean, of course, even though) Nad is bi. Doesn't bother me, she's the best gal-pal I ever had. At this particular moment, I cannot understand why I haven't seen her for so long. Then I remember, Paul. Duh, yeah, him.

Well, I don't need him at the moment, I realise as I drape myself across Nadine, do I? I think about my sexy dance while she runs her fingers up and down the inside of my arm. My skin's gone hypersensitive and it's sending sensations like sparks into my armpit and through to my tits. I feel the nipples stiffen and glance down. Nadine's nips are firm and puckered and sticking right through the mesh of her top as well. Shit, wasn't Ivan the Terrible supposed to be getting wound up, not us? We're losing control of the situation here. I look at him and shrug. 'Pheromones!' I say.

He laughs. 'Dancing, one big group fuck, I think. It is why you and Nadine are so aroused.' I nearly choke. You just don't say stuff like that. I wriggle into a vaguely upright position (difficult because all of our limbs are pretty tangled up together) and announce that, now, we must all dance.

The main room is heaving because the big act is on. Nadine leads the way through the crowd with Ivan bringing up the rear as we wind our way conga-style to the heart of the action. 'Let's put Mr Director's theory to the test, then,' she shouts in my ear and goes for it. Nadine has two passions. A: spinning records (hip-hop, drum 'n' bass, garage, funk). B: dancing to same. When she dances, she pays no attention to what's around her, just lets it all go like she's possessed. It's infectious. I raise my arms over my head, arch my spine and shove my arse out backways. Behind me I feel a body move in close and spoon in.

Ivan? Gotta be, his tempo's all wrong. I don't care. I find the rhythm in his body and move with it, gradually bringing it into my own groove. I can feel his heart beating as I slowly increase the depravity of my dancing. His cock hardens against the cheeks of my rotating arse and I begin pushing harder into his groin. The Man's theory must be right because we've attracted quite a crowd. I turn to say this to him and ... whoops. It ain't Ivan at all but some bare-chested, shaven-headed youth. Early twenties. Sweaty-sexy in that fit-but-undernourished look some white lads achieve. In the brief flowering between spotty adolescence and acquiring the beer belly.

My fanny kinda flutters, a mixture of excitement and panic. Ivan is jigging near me with a big lascivious grin all over his face. He leans across and shouts in my ear. 'Clubbing, hah! Big group fucking, I say.' I humour him by smiling and nodding and turn to Nadine. I can barely see her. She's completely surrounded by a harem of loved-up sweaty boys. I guess that her pill has come on, too, because she's away now. She looks at me and shouts, 'The Man is right. One big shag, innit?' Then she throws her head back and screams. The floor goes berserk.

An hour later and my pill's wearing off and I'm starting to feel a bit uncomfortable with things. I'd been picking up a slightly scary vibe from a clutch of hard-faced, hard-eyed girls lurking near the edge of the dance floor. Well, they all have their hair pulled up really tight on the top of their head the way hard girls in school always did. That was scary enough for me. I dance up to Nadine and holler, '*Toilet!*' in her ear so she won't think I've just gone home or something. I swim my way through the throng in the main room and attach myself to the end of a queue snaking endlessly down a corridor draped with fur fabric. I figure that, as the toilets would be close to the exit, they'll be close to where the bouncers hang out. So, if anything kicks off, I should be relatively safe. I'm there minding my own business when a pair of the hard-faced Ponytails appear. I decide to close my eyes, thereby avoiding eye contact.

But I can hear them all right though. Apparently, the sweaty white yout' are with them and they think that Nadine and I are thieving. Oh puh-lease, I want to say. Women just don't do this any more. You're all being very juvenile and it's definitely against every rule in clubbing to behave so. I want to say this, but, naturally, I don't utter a word of it. In fact, I keep my head down and feel my way along the sweaty fabric-coated wall with my hands in the hope that the Ponytails will assume I'm completely out of it. I start questioning the wisdom of my head-in-the-sand strat-egy when I hear Nadine's voice in growling mode. I open one eye and catch her engaged in competitive face-to-face snarling with the Chief Ponytail.

My money is gonna have to be on Nadine, a practi-sed snarler in these circumstances, and I guess Secur-ity's is too. He comes galloping down the corridor and breaks them up right off. He holds Nadine against the wall while the Ponytails troop back to the dance floor. Lead 'Tail swaggers out last and, as she passes Nadine, she pokes her in the cheek with her index finger. Oh, bad move! I watch Nadine kinda tip her head back and then close my eyes again. I hear the crunch of Nadine's forehead colliding with the girl's nose but luckily do not see it.

So, the next thing I know is that the hard girls are all still in the club, no doubt being tended by the designated first-aider, while me and Nadine are out on the street. It's 4 a.m. I'm in a bikini top, my coat's inside the club and Nadine is hammering on the chest of a mountainously impassive bouncer, demanding to be let in to reclaim her vinyl. He ain't having any of it. He tells Nadine to come back tomorrow, or words to that effect, when she's calmed down because, if she goes back in, he knows she'll go straight for the jugular of Ponytail bitch. I'm inclined to agree, but Nadine tells me that she's done two pills so she isn't straight enough to drive all the way home yet, and besides her house keys were with her records. At this moment, Nadine is living way out in the sticks, right off the *A-Z*. Beyond the M25 even. She starts beating furiously on the (by now closed) metal club door while I pace up and down trying to keep warm and avoid the leers from the shoal of gypsy cab drivers floating on the wrong side of the barrier. We are fucked.

I have my flat keys, but no money. So the horrendous prospect of having to walk from London Bridge to Camberwell at four in the morning, wearing only a halter-neck leopardskin bikini top and skin-tight op-art leggings, looms before me. Or I accept a lift from Nad, in return for which she will expect to stay at the flat. I should say, 'Come back to Camberwell,' but I just know that Paul would find out she'd been there. And all of a sudden, I'm immersed in paranoia about his calling it *his* flat and that stay-as-long-as-you-need stuff. Shit, he didn't mean it, I know but –

Suddenly, Nadine lets out a big whoop. Ivan is standing there with her record boxes clamped under his big, strong, Russian arms. Our hero! Then Ivan says that he lives in Clerkenwell and we could all go back to his place if Nadine would give him a lift. Nadine decides that she can handle London Bridge to Old Street and, *wunderbar*, everything is sorted! I'm absolved from the need to make a moral decision.

Ivan has this really cool flat. Very, very chic. It makes Paul's look exactly what it is – a tacky little conversion done on the cheap, window-dressed with a splattering of recherché colour-supplement style. Ivan's got the real thing. A huge, high-ceilinged studio – must have cost a fortune. I'm beginning to believe that maybe he *is* some big-shot director after all. Nadine makes herself at home and starts chopping lines on this Perspex cube thing he has for a table. I stroke her arm gently and ask her if she feels better after her little contretemps. Nadine gives me her huge, sunny smile as an answer, then turns to Ivan and says, 'So, Ivan. These films you make. Like, what are they?'

He finishes hoovering up with an enormous snort and then says glumly, 'Forgotten ones.' I've perked up considerably, so now I don't want him going all melancholic on us. I decide to lighten up the atmosphere and jump to my feet, saying brightly, 'Come on, then, Eisenstein, direct me!' Ivan looks at me with a strange expression on his face. Somewhere between pain and hunger. Nadine picks up on where I'm coming from and joins in. 'Yeah, c'mon, Ivan. Do some directing stuff.'

Ivan sits back shaking his head while Nadine bounces round the room putting music on and wheedling, 'Hey, Ivan, you could make a very sexy film with me and Zita.' She struts over to the couch, wiggling her nonexistent hips suggestively, then straddles my left leg and begins lasciviously grinding her crotch into my thigh. 'Is this how you do it, Ivan?' she pants, in a parody of a blue movie.

Ivan helps himself to another line and mutters, 'No, you look as if you are playing. You must look like you are enjoying yourself. Even when you are not.'

Nadine laughs. 'Oh, that'll be easy for Zita. She does that all the time.'

I realise what Nadine has just said and poke her

sharply in the ribs. She retaliates by whipping my legs out from under me, yanking me off the couch and pinning me to the floor. I tell her to sod off but Nadine just wriggles herself about till she's lying prone on top of me. I try to loop my feet round her hips to wrassle her off me, but I can't get a grip 'cos she's so lithe and agile.

I'm about to give in when one of Nadine's favourite tunes comes on, 'Bump & Grind'. Next thing, she's doing just that. Her bony pubis is bashing and wriggling against mine like pretend dry humping. The silliness of the situation gets to me and I can't help joining in, in perfect time to the music, of course. Soon, we're both puffing and snorting and laughing hilariously as we do a horizontal tango. One of my breasts has slipped out of my bikini top but I can't move my hands, which Nadine has pinned to the floorboards, to pull the material back over it. My nipple has gone disconcertingly hard. Next thing, Nadine takes it between her teeth and, giggling, nips me. If that's the way she wants to play it . . . I manage to pull a hand free and get a grip on her vest and yank. I get the garment over her head and, while she's distracted, manage to twist her off me. Nadine is crouched kneeling on the floor, grinning at me fiercely and panting. We've got Ivan's attention now, though. He's produced a tiny miniature camcorder from someplace and squatted down right next to us, close enough for me to notice that bulge again, straining the confines of his leather trousers. 'Very good. I think now you are in character, girls,' he says. 'But give me more action. Go, go, go!'

Nadine must be still fired up from the Ponytail situation, 'cos she does. Go. She hurls her top into the corner of the room and, bare-chested, comes at me again. Like for real now. Within seconds, she has my bikini bra ripped off and we're wrestling topless with each other, thumping against the floor, bashing against the furniture. I say we, but in fact, I'm giggling and squeaking, 'No, Nadine, no,' while Nadine simultaneously tickles me and puts me into some kind of advanced judo hold. She is fit. Within seconds, she has me back down on the floor. In the scrum, I can distinctly feel her pert, taut nipples pressing into my chest, her hard belly flat against mine, and her hand working my Lycra leggings over my hips. Hey, what?

I'm getting angry now and intend to say so, but I'm so puffed, I can't find the breath to tell her to *stop right there*. So I wriggle and roll with maximum vigour to escape her snatching fingers but the result is my wriggling actually enables her to pull my pants down over my bum, the bitch. I'm extremely annoyed but, I realise with a shock, excited as well. I've never been forcibly undressed on camera before and the sensation is confusing. It must be that fucking pheromone thing again. Like, my normal responses are frozen. Nadine uses the opportunity. She jumps off me and hauls my leggings down over my knees, just as a female voice says, 'The remake of *Blow Up*, is it, darling?' in a strangely familiar, condescending tone.

What the fuck? What is Saskia St John-Smythe doing here? She's supposed to filming somewhere out on the remotest tip of Cuba.

4

We're whizzing westwards along the Westway, the speed limit totally ignored. Nadine has only one speed: as fast as her rust bucket red Capri will go. I have this excited butterfly feeling in my tummy, part hysteria at her driving and part guilt. l know I should be trotting dutifully home to Camberwell and doing something sensible. Like finishing that CV. But I'm still buzzing about the whole evening and when Nad said, 'Back to mine, then?' it seemed the natural thing to do. I feel like I'm off on holiday, the same spaced-out up-all-night feeling when you have to make an early flight. Perhaps that's how Celia had felt.

Celia, ah, yes. The memory of the Celia part of the evening turns the butterfly in my belly into a block of ice. Celia Draycott, internationally famous executive producer and mate of Clare Dodderidge. I sink further down in the bucket seat and cringe. Please, God, don't let her tell Ms CD I was lying on her living room floor, naked but for a thong round my ankles. The whole scene plays inside my head in glorious, vivid Technicolor: Nadine standing, bare titties heaving, in front of me, Ivan kneeling a few yards away with his camcorder while behind him stands his elegant wife, pinching the bridge of her nose and looking rather wearied. I'm thinking, Are they swingers? Is she gonna produce a gun from out of that Kelly bag? The whole thing reeks of some bizarre sex-crime scenario: me and Nadine the unwitting stars in an international co-production snuff movie. I can hear Paul saying, 'Told you so!' to my coffin. 'Rule Number One: never, ever go back to some complete stranger's with your best mate and end up wrasslin' nekkid on a rug.' Especially when his wife is about to arrive home.

I hear Ivan's voice say, 'Celia, sweetest, you are back tomorrow.'

Celia just stands there like a fashion plate from a magazine for the thirtysomething woman and says, very evenly, in her dead-ringer-for-Saskia meejah voice, 'It is tomorrow, Ivan. I got an earlier flight. If you ever bothered to check your voicemail –'

Ivan interrupts her, 'Yah, yah, yahing', and gets to his feet. 'Darling, you are home.' And he embraces her. Then, as almost an afterthought, he introduces us to his wife. He doesn't sound a bit embarrassed.

'Hi,' says Nadine. I smile wanly and wave a limp wrist towards Mrs Ivan. She doesn't bat an eyelid. I must admit she's good. This woman makes regular ice maidens look positively tepid.

'Do excuse me, girls. I'm sure your project is very interesting,' she says smoothly, 'but I've just flown overnight long-haul and I am bushed.'

Totally weird. I mean, I just don't get this. If I walked in on Paul and he was filming two nearly nude females sprawled over the marital kilim ... Well, suffice to say I would not be so sanguine. She just ruffles her hand through her ash-blonde bob and offers us tea.

Before I can politely decline, Nadine says, in this strangely phoney voice, 'Thank you! Tea would be lovely.' I'm making all kinds of let's-just-go faces at her but she shrugs at me while Celia disappears to the kitchen.

When she's out of the room, I grab for my clothes and hiss at Nadine, 'What are you doing?'

Nadine pulls her vest back on and rolls her eyes at me. 'Zita, c'mon, she's gorgeous!'

I cannot believe she's serious. I snap back, 'She's also married, Nad!' Nadine smirks and says, 'Jesus, Zita. I always forget how naïve you are.'

Naïve, *moi*? I am not having that. We're sitting next to each other on the sofa conducting this 'I am not naïve/yes you are!' argument with each other in whispers when Celia arrives bearing a tray with four little bowls like you get in Oriental restaurants. She pauses by the Perspex cube table thing and her mouth makes a wiggly line when she sees the powder and rolled up notes scattered across it. I don't move a muscle. It's Nadine's idea to stay, so she can deal with the social niceties. But Nadine doesn't have to do a thing, 'cos Celia just kicks the table out of the way before bending at the waist and setting the tray on the floor before us. She then folds her legs up underneath herself and sits gracefully on the floor saying, 'Green tea. I'm afraid I don't have any other.' And she pours some out into the little bowls.

I have to work consciously at keeping my jaw from dropping when Nadine starts up with her 'Wow, you're so supple. You do Pilates?' routine. I make a mental note to tell her that her chat-up line stinks and I'm just beginning to think that the evening can't get any stranger when Celia sends Ivan into the kitchen to find her fags and snaps, 'Of course, you won't understand the impact of *Eva Baby*. You'd probably have been in infants at the time.'

We stare at her, bemused, while she lectures us on *perestroika* and *glasnost* and how important Ivan was. He won awards for some ground-breaking movie called *Eva Baby*. His one great contribution to world cinema. He really was a big-shot director. Was. Once, in the eighties. His problem is he peaked too early, he never followed up. Fuck me. Is this woman doing a ballectomy, or what? There's an almighty crash from the kitchen. Ivan imploding, I think. He strides back in, hurls the fags at Celia, then says in a voice trembling with emotion, 'Forgive me. It is impossible for a man to stay in company while his wife emasculates him. Goodnight!' With a little nod of the head, he turns on his heels and stalks away. He stops momentarily, turns back and adds, very formally, 'I mean, of course, good morning,' before finally leaving us alone with Madame Ball Breaker.

If Celia's intention was to scare away the competition, it's worked, on me at least. And, once Ivan's gone, Celia doesn't seem that interested in us. Well, me, to be precise. Nadine is still doing her full-on Nadine-sex-machine charm offensive and Celia seems, well, not exactly interested but certainly flattered and amused. Nad *can* be very charming and she's never been a one to leave empty-handed. 'Result!' she mouths to me when, as Celia politely turfs us out, she manages to get her business card: Celia Draycott-Punin, Chief Executive, Slo-Mo Films International, Greek St. Oh, fucking marvellous, I think, as Nad's Capri noses westwards, leaving the remains of the rosy pink (false) dawn of my truly scuppered career behind. I haven't the faintest idea where I'm going. Off out into the sticks, out into the wilds. Beyond the M25 anyway.

I've never been to her current place before. Nadine has a history of moving around. She has some deal going whereby she caretakes empty property in danger of being squatted. I've just got used to her address changing annually and accepted it as a matter of fact. But we seem to have been driving for ages.

'Nad?' I ask 'Where the fuck are we?'

Nad grins and yells over the rattle of the engine, 'Told you. The cunt-tree!' And we suddenly shoot up a sliproad off the M40 and, before I know it, it's just vegetation and we are in the middle of fucking nowhere.

She clocks the dubious expression on my face and starts laughing. 'Jesus, Zita, you've been living in suburbia too long. Trust me.' Nadine saying 'Trust me', I have learned from bitter experience, is not a good thing, but suddenly I realise that we must have arrived somewhere, because Nadine slews the car into what looks like a gap in a hedge. We bump along a narrow unmettled track before scrunching to a halt in front of a crumbling Gothic heap that must have been last occupied by the Addams Family. 'Tanglebush Towers,' she says proudly, 'Welcome to my lovely home!'

I follow her up a beautiful, cobwebbed, carpetless wood staircase to the first floor. The house has a deserted feel, but it's strangely welcoming rather than spooky. Nadine's room is huge and minimalist, but not in a way that Paul would understand by the word. She dumps her record cases and starts skinning up while I crash on her king-size mattress. It's the only piece of 'furniture' in the room, besides a vast stack of CDs, tapes and records, her mixing console and speakers and a pair of overstuffed clothes rails. The morning sun is slanting through the (curtainless) windows and everywhere looks bright and airy, if a trifle dusty. Tree branches are waving gently in the breeze right outside, making dappled patterns of light and shade on the opposite wall. I love this place immediately and tell Nadine so.

'Yeah, it's cool,' she says noncommittally. She lights the joint and brings it over to join me on the bed and we lie silently for a while, smoking and watching sunlight dance round the room. I stretch out luxuriously and wiggle my toes. Nadine gently prods my side. 'You'll have a bruise in the morning,' she says. 'I got a bit rough back there, didn't I? Let me check your back.' I smile in forgiveness and roll over on to my tummy and allow Nadine to untie my halter top. I lie there listening to the birds trilling and tweeting outside while she strokes and tickles my shoulders. After ten minutes of this, I'm totally relaxed.

Although I'm not sleepy, I wonder if I should get some. I murmur something like this to Nadine, who says, 'Just get under the duvet, then.' I wriggle under it while she stands up, pulls off her mesh top and steps out of her low-slung baggy jeans and knickers. I watch her pad round the room, nude, sorting out her things, and think how graceful and lissom she is. Then she is kneeling naked beside me on the mattress and pulling the duvet up to get in. I look up at her skinny, dark skinned body, neat and delicate as a schoolgirl's. Her pubic hair is a dense mat of curls. Tanglebushed, I think to myself. Next thing, she has slipped in and cuddled up beside me.

'You'll get thrush if you leave your leggings on,' she says.

'You've been trying to get them off all night,' I murmur.

She starts tugging at the waistband but I can't be bothered to object. She's probably right about the thrush. I lift my hips off the bed and Nadine sweeps the leggings down and over my feet, somehow taking my thong with them too. So now we're lying next to each other naked. Now, although me and Nadine can get quite openly physical with each other in front of other people, I've always thought of it as a joke thing. We've never actually done anything together in private. In fact, I've never ever *done* anything with *any* girl, though Nadine doesn't necessarily know that.

However, it seems highly unsophisticated to make an issue of the situation, so I stay face down, trying to work out how best to play things, when I feel the palm of her hand smooth softly over the base of my spine and round my buttocks. Nadine begins rubbing my arse comfortingly. If we can keep it at that, things'll be fine, and I can float serenely off to sleep. Nadine's fingertips brush lightly up and down the top of the cleft of my bum. It's not unpleasant and I snuggle deeper into the mattress and murmur a little sigh of appreciation. I guess I must have drifted away, enchanted by the sounds of nature from outside or something, because the next thing I realise is that Nadine's hand has drifted somewhat further down and she is alternately teasing the tuft of hair round my pussy lips and fingering the crease where my thighs join my crotch. The problem is, my legs have parted to allow her to do this while my groin is pushing imperceptibly up and down into the mattress. I realise with a shock that I am beginning to get turned on.

Unwittingly, I immediately roll over to tell Nadine this and that she must stop now. We're face to face, only inches apart. Again, I'm fully intending to say *stop right there*, but somehow, it won't come out. Nadine just bends forward and kisses me lightly on the lips. Just a peck on the mouth. I'm still trying to get the instruction to *cease forthwith* out but, instead, my mouth puckers up and, annoyingly, kisses her back. Suddenly we're lash-locked and brazenly smooching each other. Her fingers have found my pussy again and are playing saucily around the general area of my clit. Unlike Paul, she doesn't prod or poke, but begins an interesting circular movement which is, I admit, not unpleasant and, in fact, seems to have stimulated this automatic opening reflex in my thighs. Nadine runs a finger down my groove and slips it into my extremely moist hole. My body stiffens in surprise and we pull apart and look at each other.

Watching me the whole time, Nadine rolls me over on to my back and kneels astride me. We've got that mirroring thing going again. She's biting her lip, I'm biting mine. Then she slowly bends forward and kisses me again, little pecks down the side of my neck to my throat till she gets to my nipples. I smile at her, friendly, and Nadine smiles back. Nadine does a smooch on one and then on the other. I have quite large, quite responsive nips and, suddenly, it's Mexican hats time. I know this is probably where it should stop but – maybe it's the remnants of the pill – I am enjoying the attention. I decide to give it just one more minute and stretch my arms back luxuriously over my head as Nadine suckles my tits gently in her mouth, one at a time. Her fingernails scratch lightly up and down my armpits, which is sending a signal into my tummy, which seems to be telling my hips to rock slightly, but nonetheless rhythmically, so that my mons is bumping up against hers. I can feel our tanglebushes brushing and snagging together. I think of that funky little horizontal tango we did at Ivan's only a couple of hours ago. Was this what it looked like? I wonder what he'll do with the video tape. We really ought to ask him about that. I'll talk to Nadine about it later.

Nadine continues kissing down my belly until she reaches the top of my slit and she starts snogging my pussy. I'm thinking I should remind Nadine I'm not a lesbian and we should definitely not be doing this 'cos we're just mates, but my mouth keeps swallowing saliva rather than forming words, so I figure, as things've gone this far, it would be churlishly unmatish to interfere right now, and, anyway, she's being unbelievably creative with her tongue, when, in one of my life's Before-I-Knew-It moments, my arse is lifting right off the mattress and I'm pushing myself into her face and the birds are twittering and it's way too late and, ohhhh, a long, soft murmur wells in my throat and I'm coming. A slow, drawn-out and agonisingly intense come. My first in weeks. My first with a girl. Ohmygod, I'm a lesbian. I'll worry about it tomorrow.

5

I wake up alone in a strange bed. Story of my life these days. I can hear birds doing that 'Woo woo-woo woo' thing, the sun is streaming in through the windows and although, as you may well have gathered, I'm not really your outdoorsy kinda gal, at least I know that means they're not owls.

Don't panic, this isn't one of those 'Where am I? What happened?' scenarios. I know exactly where I am. I am in my sometimes best friend's bed in some stately home someplace that doesn't figure in the *A-Z*. And I know exactly what happened. I did the all-girl version of the wrestling scene in *Women in Love* for an (allegedly) famous Russian film director and there was something else too. Oh yes. I fucked my best mate. Or she fucked me. Whatever. Either way I have just broken two of the cardinal rules. One: never, ever sleep with friends. Two: never walk (and certainly don't frolic half fucking naked) in front of a camera. Time to worry, I guess. This is all Alison's fault. And don't you go feeling sorry for her, either, because it is. It's the domino effect. Alison breaking that first rule has fucked everything up. We have Anarchy.

So, priorities. First, wash. I stink of sex and I can remember enough of the pheromones conversation not to endanger myself by venturing out into a place wherein wildlife lurks, at least while my body reeks of them. I might get mounted by a stag or something. I find a bathroom that looks serviceable next to the door with the sign painted on it saying DON'T GO THERE in two-foot fluoro letters. Interesting, but I've broken far too many rules this weekend, so I decide to pass on investigating and head into the bathroom. I risk heart attack through shock and squat in the chipped enamel bath trying to aim a jet of water from the big clunky bathtaps at my fanny. I succeed far too well and shoot up pretty smartish. 'Wooh.' Was that me? I splash more freezing cold but mercifully rust-free water about myself when I hear another 'Woogh.' It's coming from outside. It is exactly like the sound I imagine a rutting stag would make. Pheromones!

Apart from the fact that I have a raging cocaine hangover and the wooghing is quite painful, it's completely doing my head in. This is one of the many reasons I don't do rural. At least in town all the noise is a constant pleasant hum. Well, a roar, perhaps. But there's so much of the roaring that you don't notice it any more. Whereas in any place green and leafy, the slightest little squeak and you pee yourself. Going on the know-your-enemy principle, I decide to investigate.

I take my courage in my hands and stand on the lip of the bath with one foot on the window ledge so I can just about peer out of the broken bit of the cobweb-shrouded window. I can see a small patch of overgrown green and little else. I'm about to give up, when an image of the most beautiful boy in the world appears beneath the waving branches. Beautiful and naked. I do not lie. He is your perfect golden-limbed, six-pack-bearing, muscle-rippling Greek god except for one very important factor. Unlike your average Greek god, he has a cock that comes into the you'll-never-fit-*that*-in-*there* category. I watch it bounce around as he strikes various martial-arty-looking attitudes. Pose ... Woogh. Pose ... Woogh.

Woogh indeed. The combination of naked god and

great height is giving me a definite fanny rush. 'Hey, I'm not a lesbian after all!' I say to myself as I lose my balance and tumble backwards into the bath. As you know, since the Alison Incident, I have developed terrible vertigo but I resolutely overcome my fear to clamber back up. Naturally, my vision of loveliness has disappeared. For ever, knowing my luck, I think glumly. Probably a mirage, something my unconscious has conjured up to taunt me about the Nadine situation. Nevertheless, I cling on grimly for several minutes, hopefully scanning the view before returning to priorities: first, wash; second, clothes. Mine stink and, anyway, seem a tad inappropriate for the country. I slink back past DON'T GO THERE to Nadine's room and peruse one of her clothes rails for something suitably rustic. I notice a cherry-red strappy minidress that's been thrown across the top of the rail, like it's recently been worn and discarded. I sniff it, but it smells fresh. It's made of fine cord, OK, which is about as rustic as I'm prepared to go. A bit tight, but it'll do.

I can hear music of the shouty-pointy-finger variety, which means it's fairly safe to assume that Nadine is in the house, and I set off to face it. I manage to find my way back to the grand staircase, noticing that the place has more than a whiff of Miss Haversham about it. I eventually locate Nadine in the kitchen, lounging at a huge pockmarked wooden table, her head nodding to the beat.

It would be nice to say something spontaneously, wittily blasé now. Something that would get matters straight between us. But last night, this morning, or whenever, has left me feeling a tad awkward. And a teensy bit guilty. Shit, the honesty-about-fidelity clause was one of mine. Do I have to tell Paul? Does a girl count? What are the rules? I contemplate Paul romping with his best mate. Would I be jealous?

Hmmmm, curious but possibly not jealous. Especially if he was lonely. So, therefore, a bit of affection from *my* best mate won't really matter. To him, at least.

Nadine smiles her tiger smile, pours out some coffee and pushes it across the table at me. I say, 'Thank you' casually, except it comes out like a bleat.

Nadine lights a fag and says, 'God, I hope you're not like this with men.'

I blush (hey, I *never* blush: it's one of my characteristics) and manage to say, 'Like what?'

Nadine puts her fag down and does this big-eyed ickle-girl routine. 'Thankoo.'

I blush deeper and eventually stutter, 'I'm embarrassed, Nadine.' She just gives it the raised eyebrows so I'm like, 'Nadine, we had sex last night,' but Nadine merely shrugs and blows out some smoke and looks all cool. She's bugging me now. I blurt out all in one go that the sex was OK and everything but I have no desire to feel her tits or go anywhere near her cunt and I'm not a lesbian or even bi. This is my way of clearing the air without hurting her feelings. There's a rustic silence disturbed only by the tweeting of birds. Then Nadine just bursts out laughing and starts singing, 'I deflowered a virgin ...'

I help myself to one of her fags and tell her to fuck off and, although I still have a nagging feeling of worry, the equilibrium is kinda restored. Issue number one dealt with, I turn to the other pressing situation. The video evidence. Nadine snorts and tells me I worry too much. I've been hanging with Paul too long. So what if there's a tape of us arsing round? Who cares? Nadine is so annoying sometimes. Of course, I can't admit that I care, and I don't. Not really. It's just that whole reputation thing, you know, and if I remember rightly Mrs Ivan was a producer and that could impact on my bourgeoning career greatly. I say all this to Nad and she looks very thoughtful then says that she'll give me a lift back to town on Monday and we'll go and visit Ivan and get the tape off him. I'm, like, 'Tomorrow?' and Nad goes, 'Yeah, tomorrow. You can hang out here for the rest of the weekend and chill.' This means another night sleeping here, which raises certain questions, but I don't know how to phrase them. So I don't. But Nad reads my mind and says, in this indulgent way that I'm not altogether sure I like, 'Don't fret, Zita, babe, I won't bother you.' Then adds, with a sly smirk, 'Not unless you want me to.'

There really is no answer to that so, to change the subject, I ask Nad how come she's living in the middle of nowhere in this great big fuck-off mansion. Now, I said that Nadine has some deal whereby she lives rent-free in empty places that are likely to get squatted. The rationale goes something like this: it's tedious, expensive and time-consuming to evict squatters, so get in first by letting your better-quality squatter type occupy the property legit on condition that (a) they keep others out and (b) they go when asked. Usually, that's OK. If you are prepared to go, that means you're reliable, so you'll immediately get offered another property to 'caretake'. Once you get established on that scene, you've got a never-ending supply of freebie accommodation, often at quite desirable addresses, even if things might be a bit basic in the wash-and-brush-up department. For a natural nomad like Nadine, it's ideal. Except, normally, she's a townie through and through and wouldn't consider a postcode that so much as crept into double digits. I point this out to her and Nad takes a drag on her cig and says, 'I fancied summer in the country for a change. They're selling the land for executive housing or something. When the deal goes through, they'll demolish Ol' Tanglebush Towers and I'll be back in central London for the winter.'

I feel another flush spreading up my neck. The mere mention of Tanglebush brings back a dangerously vivid memory of our entangled pubes, and that reminds me of the sensation of my mons dry-humping anxiously against hers. Was it just the E or did I actually enjoy that as much as I'm afraid I might have done? And everything else that led to. I feel very aware of my naked fanny under the cherry-red minidress. I'm not wearing any knickers. (I draw the line at borrowing friends' undies.) Nadine's hooded eyes study me with amusement, like she knows exactly what I'm thinking. Desperately, I search for something to keep the sexually neutral spin of our current conversation going. Luckily, I hit on the flaw in Nadine's arrangements. She must spend a good deal of her time away from this place, doing DJ stuff like buying records, finding gigs, playing them even. She'll be away for days at a time, knowing her.

'Hang on a minute, Nad,' I say. 'Technically, you shouldn't ever go out, 'cos you'd be leaving the place vacant. And that's against the lease. What if Tanglebush Towers gets squatted?' I finish triumphantly, even though I stumble slightly over the Tanglebush bit. Nad affects a bored look and eventually says, 'I thought I told you about Sigh.'

'What's Sigh?'I ask, thinking she's about to explain some arcane housing law to me. 'Cy,' answers Nadine, 'is who I share the lease with. He's a scenic painter but, since we've been out here, he's decided to get into his art. He's made the stables out back into a studio and just hangs out there, painting, now. He's gone all feral, never goes out any more. I can come and go pretty much how I please.'

Aha. That would explain (oh, be still, my beating heart) the Greek god I saw from the bathroom. I ask Nadine what this Cy looks like and she raises her eyebrows at me 'Why?' I describe my vision and she shrugs and says, 'Yup, that would be Cy. He's into nude t'ai chi. Cy's into nude, full stop. We hardly see each other, so why should I complain?' She studies me for a moment. 'I guess you won't.'

I feel yet another blush coming on but masterfully bring it under control and add nonchalantly, 'What red-blooded heterosexual gal wouldn't?'

Nadine pulls a moue. 'Yeah, got quite a fan club, our Cy.' She gets up then and says, 'Look, if you really want to get back into town and pine for Pauley baby, I'll take you.'

I get a sudden image of Paul all cosied up with Saskia St John-Smythe in Cuba and say, 'No you're all right, Nad. Monday will be fine.'

'Good. I got work to do. Make yourself at home. Catch ya later,' she says and ambles out of the kitchen. Left to my own devices, I decide to venture outside and dare to examine the countryside at close quarters. The sun's blazing and the day's turned out very hot for May. The garden is completely overgrown but I can vaguely make out the remains of what was once presumably a formal patio and lawn. There's a sense of all the nature having once been under control even if now, to quote a Nadine phrase, it has gone feral, with bees buzzing and butterflies fluttering and birds, inevitably, tweeting. I walk over the springy grass in my bare feet, enjoying the feel of it between my toes. In case anybody (such as this Cy guy) might be watching me, I adopt a languid, dreamy, yet essentially classy look. You know, *Vogue* Nature Girl (all green wellies and no mud). Very improbable. It doesn't last long. After a couple of circuits, I'm getting bored of being whimsical, when I notice a narrow track at the far end of the garden. I decide to investigate before I go back to the house and catch up on my sleep.

The path turns out to be anything but a pleasant country stroll. Tanglebush certainly lives up to its name. There's green stuff growing everywhere and, pretty soon, I'm surrounded by a rampant jungle. In fact, I can hardly see the path I've come down any more. I'm gingerly parting brambles and fighting the urge to holler for Nadine at the top of my voice when I'm startled by something I swear is Bambi flitting across the track about ten yards ahead of me. Except this Bambi has a definitely girly giggle and skinny girlish tits to boot. In fact, Bambi is about nineteen and stark naked. Hey!

After the initial shock, I notice the path sort of opens out where Bambi disappeared into the under-growth. I decide to go with the whole weird Alice thing and follow the critter. I force my way through a load of scrubby weeds but I'm disappointed. No enchanted rabbit holes here. I'm about to shuffle out backwards when I notice through a gap that there is a grass clearing. I freeze. In the clearing is a strange tableaux of two figures, one of which is the naked fawn I saw a minute before. The other is equally naked, and impressively priapic, too. And forcing his swollen priapus into the fawn's mouth. I know the proper thing to do would be to retreat and leave this satyr and his nymph to get on with their little Arcadian copulation rite in private but, well, if I move, they might hear me. And that would put them off their stride, OK? So, obviously, the politest action is to sit tight and keep a low profile.

I squat down in my little thicket and decide to sit it out. I don't want to play the voyeur, but, while I've got a floor show, I might as well watch it. I take a good look at the girl. Don't get me wrong, I'm interested to see what fawns are built like, that's all. Fawns, as it happens, are skinny. Skinnier than me. Too skinny in my opinion. Even kneeling down her belly is concave. Surprisingly, her skin is really pale. Even from this distance, I can see the faint blue tracery of veins across its surface. Can't make my mind up about the hair. I don't normally rate red hair – I associate it with Alison – but this girl's hair is really long and straight, the kind of dark-red mane that crackles and flares in sunlight. It's impossible to tell what her face is like, but she must have a fucking big gob to swallow all of *that*.

That belongs to a Golden Boy who has to be the mysterious naturist I glimpsed earlier, Cy. Nad must be right. Judging by his all-over tan, he doesn't spend a great deal of time fully clothed. Cy's hair is in kinda dirty blonde locks, falling over his face in long, sweaty tendrils. He has a neat, muscular body, smooth and relatively hairless. I should imagine that any hair that he does have is of the soft and downy variety. I notice his buttocks are rounded, but hard-looking. My own are beginning to ache, so I relax my squatting position so that my bum is resting on the ground. Each time he thrusts his cock into the girl's gaping mouth I see the muscles tighten under the skin. I wriggle, conscious of a spreading moistness. Shit, I don't want to stain Nad's dress (how would I explain that?), so I hike the skirt up over my thighs so my bare skin rests on the mossy earth. I can feel the moist, delicate tendrils just brushing my arse and my cunt.

Cy pulls his cock out of the girl's mouth and roughly pushes her round so that she is facing away from him, on her hands and knees. Nothing is said. He takes his cock in his hand and guides it between her buttocks, mounting her from behind. She winces slightly as she takes it fully up her and then they begin a slow, regular heaving. They're soon into a strong, vigorous rhythm, the girl working backwards against Cy's thrusts to take him fully inside herself. Automatically, I push downwards too and then jump as the cool, springy vegetation squishes into my fanny. Ohhh, don't want any creepy-crawlies in there! I reach down and brush myself with my right hand. My fanny lips feel all plump and open between the damp, curling hair.

This whole tableau thing is so strange and other-worldly. It's not like I'm really present, more like I'm watching myself in a dream. I feel a mystical empathy with that couple fornicating in their grove and, it's weird, I want to be part of it. I feel all earthy and hungry and animal. I realise my fingers have parted my lips and one has slipped in. I'm shocked at myself – I never do this to myself normally: somehow it feels sorta Alisonish – but I know I'm not gonna stop. Soon, I'm stroking across my clit with the same languorous rhythm that Cy is pushing his stunning dick in the girl's pussy. The harder the satyr shoves, the harder the fawn moans. The harder she moans, the harder I want to finger myself. The harder I rub it, the more deliciously engorged my clit becomes till it is plumped fully right out of my lips. I'm surprised and excited by how deliciously, dirtily big I am. I must be crazy, doing this to myself out in the open. I finger and feel and rub it more brutally, my eyes locked on to the guy's pelvis banging ferociously now against the girl's skinny arse, hungry for a glimpse of his slick, shiny cock each time he withdraws. Ohmygod, I'm panting. Go on, fuck her. Please. I'm nearly there now, fuck her hard. My thighs are doing the splits and I'm aware they're trembling violently. I know I've gotta shift my weight when, shit, a twig snaps.

The pumping figure slowly turns in my direction without missing a beat, his mouth turned up slightly on one side, giving his beautiful face a demonic, scary air. It's the same dark, angry look Paul had when we were playing the prostitute game. Cy seems to be looking straight at me angrily through half-closed eyes. Oh, fuck, can he see me? Me, alone in the wildwood, snooping on strangers' sex games while frantically frigging myself off. The same fear rush I felt when I was gaffered to the kitchen table and Paul entered me and I really wanted to let go sweeps through my belly to my cunt. My hand freezes just as Cy's legs begin to buckle and his body jerks and spasms as buckets full of his semen pump into the girl's puss. Oh, shit, if I hadn't stopped, I would have come at that very same moment, too.

I become aware of the sharp little stones digging into my knees and I move my weight to my bum. Surreptitiously, I brush away the dirt and gravel with a niggling sense of guilt at my voyeurism. I sit there, trying to control my breathing, watching as he slides out of the girl's cunt. She clambers round on her hands and knees to take it in her mouth, greedily sucking juice from the still erect cock. Then, when she has done, Cy turns on his heel and walks off without a word.

I stay hidden in my thicket, trying to figure out what was going on. It wasn't like the game me and Paul played, 'cos, when that ended, Paul went back to normal. I come to the conclusion that Cy just doesn't like the girl very much and, I'm ashamed to admit it, 'cos I know it is a total no-no and breaks every rule of sisterhood, the thought actually makes me smirk.

I sit there waiting for the girl to go but instead she walks over to my bush. She calls out, 'It's OK, you can come out now.' My face burns red as the dress. How did she know I was there? And, fucking hell, did she know what I was doing? There's no point just sitting stupidly in the middle of a bush, so I shuffle out and stagger to my feet, making a big deal of brushing dirt from Nad's dress, willing the flush to subside. (I mean it, I do *not* blush normally, but today . . .)

Anyway, she's taller than I imagined. I look up into her freckly face with its retroussé nose and smile sheepishly. She's annoying me. For someone who's bare-arse-naked and has just been witnessed fucking the fattest dick in the world, she seems remarkably unfazed. I feel obliged to offer some kind of explanation but, before I can say a thing, she goes, 'Hope we didn't embarrass you. You get used to no one being here. You know how it is.' Before I can say anything, she's turned her skinny back on me and starts jogging away. I call after her lamely. 'But I could be anybody.'

She stops and glances over her shoulder, smiling now. 'I'm not being funny or anything,' she says, 'but I don't need to know who you are.'

Aha! She wants to play it like that, does she? 'I could be a neighbour. The police,' I say darkly.

'I *know* who you are. One of Nad's girlfriends. You're wearing the red dress,' she shouts as she runs away though the dappled woodland light, Bambi-faun again.

I'm wearing *the* red dress? I watch ginger bint, who I have decided is a fucking werepig, run away from me and I have to struggle to suppress the urge to pick up a rock and hurl it at her head. I could kill Nad. No wonder she said nothing about my wearing it. She must give it to all of her shags to wear. Well, women shags, at least. What to do the men shags wear? I concentrate on the issue in hand. I'm not having this. I storm back to the house to demand that she take me back to London right now, this second.

By the time I find her, Nadine has quit with the shouty music and is sprawled out on a huge pile of cushions spread across the parquet floor of the main room, the French windows wide open to let in the afternoon sun. She just lies there, smoking a blunt and looking at me while I launch into a rant that begins with the dress and diverts via Ivan and my suspicion that Paul is screwing his producer in Cuba to the fact that I'm stuck in his flat and I'm lonely and I don't want to end up like Alison and I don't know what I'm doing with my life. My voice gets higher and higher until eventually I burst into tears. Ohmygod, what is happening to me?

Nadine gives me a big hug and sits me down, wipes my snotty nose and hands me the spliff. She strokes my hair and tells me everything will be all right. I whinge a bit more that everything will *not* be all right but Nad shushes me and tells me that, when I shut up, she will tell me exactly how everything will be all right. When I've stopped hiccupping enough, I lean against her while she begins.

On Monday we will go to Ivan's and retrieve our video from him. While there we will persuade him to direct a promo video of Nad doing her stuff, which I will produce. Nad will then get Celia to promote it, thus giving her exposure and me a calling card and a shared credit with a famous film director. By the time Paul gets back, I'll be the uberbabe producer of the hottest promo video in town. When I raise my eyebrows about all this, especially the Celia bit, Nad smirks. She carries on, 'Zita, trust me. Anyway, what have we got to lose?'

I lie on the floor and ponder Nadine's 'Everything Will Be All Right and We Will Rule the World' plan while I allow my handmaiden to minister unto me. Herb tea, spliff, massage of my shoulders. I am now stretched languorously out in the sun, the Dress scrunched up round my neck, while Nadine tickles my back. Hey, she's an adult. I've told her the score. I may be leading Nadine on a little, but this is a purely platonic massage I'm getting here. And it's a beautiful, mellow early-summer afternoon, the fading rays just kissing my naked skin, and everything is golden and ripe. I reprise that golden, muscular body bucking and arcing as Nature Boy spurted his seed into the fawn. It seems less dangerous now, more rude and earthy. Somehow, I wanna tell Nad how I've been a bit of a slut out there in the woods.

'Nad? Does anybody else live here?' I ask, rolling on my back. 'Anyone lanky and ginger?' I continue. Nad rolls her eyes 'Oh, you met bubblebrain Elaine. Some kid who hangs round Tanglebush. She's latched herself on to Cy, follows him about like a lost dog.' More a werepig, I think. But hey, I can see how this Tanglebush does kinda grow on you. I stretch my legs and wriggle my toes. Nadine is smiling. Oh fuck, just this once, I'll spoil her. I smile back indulgently and, allowing my thighs to fall apart, I dreamily watch Nadine's curly locks disappear between them.

6

Something very strange is happening to me. I have this bordering-on-the-hysterical feeling of being out of control. Could be the orgasms. Could be I'm morphing into a shag monster like Alison. Could be it's the weather, 'cos something very strange is happening there, too. It's hot. Not just very-pleasant-for-the-time-of-year hot, but hosepipe-ban-in-May/global-warming-warning/screaming-headlines hot. It's also Monday, and me and Nad are sitting in the traffic on the Euston Road. The Capri doesn't have even so much as a sunroof and, although we have the windows wound right down, we are both oiled with sweat. Could it be that the hysteria is actually carbon monoxide poisoning? Could be, or it could be that the unfamiliar hysterical feeling I have is in fact happiness. Yes, I know it's completely uncool, bizarre even. Think about it. When was the last time someone over seven said to you they feel really, really happy? Just doesn't happen. Or, maybe it happens to you all of the time and I just hang out with miserable fuckers. Whatever. Point is, I'm choking on fumes in a honking, squealing, bad-tempered line of London traffic and I feel a strange, otherworldly happiness. I've had a really good weekend and me and my best friend are now on our way to pitch a project at a famous film director. Cool.

It doesn't last, natch. After leaning on Ivan's doorbell, pounding on his door, throwing stones up at his windows and screaming his name long enough to have the Neighbourhood Watch get antsy, Nadine and I decide that Ivan either isn't home or, at least, isn't home to us. It was all a hallucination. This Ivan doesn't actually exist. The whole weekend has been a dream. I pinch myself. The happy stuff is wobbling.

Besides, a nagging voice is telling me I should be chasing that job at Big World Media. And then there's the little number that keeps saying maybe it was for real, maybe you did meet a famous film director, maybe you and your best mate did roll around on the floor for him, half naked, while he videoed you. And, if that vid exists, I really ought to get my hands on the tape this Ivan guy shot. Maybe I'm just a natural worrier, but I keep picturing the unlikely scenario of it becoming a hot chickflick porno tape, and somehow Saskia St John-Smythe seeing a copy and her braying, full volume, at all the crew I've ever worked with, 'Oh, my God, dahlings, that silly tart Zita! An even *bigger* slapper than Argh-Argh-Arghlison!' So I grumpily decide to wait a bit, case he shows up, while I listen to Nadine's plans for world domination via her music video.

Eventually I interrupt and ask, 'Nad, what exactly is this video for?'

Nad gives me a narrow lidded stare. 'What do you mean, what is it for?' She mimics my voice on the what-is-it-for part to make me sound all mimsy.

I'm getting irritated. I know about this stuff. 'Look, Nad, it's a reasonable question. You're talking about approaching an internationally renowned director to make a video of you. You should at least know why.'

Nadine kisses her teeth and goes all homegirly on me. 'You calling me a fool, fool?' Nadine's tone is ambiguous. She's prodding to see where I'm coming from.

I am in fact coming from bitch universe. I adopt

full-on Saskia St John-Smythe. 'I'm saying that you're talking about making a promotional video, a marketing tool. So you should at least fucking know what you're selling and who you're selling it to.' I guess this is why you should never sleep with your friends. With just-friends, you leave stuff unsaid or you say things in a nice way. With more-than-just-friends, things get different. Anyway, for me, at least, I can't see much point in beating round the bush with someone who's just had their face in it.

Nadine stands up and starts pacing. 'You know that mix I was working on yesterday?' I nod, assuming she is referring to the shouty music she was messing with most of the afternoon. 'My new mix, "Outlaws". Even if I say it myself, it's good. Fucking incredibly good. Why's it good? 'Cos I'm good. Now, how are people gonna know I'm good?' I squint up at her and shake my head vacantly. Nad's voice comes out fast. 'OK, I've gotta get gigs for that. I've got mix tapes which I send to people. Only thing is, on a mix tape they can't see that I am also fucking gorgeous. And anyway, how many people will hear me at a gig?' She doesn't give me a chance to answer. 'A couple of hundred, few thou at best. The world can't all see me live. So, I want a video. I know what I'm selling, Zita. I'm selling *me*. And I know who I'm selling to. Everybody.'

She glowers down at me, the sun slanting off the edge of her cheekbones and her tight little titties heaving in justified anger. I light a fag, nodding wisely. 'You're right about one thing.'

'What's that?' she asks suspiciously.

I blow a plume of smoke out, before smiling up at her. 'You are fucking gorgeous, Nad.'

She squats down in front of me, trying to suppress the smile I know is going to light up her face any moment now. 'Are you flirting with me?' she asks sternly. I don't need to answer because a big Russian-shaped shadow falls across us. We both look up and it is, indeed, Ivan. He has ditched the leather trousers and flowery shirt and is wearing a rather subdued T-shirt and cargoes. I think I preferred loud, proud Ivan to this.

'Hey, it's Gap Man!' says Nadine by way of greeting.

Ivan just looks at her balefully. 'Gapman? Who is this Gapman? Is he like Nowhere Man?'

Nadine and I look at each other. 'Nowhere man?' I mouth. Nadine rolls her eyes and says, 'The Beatles. It's a Russian thing. Don't worry.'

I worry about the wisdom of using a man who makes Beatles references to direct a video featuring Nadine and her wheels of steel but, once I've got the camera tape in my hot little fist, I really don't care whether we persuade Ivan to shoot Nad's video or not. Then I feel mean about my attitude. Nadine has been sweet to me all weekend, so I try to make it up to her by laying on the flirty dolly dyke routine with a trowel. I've junked the red dress in favour of my animal-print bikini top (quite practical in this weather, apart from my back sticking to the vinyl of the Capri's bucket seats) combined with a dance-hall queen micro-mini borrowed from Nadine. I surreptitiously pinch my nipples and take care that I'm hunkered up close enough to Nad for my now rather obviously pointy bits to be prodding firmly into her upper arms. Ivan is nodding sagely at my cleavage while Nad gives him the bones of the proposal. I make sure that I drag my tit tips back and forth several times across her bare skin.

It works, in that we manage to persuade Ivan to come and have a drink with us. We shoehorn him into the back of the Capri, drive around a bit, and when he starts pleading to get out, settle down on some rickety wooden benches outside a café in Shoreditch and set about trying to rekindle Ivan's fire. But at first he just sits there, looking all grey and being a total Eeyore. 'Why do you want me? I am a has-been!' Et cetera, et cetera. I realise this is gonna take a rather more sophisticated deployment of the Nadine/Zita Dyke Love Show.

Now, though we have actually done this a million times, in all the previous million minus one times, I wasn't actually shagging with Nad. So, perhaps on this occasion, the performance has a little more veracity than usual. Nad and me are sitting together on the bench, me with my left leg flopped over her right. Nad is playfully scratching my inner thigh, just running a fingernail under the hem of my, or rather her, skirt, while initially she does most of the talking. I can feel little goosebumps starting to form on the skin. There seems to be a direct connection between the nerve endings there and my breasts, because their tips have gone all puckered and sensitive again without even so much as a tweak this time.

The traffic thunders past on the Shoreditch Gyratory while I'm feeling all languorous and woozy. It half annoys me. Nadine seems to know exactly how to hit the spot every time and doesn't seem to mind exploiting it. I mean, I know *she*'s a bi-girl but I think it's a bit of a cheek to assume I am, just on the back of a casual weekend fling. But, as I'm committed to helping her hook Ivan into this project, I guess it's going to be go-with-the-flow time yet again. I twist my ankle round the back of Nad's shin and lean back on my arms, my tits thrusting proudly out towards the world in general and a group of young, bare-chested workmen laying a cable on the other side of Curtain Street in particular. Then I join the pitch. It's a slow burn. I can feel the skin between my fanny and my arse begin to tighten as Nadine's nails continue to scratch while I contemplate the workies' denim-wrapped bums and try to concentrate on what I'm saying.

My spiel is getting increasingly breathless as I'm telling him that we have a wild location (Tanglebush Towers) and an art director (thinking, of course, of Cy). I hear Ivan's interest first smoulder, then glow, until, suddenly, whoof: he ignites and goes all incendiary. He starts rattling out a stream of fabulous ideas. I note that he has an alarming tendency towards the grandiose but figure that, for the time being at least, it's just important to give his imagination head. Besides, it's infectious.

Nadine has stopped the fingerwork and is listening intently. 'You'll do it, then?' she asks.

He shrugs. 'Maybe possibly.'

Fuck me, that is as good as a 'Yes.' My out-of-control happy feeling returns. I dive straight in and pin him down with a date to come to Tanglebush and see for himself. Wow, Nadine was right. I am a producer.

Nad drives me back to Camberwell, singing her funky version of 'Let the Sun Shine In' at the top of her voice and, high with our joint success, we're alternately ranting and giggling deliriously. When we get to the flat, my unfinished CV is still up on the computer screen. I quickly type the *Outlaws* project into it. I figure Ivan Punin's name there isn't gonna hurt. I check my email. Nothing from Paul. The place feels sorta dusty and lifeless, so I don't object when Nadine throws open the blinds, still singing her stupid song, and does indeed let the sun shine in. She throws her arms up, and, backlit, she dances into the kitchen, her hair standing out in the light like a fuzzy halo. She flings open the Smeg door and continues her dance routine, fridge lit and bathed in clouds, like the opening credits to a Bond movie. It's only when the fridge starts making alarming gurgling sounds that I giggle. 'Nad, no fridge dancing! It's against house rules.'

She turns to me. 'Yours or Paul's?'

She kicks the fridge door shut, clutching a coupla Bacardi breezers. 'House rules? I don't understand why you put up with that stuff.' There's a silence while we swig our drinks, then Nadine adds, 'Seriously, Zeet. Why are you stuck here while Paul's on holiday?' I murmur something about it ain't a holiday, it's work but Nadine sits up and goes, 'Work, holiday, it's Cuba. Look, why don't you move into Tanglebush while he's away? You can have a break, too.' I'm sort of 'well, maybe-ing' in an 'I-don't-think-so-really' way when she puts her face in mine and wheedles, 'C'mon, Zeet. You don't have to fuck me all the time.'

I feel a blush creeping up my neck and hold the bottle to my cheeks to cool them. 'It's not that,' I stammer. Nad laughs and pokes me in the ribs and goes, 'Why not, then? There's loadsa room. You can have the attic.'

I'm still not convinced. 'Nad, I'm a city girl. Tanglebush is the wilds.'

Nadine starts laughing 'You're not being sent into exile. You *can* come back to London, you know.'

While Nad goes on about how much of a laugh we'd have/how it would be easier to co-ordinate *Outlaws* on location/how I could get a great tan and have some space to myself, I turn the idea over. Hmmm, no email from Paul, no voice mail, either. So, Paul's busy. Well, I can be, too. Just as I finally agree that maybe it's not a bad idea, Nad springs up off the couch. 'God, Zeet. It's stuffy in here. Wanna take a shower?' I choke on my breezer and while I'm spluttering, Nadine stands up and wriggles out of her own scanty clothing. She bats her eyes coquettishly at me. 'Well?'

I'm all flustered. I mean, the weekend has been a lot of fun and Nadine has been extremely sweet and attentive but the workies have reminded me of what I'm supposed to be missing as well. How do I remind my best friend, who has only recently given me a particularly satisfying orgasm (well, two, actually), that I'm definitely heterosexual? If I'm gonna move into Tanglebush for a time, I'd better sort this out now. I don't want there to be any weirdness between us. Nadine's fun and I'm just getting used to hanging with her again and I don't want to fall out and end up with another six months of no contact. And, I've realised, there's no way I want to spend the next ten weeks moping around in Camberwell on my own. So, I try to clear the air.

I tell her that, if me and Nad are going to work together, then we'll have to curb the dykish conjugality for the moment. That I have to be fair to her, because, after all, I'm really not that way. She stretches her neat, coffee-coloured body luxuriously out on the couch, and says, 'Yeah, yeah.' I detect something distinctly sniffy in there, so I explain to her it might be tough for her, but she'll thank me for it in the long run. She starts laughing.

I know what she's doing. I've seen enough daytime telly to recognise denial so I nod and smile back laconically. She sniggers, 'Man, I'd forgotten how incredibly fucking *repressed* you are, Zita!' Hey? First, I was naïve, now, I'm repressed? The bitchfest proper starts here. It goes something like this:

'Jeez, Zeet. As soon as you're back within Paul's influence, you do one!'

'Like one what?'

'You get all inhibited. Repressed.'

'What d'you mean?'

'We fucked, that's all, we had some fun. Leastways, I did. I thought you did, too. Mind, you can never be quite sure about Zita having fun in bed.'

'Now hold on, Nadine . . .'

'Look, we took our clothes off and had a good time together. You wanna do it again and I'm in the mood too, fine. You don't wanna do it again, that's fine too. No big deal.'

'What's all this got to do with Paul?'

'I'm not a control freak. You can do what you like.'

'Paul's not a control freak!'

'You start seeing Paul, you drop me like a stone. The moment he fucks off, you're on the phone to me again. I could have told you to fuck off. But I didn't 'cos I like you. I shagged you 'cos you looked kinda sweet and like you needed it. OK, I wanted it too. But Zita, I hate to break this to you . . . [Snigger, snigger.] You are my friend but you ain't the most fantastic lay in the world and I won't throw myself off a bridge if we don't ever do it again . . .'

'Excuse me? I was just suggesting we keep a proper professional distance.'

'Like I said, Zita. Repressed.'

Nadine is, of course, talking bollocks but I realise retaliation will just result in all-out war, so I bite my tongue and let her carry on. She even says that, when we had the fight in Ivan's, I was enjoying it and I was turned on, but that I'm frightened of losing control. I make myself laugh at that one, even though I am fucking furious. I told you nothing good comes from sleeping with your friends. I say, in a somewhat friendlier tone than I feel, 'Look Nadine. It's OK if you're pissed off with me. I just happen to think it's unfair of me to lead you on or anything.'

I know that hits home 'cos Nadine goes, 'Aha . . .'

So, in case she hasn't understood, I add, 'You know, with me not being bi?'

She goes, 'Aha . . .' again and continues to make 'Aha' sounds at pertinent intervals throughout my little speech about not wanting to spoil our friendship until, in the end all of the Ahas join up into an Hah-hah-hah-hah and I realise that she's laughing. And not just tee-heeing: it's great-deal-of-hilarity laughing. She's rolled off the couch and is squirming around the floor.

I'm, like, 'Nadine, I'm being serious.'

She staggers upright, wiping her eyes where her mascara has run, and says, 'C'm'ere, babe,' and yanks me towards her. Then, she plants a big kiss on me. 'Look, thanks, Zita. Thanks for everything: Ivan, the project. You're my friend. I mean it. Just ease off on how irresistible you are, OK?' she adds, looking deep into my eyes, before adding, 'Hey, wanna take that shower?' Just as my jaw drops, she gives me an old-fashioned look. 'I mean, to freshen up.'

Well, OK, I am kinda sweaty and so I allow Nadine to lead me into the shower, where she washes me and herself without once taking advantage of our shared nakedness, even though it's a bit of a squash in the shower cubicle. My nips, being pressed up against Nad's rather pert little opposites, annoy me by tightening, completely of their own accord, and then my thighs accidentally part a little while she is soaping my pubes. Nadine gives me that old-fashioned look once again and tuts and, completely unnecessarily, reminds me I'm not bi. Then she takes one of Paul's massive bath towels and begins patting me dry. I close my eyes. It's like being licked by a kitten. My skin tingles and I feel the bit between my holes begin to tighten again, just like when Nadine's nails scratched my thighs in Shoreditch.

Shit, she's doing all this simply to make a point, I know. Well, she's wrong. It doesn't make me repressed just because I agree with Paul and not her and she ain't gonna prove otherwise. And just 'cos I let her be affectionate towards me the once (OK, twice) doesn't make me bi, either. You can't just go round doing whatever you feel like. You need structure in life. There are rules. Not convinced? I got just one more word to say on the matter. *Alison.* It's a matter of self-control. I clench my cunt muscles tight but this only makes me realise that there's a bothersome level of creaminess down there. Nad continues to dry me with kitten-tongue intensity until my legs begin to shake and I have to lean on her shoulder for support. By the time I'm dry, I'm beginning to feel like a rung-out rag. If Nadine was just to . . . But she simply hugs me and gives me another, very chaste, kiss.

'Zita, you gotta be what you gotta be, babe. Whatever you gotta be, it's OK by me, as long as it's true to your real self. I'm glad you're going to stay at Tanglebush awhile. Make use of the attic for as long as you want.' I nod OK rather seriously. Temporarily, for some reason, I'm finding it difficult to speak.

After we're dressed in silence, Nadine asks me if I'm going back with her. But Paul's cute little yellow MGB Roadster is mouldering all alone in her garage. I figure she deserves a holiday in the country too. I grab some essentials and dig out the car keys, stuff the MGB with bin bags full of clothes and bedding and head off back to Tanglebush while Nadine goes to Brixton in her Capri to swap money for vinyl. As we part, she grabs me and gives me a big smudgy lipsticky kiss and I swear I hear her muttering 'clit tease' under her breath. But it's OK, we're friends again.

I'd forgotten how near to the ground a Roadster is. It's like a motorised skateboard. I've got the top down and Nadine's skirt has ridden up so that the sun is making my thighs itch. I'm waiting at the lights by Vauxhall Bridge, staring down and assessing the damage, when I get the distinct impression that I'm being watched. I look over to my left, right into a set of Skania wheel nuts. Ah, lorry drivers, my favourite. I remember I'm not wearing knickers. I raise my gaze into the driver's leering face and smile demurely. Then I slide my bum forward to give him a sustained flash of bush. Just as the lights change. Mr Macho stalls his truck while I roar off whooping. Brilliant. Forty-eight hours with Nadine and I'm Riot Grrrl! Yep, could be a long hot summer!

Alone in Tanglebush, I have a snoop. I discover the attic. It's massive and airy and clean, and empty but for a double mattress and an old Lloyd Loom wicker chair. The ceiling kinda slopes down at the edges but that doesn't matter 'cos the rooms are so big. In the corner of the main one is a sort of glazed turret affair that is almost large enough to qualify as a room in its own right. It's certainly big enough to take the mattress. I think it will be kinda neat sitting up here with a bird's-eye view of the Tanglebush estate, so I drag the mattress into it and throw open the windows to let in the air. A lot of the view is obscured by an enormous tree with branches that extend almost up to the window. It's so cool, sitting on my mattress listening to the leaves swishing in the breeze, like being in a tree house or something.

OK, enough whimsy for now. Back to basics. There's an *en-suite* bathroom with an antique shower and a huge, ancient toilet on a plinth that really qualifies for the word 'throne'. The shower clonks and grumbles, but eventually spurts water. This'll do nicely. It crosses my mind that Nadine has a point. After all those months of cohabitation, maybe I could use my own space. Feeling like an excited eight-year-old, I stake out my new den, do homey stuff like unpacking, throw a sheet over the mattress and other stuff. When I'm done, I'm so hot and dusty, I have to have a shower. Afterwards, I don't dry myself, but let the moisture evaporate off my naked body into the warm, dry air. I think I'll stay undressed, for the time being. After all, it's the style here, isn't it?

I sprawl out on my bed and 'txt msg' Paul. I know it's juvenile but I don't have a WAP phone and I daren't mess with Nadine's computer, 'cos she uses it for her music. And anyhow, I think text messaging's kinda sweet. 'P. GT GR8 NU POP VID JOB! FMOS DRCTR!! ME PRDCR!!! MS U. LUV Z.' There. It's like having a teen romance. I decide against mentioning I'm saying at Nad's. Or that I've borrowed his car. Stuff, quite frankly, he doesn't need to know about. He'd only worry needlessly. And he's busy enough without me selfishly causing him any unnecessary concern.

Work over, I stretch out and take in the view of the crowns of distant trees waving against the fading light of dusk. Hey, this is a lot less claustrophobic than Camberwell. I relax and think about my day. It's been quite a full one. Euston Road and the flirty little act in Shoreditch and the workies and the lorry driver and Nadine's kitten-tongue drying technique after the shower. The combination of memories all seem to have reactivated those languorous, post-pill sensations that were swirling around earlier on. My fingers idly wander south and, before I even think about it, they've parted my pussy lips and I'm stroking my own kitty.

She purrs in appreciation. I don't normally do this but I'm kinda irritated by what Nadine said about my being too controlled. Where did she got that from? Me, Zita, uptight? I spread my thighs and show my cunt to the sun setting slowly over Tanglebush Towers, one finger lazily circling my clit. Then I slip a finger down and rub it over that little patch of skin between my holes, the bit that has been causing me bother all day. It contracts, bringing the bud of my arsehole invitingly up towards my finger. It's moist with pussy juice streaming down from my cunt.

I'm half-consciously teasing round my arse when my hole opens like a blossom. Oh, God, this is rude. I stop. Then I hear Nadine lecturing me again and I let the tip of my finger slide right in and the muscle immediately contracts around it. I lie back and rest my feet on the window ledges and finger my orifices lazily with one hand while I vibrate my rather tense clit with the other. Fuck, this is good. I enjoy picturing myself, lying here, languidly fingering myself for what seems like hours, enjoying the soft swish of the leaves and the ache radiating slowly out from my groin until my whole body is swooning sluttishly and I'm shamelessly panting and pushing and bucking my hips at the emerging stars and I allow myself a gorgeous, private orgasm.

Somewhere, a nearby owl offers a celebratory hoot in response to my own low moan. Mmmn, maybe I can go feral too?

7

I've never been the outdoorsy type. All that wilderness. Anything buzzing within twenty feet of me normally has me grabbing for the nearest thing toxic and ozone-depleting in a spraycan. Well, that was the old me. The new me is lying flat on my belly on the used-to-be-lawn bit of garden in front of the French windows, watching some feely-boppered insect thing climb up a blade of grass, sniff the air, then climb back down again. Normally I'd be screaming 'Kill the roach!' and reaching for that can. Now, I'm quietly contemplating the little beastie. I almost think it's cute. As long as it doesn't suddenly take wing, or anything. See, how country is that? And my tan is coming along nicely. Which shows that we've done fuck all about the promo.

I've hardly seen Nadine for days and I'm starting to brood about that application for *Massive* still stuck to the Smeg. I'm just thinking maybe I'll just chill here for a bit longer, then go back home and deal with business, when something starts buzzing underneath me. Fortunately, I realise it's my phone before I stomp on it. It's Nadine saying that she's hooked up with Ivan and she's on the way back with him now. Yeah, right. She says jump and I'm supposed to go, 'How high?' It'll take more than that to panic me into action. Then, when I check the rest of my messages, I find this little number from Paul.

'SEXY PRDCR LADY! SUCCESSFUL WOMEN MAKE ME SO-O HORNY!!! SUBMITTED THE BWM APPLN YET?'

Fuck, I'd forgotten I told Paul about the project – and what's with the message? Paul just doesn't do playful innuendo. A thought bubble floats into my brain. What if someone else sent this message? Someone else who had access to his phone? Someone like Ms Saskia St John-Fuckbag-Smythe? Pop, the bubble bursts and I'm covered in shit. Shitty shit shit. Paul's bound to have told her and, if that woman's got the slightest inkling of the project, then I've really got no choice. I'll have to do it. The prospect of her gloating and telling people I'm flaky, that I don't deliver, is beyond contemplation. Reluctantly, I recognise it's time to pull a digit out. I glance over at the stables. Guess maybe I might just check out the possibility of getting me an art director.

I stand just inside the door blinking and getting used to the darkness. It's kinda spooky in here. After a minute or so, I'm able to make out that the skeletal shapes hanging from the roof beams are, in fact, old bike frames and what looks like a giant rusty screw is presumably part of some antique farming tool. In the dim, dusty light I can see huge canvases propped up along the far wall. They all look pretty abstract to me except that, when I squint a bit, the squiggles start to resemble dancing figures. I take my shades off. Duh! And take a few more steps into the heart of darkness. 'Hallo?' I shout. No answer, so I walk closer. Suddenly, one of the dancing figures jumps out at me. I scream. The dancing figure screams back. Or, rather, squeals.

Now, did I explain what a werepig is? I don't believe I did. It's very straightforward. You know the way werewolves are people who once were wolves? Giveaways being eyebrows that meet in the middle and a propensity for howling at the full moon. Well, it's exactly the same deal with werepigs, except they're people who were pigs. Identifying features include snouty noses, pinkish skin and a tendency to grow trotters and snuffle at the sky come midnight. This one has tried to disguise itself by covering itself in emulsion paint and masquerading as a work of art, but werepig it most definitely is. When my heart slows to a less troublesome pace, I say, 'Elaine. Your mind is not your best feature, is it?'

She laughs, one of those rising-scale tinkly laughs, and bats paint-clogged lashes at me. 'Oh, I get it. You're trying to insult me. Right?' I laugh back, 'Hah-hahhahhahhah,' carefully getting the rising inflection too, then add flatly, 'Elaine, am I trying?' But she's no longer paying attention. She's turned away from me and is bent over, stirring something in a very witchy way. I ask what she is doing and she just smiles and beckons me to come and see. Jesus, this girl takes winsome to extremes.

I take an exaggerated just-humouring-you stride towards her and raise an eyebrow expectantly. Next thing, I'm standing in a fast-growing pool of blue gunk. Fast-growing because it is glooping between my tits, cascading over my belly and funnelling down between my legs. '*Hahhhh!*' I gasp, looking down at my ex-leopardskin bikini. 'This had better be water-soluble!'

Elaine shrugs bony, paint-spattered shoulders at me. 'Can't see why you bothered wearing it. Nobody else round here's a prude ...' Now I'm a vain, naïve, repressed prude. What *is* this? Deconstructing Zita Week? For the record, I sunbathe in my bikini not because I am a prude but because I *like* having white bits. Any floozy with a sun bed can have an all-over tan. I open my mouth to say this but nothing comes out. How do you start with a weirdo airhead who has just tipped a bucket of blue paint over your favourite sunwear and then called you a prude?

'C'mon, quick. Lie down and press yourself on to the canvas.' A voice wafts from somewhere up among the farmyard implements. 'Before it dries.' I'm trying to pinpoint its source among the roof beams when Elaine grabs me. She shoves me on to a white canvas laid out on the floor I hadn't previously noticed. I, of course, shove back but slip on the paint and end up on all fours. Elaine is laughing like a maniac at this point. She grabs my arse and tries to shove me down flat, but I go straight into martial-arts mode (those two weeks before I dropped out of the self-defence class at Hammersmith Community College were not wasted). I wriggle round to face her but her fingers are still snatching to get a grip on my hips. She grabs the elasticated thong of my briefs, which stretch and stretch till, inevitably, they snap.

This is the point when Nadine and Ivan arrive. They discover us doing the all-female, all-kickin', all-screamin', paint-wrasslin' tag-team routine. Oh, yeah. I am still partly clothed in my poor ruined bikini top, but Elaine is apparently following local custom and practice. A coating of crusty paint aside, she is nude. So, we are doing the bare-arsed-naked-ladies kickin', screamin', and wrasslin' routine. That old number. And there was me, worrying about Nadine saying I was repressed. 'Hi, guys,' I say, as nonchalantly as possible, then launch into damage limitation. 'Ivan, meet Elaine. Elaine, Ivan. You and Nadine know each other, right? OK, high concept. The raw tribal primitivism of dance culture . . .'

I think, under the circumstances, I give a pretty good spiel. I'm banking on appealing to the Ken Russell within Ivan's psyche. He loves it, which is the most important thing. I studiously avoid catching Nadine's eye throughout my entire pitch but I think the situation is so incomprehensible to her that even she half buys my explanation that we were working out an idea for the video. I wave in the general direction of the roof beams. 'Cy, *the art director*, wanted to try ... something ... small crew ... all have to do it together kinda thing. And here we are trying ... it.'

Nadine gives me a go-on look and asks, 'And *it* is?'

I beam at her. 'You do your stuff, and all around you, nude painted people go wild!'

I nod at Elaine and call, 'Thanks, Cy. Speak to you later,' up into the roof void ('cos I know he's lurking up there, somewhere). Then I tell Ivan and Nadine breezily that I'm going to take a shower. I suggest Nadine give Ivan the guided tour and arrange to meet them in half an hour on the verandah. Fuck, I am so good under pressure.

When I catch up with Nad and Ivan, I'm still so speedy, I go for it. I don't feel self-conscious any more. Being dressed helps but, once someone has seen you naked and covered in paint, it kinda loosens your inhibitions. I take a deep breath and dive in. I tell Ivan how much I loved *Eva Baby* (total lies, I've never seen the movie) and how I think working low-budget will suit his style and how he'll have total artistic control with it being such a small crew and everything. It'll be like a party. It'll be a rave, a ...

Ivan, who has been staring kind of moodily into the garden, holds up his hand. 'Zita, OK. Stop. I will do this.'

I struggle to curb the incredulousness in my voice. 'You'll do it. Just like that?'

He gets to his feet and starts pacing up and down the verandah, his eyes looking out beyond the horizon. 'Yes. Fire. Dawn light. Sacrifice. I will do it. Nadine is an inspiring artiste. This is a great location. We can do it. We will have ... *fun!*'

I'm a little concerned about some of the more grandiose aspects of Ivan's vision. At one point, he describes what sounds like a heavy-metal Viking rape-'n'-pillage flick. I gently point out budget constraints and we manage a compromise. It will be more your pagan, animalistic, sacrificial, handheld camera, arthouse flick. Oh, and he wants nudity. Lots of nudity. He actually liked the 'living paintings' bullshit I came out with. Well, there's directors for you.

So I'm a producer. A *real* producer. Now all I've got to do is persuade Cy that *he* is the art director, build a set, borrow some lights, sort out the music playback, lay on some catering, recruit a crew and assemble a cast, all of whom have to be persuaded to appear on screen naked. By next week. Easy.

Partly as a salve to Nadine and partly in an attempt to begin the crew and cast part of my mission, I accompany Nadine to another gig. (I'm saving the Cy part for later.) Between us, we manage to snare three ex-girlfriends of Nad, a coterie of resting actors, and an assortment of moshers from north London. Piece of piss, really. Me and Nad just stand at the edge of the dance floor and stare, hard. Whenever anyone comes over and asks what we're looking at, we smirk, 'Oh, just imagining you back at ours, naked and covered with paint.' It's a fantastic chat-up line – try it sometime. Anyway, suffice to say the ones that are up for it are in.

When we get back to Tanglebush, I tell Nad that I want to do some producery-planny things and, instead of going into the house with her, I do a lap of the gardens. She just shrugs and gets off. Really, I don't want to get into any me-proving-I'm-not-repressed-thing (of course, I'm not). I also want to avoid any embarrassing parting-outside-the-bedroom-door stuff, so I'm giving her a head start before I crash myself. It's inky black out here but that's one of the country things that are beginning to grow on me. The dark here makes everything soft and mysterious. It's almost intoxicating. It's also still incredibly warm, too, and, as I walk, I begin to notice that I am feeling somewhat chafed: the original seventies hot-pants ensemble I am wearing, though funky in the extreme, is made of something akin to Nylon (no wick-away fabrics then). At first, I start pulling at the shorts where they have ridden up the crack of my arse, thinking I'd better go indoors and take them off. But I think the night is so beautiful, somehow, I don't want to waste it by going inside. It strikes me, what the fuck?

I strip slowly, enjoying the sense of peeling off the layers, and stand in the dark, quite pleased with myself. There's no threat, just a sense of security and oneness. The balmy night air is like velvet on my flesh. I even catch myself sniffing it. There's an earthy green smell which I'm not totally sure I like and I'm trying to figure out what it is when something goes *wooh*. Fuck, a creature flaps silently down the old lawn and glides away into the blackness. Hey, only that owl. I relax and walk around a bit, enjoying the warm night air on my skin and the feeling of being all elfin and natural. I even prance about a bit on the lawn like a naked Tinkerbelle. I can be Nature Girl and shed my inhibitions, too. Not that I *am* inhibited, mind, but Camberwell does seem to be full of a lot of dos and don'ts, I admit. I'm beginning to get into Tanglebush. Somehow, out here, so far away from people, normal rules are kinda suspended. You could go a little wild here, I reckon. Not mad or angry or anything. Just . . . feral. I surface from my reverie to find myself standing outside the stable block. From within it, I note, a faint light doth glimmer.

There's the dull murmur of conversation, too. I listen carefully. I can hear Cy's husky voice and Elaine's tinkling laugh but there seem to be other people as well. I'm curious what Cy might be up to at this time of night. I've also not forgotten I've still got to sort out the details of his being the art director on the shoot. Fine points like his agreeing to do it. I'm actually turning the big, old-fashioned latch on the door when I remember I am *au naturel*, a nymph without her clothes. I replace the latch, intending to retrace my steps and retrieve my clothes from the bushes, where I so wantonly and imprudently dumped them a few minutes ago. Unfortunately, the latch is some ancient, rusty original that squeaks and groans like a sick cow as it drops back into place.

Everything freezes. The conversation inside ceases immediately. Next moment, there is the soft pad of bare feet, the door swings wide and the situation is flooded with light from the kerosene lamps inside. About half a dozen fully clothed strangers turn and stare at me.

Whatd'ya do in this kind of scenario? I am referring, of course, to the calling-round-on-your-neighbours-stark-naked-in-the-middle-of-the-night scenario. My arms instinctively creep over my tits and bush in the classic suddenly-all-my clothes-fell-off pose. That instantly annoys me. I've already been called a prude once this week, and that's enough. Instinctively, I know the only solution is to brazen this one out. Oh, fuck. I drop my arms and stride in nonchalantly, displaying my white bits with pride, saying bouncily, and probably somewhat louder than need be, 'Hi, Cy. Just called round to see how the painting's getting along.'

OK, now this may not be the cleverest response in the world, but can you think of a better one? My entrance is greeted with a stunned and very complete silence. After a million-year-long pause, Cy eventually drawls, in a suspiciously posh voice, 'I don't believe everyone's been introduced.' He gives me a look that I can best describe as haughtily amused condescension. His dinner guests' eyes are playing a tennis match, ping-ponging wildly between admiring wonderment at my nakedness and a curious appraisal of his sang-froid. Or is it the other way round? Either way, I get a definite flutter when they look at me.

I remember Nadine's reference to the Cy fan club and it occurs to me that there may be the slightest implication that here stands yet another member. 'Oh, I was round at Cy's the other night and, y'know, *another* naked woman called round.' I can see it there on everyone's face, Cy's included. Perhaps this arrogant bastard simply *expects* women to fall at his feet in wondrous admiration. Perhaps he's become too used to dealing with the Elaines of this world.

Well, fuck him. I really have had about all I can take of the insufferably smug occupants of this fucking house. A spark of indignation ignites inside me, galvanising me into action. Well, that, and holy terror. I decide to seize the initiative. Let me remind you, I am not a prude. I do not have a body-image problem. In fact, I quite like being looked at. But, if I'm going to display myself, I shall do it with verve and style. So I stand there and adopt a laconically challenging, hand-on-hip pose. One that says you are fucking with the wrong gal here. I just need some gum to chew to complete the effect.

After a further prolonged silence, I snort cynically and stalk blithely past the slack-jawed contingent towards the dark, unlit rear of the studio. 'That work we were doing? I can see where it's gotta go now,' I drawl back. 'Oh, don't mind me, dahlings.' See, I can do dismissive with the best of them. Like I do bluffing, too.

I leave them all pondering that last little statement and rootle purposefully among the assorted paintings until I manage to locate what I think is the canvas I was rolled upon earlier. I drag it out, with some difficulty, then indulge in a bit of walking round it making appraising umm-hmmn noises. Without even looking, I know that I have the undivided attention of the dinner party. A good deal of it focused on my arse, I suspect, but it's in good enough shape to take the heat. I shake my head and drag out several more canvases for good measure and shout dramatically 'No, no, no. Still not working.' I can feel Cy's eyes burning into my back. I walk over to where Elaine had been stirring the paint and find the multicoloured stack of household emulsion. I squat down and begin prising lids randomly off the pots.

I am saved having to make a decision about ruining what may, or for that matter may not, be an incredible work of art by one of Cy's acolytes piping up with, 'Wow, Cy. Didn't know there was a whole school of Automatism at Tanglebush.' Oh, so that's what it is. Cy cracks before I do and walks over to confront me. He tries to take the can of paint away but I hold firm. We stare at each other, eyeball to eyeball. I breathe in and very, very subtly arch my back so that my breasts swell imperceptibly towards him. The impact is bolstered by the fact that it's actually much cooler in the stable block than outside and my nips are impressively tight and bulletlike. But he continues to look me in the eyes without so much as a blink and I'm wondering exactly whose bluff is gonna be called. Then, just as I feel my own determination start to waver and panic rise within me, Cy concedes defeat. His eyes wobble, then flick down to my tits, and he swallows before returning to look me in the face. There's a moment hanging between us. I feel a frozen smile on my face and a hot flush in my fanny. I think I might have temporarily lost the power of speech again. Fortunately, Cy mumbles first, 'Yeah, Zita here has been helping me with a project.'

Aha! He knows my name. Which means that he has been interested enough to find it out. And has just admitted so in front of witnesses, which means indisputably that I win this one. I decide to go for it. I turn back to the gawping throng and sashay across to them. 'Yeah,' I concur, adopting a suitably artistic stance (sorta bohemian-uninhibited in the if-you've-got-it-flaunt-it style). Then the killer. I say, 'Cy's art-directing this music promo I'm producing, so I said I'd help him with the odd canvas. Y'know, my creativity in exchange for his, sorta thing?' There is a general rustle of interest from the dinner party. I walk back to Cy, adding, 'Yeah, the concept involves paintings coming to life. Video automatism. It's a natural extension of the work being done here.'

Cy raises his eyebrows at me and one of the dinner party ensemble (a guy who looks uncannily like Salvador Dali) goes, 'Promo? Cool. Hey, we're, umm, performance artists, y'know. D'you think there's any way *we* could get involved?'

I pause and look at the ground like I'm thinking real hard. In actual fact, I'm pondering the stunning totality of my victory. Amazing what you can achieve under the influence of blind panic. I smile insouciantly at Cy, then turn back to the hopeful faces of the performance artists. I nod thoughtfully. 'You know, maybe you can. Most of the concept's in place now but performance art ... I'll talk to the director – he's the guy that did *Eva Baby*, y'know? – and I think he'll be cool about your involvement. There's a lot of nudity, but –' I shrug my shoulders '– that's the house style.' The guys look pretty pleased about that aspect, so I close the deal quickly. 'OK, consider it sorted. I'll liaise via Cy, shall I?'

Finally, my masterstroke. I carefully pour the contents of the paint pot over myself and press myself down on to the canvas over the top of the somewhat blurry outlines that are there already. The squidgy emulsion actually feels rather sensuous on my skin and I wriggle about and stick my arse in the air for added effect, aware that I'm giving the assembly a rather gynaecological view of my crack. I don't care. Amazingly, I feel completely in control and I've almost enjoyed the whole exhibitionist experience. My God, is that uninhibited or what? Maybe I'd better cool this now. I stand up, step back and say critically, *That's better.'* Then to Cy, who's as gob-smacked as the rest of them, I add, 'Production meeting, main house, eleven o'clock tomorrow?' Dripping paint, I coolly exit past the completely overawed performance artists.

This feral stuff is easy-peasy. Game, set and match to me, I think?

8

'I'm so-o hot. My crop-top's stuck to my tits, it's so moist and sticky. My nipples have got all tender and hard from rubbing against it, I think I'll have to ... take it ... off. Ohh, that's better. I bet you're hot, too.' There's a grunting noise on the other end of the phone. 'Paul? Sorry, can't hear you.' I drop my voice to a whisper. Paul comes back gruff and distant. 'Um, yes, I'm hot.'

I stifle a giggle. 'My shorts are making me itchy, Paul, they're so sweaty. Shit, I've really gotta scratch that itch. I'm gonna have to ... loosen ... the waist-band and stick my hand down there. Ooh, God! That feels better. Oh, my fingers are all sticky now! I'll have to lick them. I'm licking them now. Where are your fingers, Paul?' I listen to the heavy breathing on the other end of the line, then lower my voice, making it catch in my throat. 'Are they round your cock? Are you stroking it with your fingers? Is it all swollen and sticky at the end? My cunt's sticky, Paul. My cunt's wet and slippy and it's –'

I switch my phone off and smile wickedly at Cy. He continues sawing his length of two-by-four until a section clunks to the ground. 'Well?' I ask. He picks up the wood and adds it to the pile of timber I have just watched him spend the best part of an hour sawing up.

'Well what?' he replies.

'Oh, fuck off, Cy,' I snap impatiently. 'You know perfectly well what.'

Cy stretches, giving me ample opportunity to admire his taut abdominal muscles and his narrow waist and his neat, firm pecs glistening with sweat. He reaches for the bottle of water propped up in the shade before replying, 'Doesn't count.'

I push myself off the half-constructed timber frame I'm perched on and demand indignantly, 'Whatdyah mean, doesn't count?' Cy doesn't answer, just takes a swig of water from the bottle. He holds the water in his mouth and walks towards me, his face expressionless. I start backing away looking around for a weapon. 'You better not be thinking of spitting that over me, Cy . . .'

Oops, I'm getting ahead of myself. I should explain. Preproduction has started with a vengeance and I'm telling ya, everything is gone mad. Nadine is working on the *Outlaws* mix full blast day and night so that I get no sleep and then, when I cannot get out of bed in the morning, she wakes me to moan about how she needs more material and disappears off to some obscure import record shack, leaving me knackered and exhausted to sort out the logistics for this nightmare of a shoot. Ivan phones me every hour, on the hour, to elaborate his ridiculous, mad, impossibly extravagant ideas and to inform me of the latest additions to his wants list. The performance artists have also taken over the shoot catering and keep bothering me with questions, like do I really, really want dead-animal tarboush as well as vegan tarboush, 'cos it's against their religion or something to cook meat. Mikey, from the house in Shepherd's Bush, who does trance parties, will be bringing a vanload of lights hot from a rave. If they finish in time. Provided his van doesn't break down. If he doesn't get offered another job on the same date. Mr Reliable there. The only ray of sunshine in this debacle is my relationship with the art department. I've been taking a very hands-on approach to my role as producer here. As you can see, this has resulted in the art department and myself developing a very mature, professional understanding.

C'mon, I'm not operating within your regular dynamics of creative teamwork. I've watched this boy naked and fornicating, don't forget. Given that Cy's been permanently stripped to the waist and indulging in loads of manly, carpentry-style exercise, forgetting our encounter in the woods has been nigh on imposs-ible. Then again, I did waltz naked into his little soirée, covered myself in paint and rolled around on the floor. Add the fact that, since I outfaced him in front of his pals, Cy has been trying to get me back. Result: me and Cy have developed a sorta game playing pro-fessional relationship. I dare him to do something, then he dares me back. Kinda competitive but good, clean fun. All this, plus Ivan, Nadine and a heatwave that just keeps building. I tell ya, it's extremely diffi-cult to make this project follow normal rules.

Anyway, we're having this ongoing debate/discus-sion about relationships, triggered by my not getting the Elaine thing. What Elaine thing? The thing that an intelligent and not unattractive creature like Cy would settle for someone as dippy as Elaine. That thing. I can't believe that Cy is content with such an unequal relationship. *He* claims that these things are never equal, there's invariably a more dominant partner. When I protest, he cites my relationship with Paul as a prime example: him dominant and me subservient. Oh, please, the justify-your-own-sad-relationship-by-rubbishing-someone-else's gambit. I can't believe he's gone for such an obvious ploy. I demand evidence.

'Zita,' he says, 'you moon around bleating, "Paul's

so clever, Paul's so successful."' (He adopts a pathetic wavery voice for these impressions of me.)

I laugh at him. 'Cy, even if that was true, which it isn't, it wouldn't make me subservient.'

Cy gives me another flash of his muscular back and resumes the wavery voice ' "Why doesn't Paul phone? What if he's fucking Saskia? Woe is me!"' I give him a that-is-still-pathetic look and he says, 'Look, Zita, if you weren't so fucking intimidated by Paul, you'd be on the phone demanding to know why the fucker hadn't been in touch and what he was up to, *now*!'

I explain to Cy, with an appropriate degree of patronisation, about the connection difficulties and Paul's workload and everything. I know that Paul is extremely busy, that's all, otherwise I would phone him any time I wanted and say anything I want to. There's no question of my being intimidated here. Cy sneers and reminds me that he's worked on more shoots than I've had orgasms and there is always time you can snatch to take a phone call.

Huh, I'm not sure I want to hear this. I start arguing vociferously that I do not *ever* moon but I'm momentarily distracted by the very butch toolbelt holding up Cy's baggy shorts, which are just, only just, clinging on to his snakelike hips. My eyes unintentionally wander south, following a soft line of blond curls that runs straight down from the dimple of his bellybutton to ...

I realise that I'm licking my lips and I shake my head, forcing my gaze from his groin up into his unblinking grey eyes. He's backed me up against the stable wall, his cheeks bulging. For someone who's about to spray someone else with water, he looks very serious. 'I mean it Cy!' I say, putting as much threat into my voice as possible. Not much, I'm afraid. His hand clamps over my mouth. All that t'ai chi has given this boy very quick reflexes. He pulls my face very close to his and, holding my jaw in a grip like a vice, clamps his lips over mine. I suspect that my nostrils are beginning to flare at this point. He forces my mouth apart with his tongue and the water he's holding gushes to the back of my throat, making me gag and splutter in a very unglamorous fashion. Most of it ends up trickling down my neck, making me even more wet than I was to begin with. The rest I spit out on to Cy's bare feet. I am swamped with the image of Elaine lapping up his spunk. When I have stopped choking, I raise my eyes. Cy blinks, twice and, though his eyes are flinty and impassive, I detect a fleeting smile at the edge of his cherubic mouth. For a moment, I remember how he turned away from Elaine, that time in the wood, and I feel a prickle of anger. He bends to retrieve his saw but, when he turns back, his eyes are twinkly and playful. 'Doesn't count,' he repeats.

I look at him blankly, then remember our dare. See, going back to our relationship discussion, when I pointed out how Paul is busy and I respect that, how I can phone him any time I want, et cetera, et cetera, Cy demanded I prove it. The proof required being for me to phone Paul's hotel, ask to speak to him urgently, then have phone sex with him. See, told you this was a professional relationship.

OK, I'll go one better. To show that I am *so* not in awe of Paul, I will take advantage of the five-hour difference in time zones so that he will just be surfacing with his early-morning erection heavy on his belly when I call. Then, I will drag him out of sleep by talking enough filth to get him wide awake and perky. Finally, I pretend to be cut off in the middle of the call, leaving him to resolve any outstanding problems in the arousal department single-handed, so as to speak.

That, I submit, is not the action of the overawed. Actually thinking about it gives me a panicky feeling. No way that doesn't count. Cy wipes the sweat from his face with the back of his arm and says, 'You could have been talking to anybody, Zita. That didn't prove anything. You could have had your phone switched off for all I know.'

I don't dignify that with an answer and start walking off back towards the house. Cy calls after me, 'Where you going, Zita? There's no need to sulk.'

I wheel round and spit at him, 'I am not sulking, Cy. I am going to the house because I need a piss.' I stalk off with my head in the air and behind me hear the sawing start up again. In case he's forgotten who I am, I call back for good measure, 'Then I have a movie to produce.' I instantly regret it, because that sounds pompous, even to me.

The sawing stops momentarily and Cy says, 'Come on, Zita! Tell the truth. You're going to ring Paul and beg his forgiveness.'

Hah, got him there. I turn and march back up to him. 'So, you do believe I called him.'

Cy smirks at me and says, 'Thought you needed a piss.'

This boy is infuriating me. I slap him hard across the face and just as I'm thinking, My God what have I done? he slaps me back. In a fury, I throw myself at him, knocking him to the ground and we roll around in the dust. I manage to end up on top and am feeling quite pleased with myself until I realise that I can't actually move. Cy has hold of me by the wrists and has bent my arms backwards so I am doing a sort of bowing swan over him. I play my trump card. 'Let me go, Cy, or I'll piss on you!'

Cy leers at me and says, 'I dare you.'

I try to move but just end up bent further over and

say in my 'Game Over' voice, 'Cy, I'm serious. Let up or I really will piss myself.' It's true. My bladder is about to burst. But Cy doesn't respond. I'm confused. Paul knows when I use the Voice that I've had enough and he stops. Well, he used to. I look into those shark eyes and it occurs to me that they're not playing by the rules. I bite my lip and clench my cunt muscles harder.

Cy starts jiggling his hips, making me bounce around on top of him. 'Come on, Zita,' he sniggers. 'Just relax. You know you want to.' I screw my face up in concentration and shake my head. Cy bucks his hips again, catching me off guard, and as I'm desperately trying to regain my grip on my pelvic muscles, a first hot spurt of pee prickles inside my jersey cotton shorts. I struggle to hold back but it's too late. The dam breaks. With a spasm of pleasure, I empty myself all over Cy's belly. The sensation is electrifying. Warm liquid wells out, flooding down the channels where my thighs press tight against his body. Cy's laconic smile is fixed on his mouth. We stare at each other in silence, like we have committed an act of gross intimacy. I've never pissed on a man before. My pussy is practically pulsing.

'So, this is a hobby of yours, I think, Zita?' I turn my head as far as I can in the direction of the voice. To my horror, I realise Ivan is striding across the lawn towards us. Oh, bollocks! Has he been watching? He has a very strange expression on his face. 'You are really very interested in martial arts!' he laughs as he gets closer.

I try to move but Cy holds me tight to him. I whisper, 'Let me up now.'

Cy digs his nails into the skin on the underside of my arms and says, 'You lose, Zita.'

I look into his eyes and feel my face burn with a

mixture of shame and anger. I grit my teeth. 'Let me up!' The corner of Cy's mouth twitches and he shakes his head. I think I'm going to cry. 'OK, Cy. You win. Let me up now.'

Cy lets go and I scrabble to my feet before Ivan gets close enough to see the patch of indecent liquid. I stand behind the altar to hide the moist patch over my groin and the wet down my legs. 'Ivan, hi! Yes. I came to see how Cy was getting on with the altar and we ended up ... Cy was showing me some, um, holds ...' I finish brightly.

Ivan shrugs and claps his hands and says, 'Fine. OK, Naked Boy. These paintings you keep hidden from the world. So, you want to show me?'

Cy gets to his feet and I notice that next to Ivan he does looks like a boy. A rather stinky, sulky little boy at the moment, I could add. Cy mutters something about his Art being private and not for general consumption. Ivan throws his head back and laughs. 'You do it for yourself then, like wanking?' Cy curls his lovely lip and he and Ivan look set for a face off.

Somehow these two just can't get on. Cy's always bitchin' about Ivan, calling him 'I-vos' behind his back, and Ivan calls Cy 'Naked Boy' just about all the time now. It's a man thing, I guess. Whatever, I grab at my opportunity for escape. 'Look, guys, I'll leave you to discuss your art or lock your antlers or whatever you need to do, OK?' They're too busy circling each other to bother with li'l ol' me anyway, so I slope off back to the house unnoticed. I take a quick douche in my clanking, antique shower and decide I'd better make some calls re the shoot, which is now only days away. I call most of the people involved, getting the usual irritating 'Don't worry, everything's fine' answers. Between calls, I try Paul's mobile. Better check he's OK.

It would be the adult thing to do. Irritatingly, I just can't get connected. By the time I speak to Paul, he is obviously up and about.

He doesn't even say anything about the conversation we had. I prod a little. Eventually Paul admits that he did have a hard-on but I guess he's on location now with the crew 'cos he phrases it like he's talking in code. It's all, 'Um yes, there was some, um, tension earlier but, um, yup I um ... It um ... has been relieved, so to speak.' Ooh, dirty boy! Thinking of Paul wanking while thinking of me wanking gets to me. In Tanglebush fashion, I am naked and allowing myself to air-dry after my shower. I'm stretched back in my wicker chair and languorously playing with my pubes, wondering if maybe he could help me, um, relieve my own tensions when all of a sudden, it's 'Gotta go' time and I'm left feeling somewhat restless and potentially rather irritable.

I stalk round the room, peering out through my window. I can hear Cy's sawing again but can't see him. Otherwise it's your usual Tanglebush rustic out there: birds, trees, blue skies and nothing much else. Then, a surprise. A dirty red fox is meandering down the middle of the lawn, looking casually this way and that, for all the world like he owned the place. I know it's a he, I can tell by his swagger. I follow him as he strolls right up to the house. I've never seen a fox before. I'm so fascinated that, by the time he disappears from view, I'm halfway out of my turret window, practically on the parapet. Ohmygod. Suddenly, I'm frozen. I'm, what? Fifty feet above the ground, a sheer drop down. I feel a strong pulsing in my innards, a feeling that's a mixture of panic and arousal. I'm terrified and wildly excited at the same time. I know I shouldn't look down but I've got to. I let my eyes drop down to the ground. Whoaaah! Electric currents surge through my body. By some act of will, I wrest myself back indoors and collapse, panting, on the bed.

My body is tingling, top to toe. There is a powerful drawing feeling in my belly. I reach down and clutch myself comfortingly. I cup my fluttering pussy in my hand. It's not like normal arousal, but my groin's alive with sensations, hypersensitive. Like that moment when you finally decide to go to bed with someone who's bad news. Danger signals everywhere, but excitement too. I realise I'm actually very horny. I want to wank myself. There, said it. I just want to have sex with myself, and my daydreams. I think about the previous time in my attic room, when I first arrived, and how good it felt. A sort of get-to-know-yourself moment. My fingers have already started working over my clit. I remember that I've leaned an old, full-length mirror against the wall, my one concession to grooming. I kneel up and look at myself. I don't look too bad. My thighs are slim and brown, my belly neat and nearly flat, my breasts are fullish but high. I spread my knees, staring straight at myself, and start to stimulate myself. It looks dirty, whorish. I like that. I know I like showing myself off. Even as a little kid, I was the one who kept pulling her dress over her head. At seven, I'd deliberately be doing handstands against the wall when the boys were looking. OK, I like people looking at me, it's true.

I'd like people to see me doing this, I think. Paul. I see his face drift past in my imagination, with an expression like the taxi driver's. The face morphs into Cy's. Shit, he shouldn't be here. Get rid of him. I think of Paul, sweaty and naked in his bed in Cuba. Three weeks without sex, big hard-on propping up the sheet. Hand grasping hard-on as he imagines my own fingers deep in my juicy cleft. Both hands on his cock, tossing and turning, wrapped round the agonisingly hard erection, while he thinks of me, naked, doing myself. I see his hungry leer. Fuck, it's Cy again, looking at me before he spat water in my mouth, looking up at me when I'd just pissed all over him. Holding his own hard-on and advancing at me.

I wrestle his face away and replace it with Paul's. That's better. My gaze follows the line of his muscular back (he's got a really nice back) down to his arse. It's rocking back and forth. His hand is on his cock. He's guiding it into a girl's cunt, mounting her from behind. I pan upwards. Paul is panting into the tousled hair of the girl he's fucking. Shit, it's blonde hair. Not my hair, Saskia's fucking hair. Fuck, if he's gonna be unfaithful in my fantasies, I can be too.

I recall Cy. I'm going to undress him. I pull up his T and nip and bite his pointy little nipples. Then I let my tongue trace a path down his hard brown belly and over the sprouting blond curls till it reaches the sagging waistband of his baggy shorts, which I deftly unhitch and drag down so his swollen cock springs out loose and hard and right in my face, deliciously aroused and very, very needful. I cup his tight, hard balls in one hand and wank the length of his cock with the glans sucked into my mouth. I can feel Cy is nearly outta control but he tears himself away and stands, looking at me. Then he steps forward and kisses me, hard and rough. He continues kissing down my throat to my swollen nips, which he takes in his mouth and bites fiercely yet delicately. His hand strokes over my belly till his fingers are into my slit and moving ever downwards towards my hole. His tongue and fingers are wandering at will and now it's me that's almost out of control.

I push him backwards and scramble on top of him, grabbing for his dick. Teasing myself, I raise myself over him and slide my clit along the length of his slippy cock while I watch his golden, muscular body writhing and pushing up to meet me. Then I move the tip back till it is against my wet, juicy hole and lower myself, oh so slowly lower myself, round that fat cock as it slips slowly into me and I finger and rub my clit as I grind against him, my eyes closed, as his cock surges and pumps away inside me just as I come too, face down on my mattress, bucking and pounding as I ram myself into my hand, my fingers up my cunt, my thumb on my clit, my fanny throbbing. Oh, I've been a bad, bad girl.

9

Elaine comes bimbling, and uninvited, in to my den. (We don't lock our doors at Tanglebush.) 'Hi, Elaine,' I drawl. 'Come on in, why don't ya?' As usual Ms Were-pig-with-the-hide-of-an-elephant ignores me. She drifts round my room till she's standing before me. Then she kneels down in front of the chair and fixes me with those big vacant eyes and says, 'Zita, I think it's only fair to warn you that you don't know what you're getting involved with.'

I can't believe this. It's the day of the shoot and I'm being warned off by an airhead nineteen-year-old space cadet. I beam at her and say insouciantly, 'Gee, thanks for the concern, Elaine. I know *Outlaws* is a big shoot but I do know what's involved, ya know?'

Her piggy brow furrows a little and she says, 'With Cy, I mean.' She does some theatrical eyeball rolling and continues, 'You don't understand. It's very...' I nod at her encouragingly and her eyes flash until finally she spits out, '... intense.' I can't help myself. I laugh. Elaine's eyes flash some more and she shakes her head and retreats. The girl is clearly insane.

When she's gone I feel a bit better. When a girl warns you off a guy it can only mean one thing – the guy fancies you. Ammunition for when I pay him back – and pay him back for what he did I am going to have to do. Bastard. I'll teach him a lesson he won't forget. Cy fancies me. Mmmn. The thought gives me a warm feeling as I stroll out into the steamy heat of the afternoon. Tanglebush is already a bit like Glastonbury that one year it didn't rain. There's people in various states of undress camped all over the place, playing bongos, juggling and generally milling about.

Seems that word has got out that there's some sort of eighties naturist rave in the offing and that Tanglebush Towers is gonna be *the* place to be this weekend. (We are handy for the M25, so that's just about right.) The performance artists (led by Dali) actually came last night and began cooking immediately. Mikey, as well as his vanload of lights, arrives with a consignment of still-buzzing weekend clubbers and enough floor cushions to corral them until needed. Nadine's coterie of ex-girlfriends fetch up lunchtime, which is handy, 'cos the north London moshers arrive just after. There's way too many people. How am I supposed to keep control? Fortunately, most of them seem to have brought their own entertainment, herbal, chemical or otherwise, so they're keeping themselves amused. Nonetheless, I'm starting to get kinda panicky. As each contingent arrives, I hand them over to Elaine, who takes them to Cy, who is happily body-painting all and sundry to look like Keith Haring stick people. It seems everyone is having fun but me. Oh, yeah, and Elaine.

Elaine, who will be the sacrificial victim, is also panicking now. Originally, she loved the concept (I'd persuaded her it meant she was in virtually every shot, which in her pea-sized brain equated to being the *star*) but now she is half terrified Ivan really means to have her slaughtered. God knows what Cy has given her, but Mikey offers her a pill to mellow her out. Half an hour later, she is happily sitting on the grass, bopping her head beatifically out of time to the frenetic rhythm of the bongo-drumming team. Which is not what I wanted, as it leaves yours truly as the only person left to produce order from this chaos.

By some fluke, we eventually get the altar arranged in one of the little glades in the woods and the lights are rigged on to old bits of timbers jammed into the crooks of trees and so forth. Nadine's decks and speakers have been cunningly built into the altar by Cy. We have two huge cables with their tails wired directly into the main power supply of the house by Mikey's mate, Stephen, who swears he is an electrician. The lights don't have any safety chains and it would only take a zephyr-strength breeze to bring the lot crashing down on the satanic worshippers below, when they would all certainly be killed by (a) concussion or (b) electrocution, even if the cocktail of intoxicants most of them seem to be imbibing don't see them off first. I start to wonder at the wisdom of saving on the indemnity insurance and whether skipping the country might still be a valid option if (as in 'when') things go pear-shaped.

By eight o'clock, the bongos are competing with Nadine's sound checks. It's just as well Tanglebush is up a private drive and half a mile from the nearest other habitation, otherwise we would certainly be expecting a visit from the boys in blue at any moment. By nine, the partygoers, I mean extras, have turned sullen. Half of Nadine's exes have left for another party while the north London boys are jabbering about how they'll be going someplace else too, unless everyone takes all their clothes off right *now*. Just about all the other extras want to know when we're gonna start shooting. I am beginning to wonder how to handle this scenario when everything is saved by Dali. *'Le tarboush est arrivé.'* Everyone, the north London boys included, dives on it. Ivan congratulates me on the catering. I merely nod my head and say nothing. Truth is, with the connection between my stomach and my brain completely severed by the tension and worry, not to mention chemical intervention purloined from Mikey, I'd totally forgotten about the matter of food.

I have a breathing space of about an hour to solve the remaining problems, the biggest of which is Nadine. Yes, Nadine. Considering this is all about her, she is being remarkably unhelpful. She has, in fact, thrown a complete strop because I have not got a make-up artist to prepare her for the shoot. I know this is really more about her own sense of self-import-ance than anything to do with what she looks like. The role of the make-up artist is as much about stoking and stroking the star's ego as anything else (and very good at it they generally are, too, let it be said). Shit, I should have seen this one coming. Any-way, Nadine is sitting, haughty and alone, up in her bedroom. In an attack of ego, she implies that she may not be *emotionally* up to a performance unless I can solve this one. While I know this is, in fact, a bluff, the danger is she will delay doing her set for so long that the now appeased extras will all get pissed off again and disappear for good. Why, oh why, did I agree to do this job?

I am seriously considering getting in the Roadster and driving the fuck away when Dali comes up trumps again. He finds me grinding my teeth and pacing and insists on sitting me down and giving me an Indian head massage, then he tells me he did a hair and beauty course before settling on art college. This guy is a low-budget dream. Catering, cast and make-up all rolled up in one fabulous package. I could kiss him and I do before pointing him at Nadine. When I leave them he is massaging her ego beauti-fully. By twelve, only three hours behind schedule, the crew are ready to roll.

Now, hang on there. Your idea of a film crew is like a small army, right? Wrong. This is low-budget (strictly speaking, no-budget) filmmaking. In our case the crew is Ivan operating a hand-held digital camcorder with Cy also filming to get plenty of coverage, Mikey mixing lights, Stephen assisting, and me, assistant director (first, second and third) and general MC. The extras are back to mid-throttle party mode (helped by a distribution of cut-price stimulants from Mikey) and ready to move up a gear or two as soon as we want. It is the moment of truth.

I feel incredibly nervous, like it's the start of a major performance or something. I stand on top of the dustbins and, at the top of my voice, give the order, 'Strip!'

A hundred people gleefully throw their clothes off and into the night. At least, those who had not already pre-empted my command. I, too, peel off my T-shirt and shorts while, deep in the heart of the wood, a throbbing, pulsing murmur begins to build. Strobes flash among the trees.'Seize the Victim,' I yell, the tenor of my voice, with it's dark, primal edge, frightening even myself.

Two dozen sweating hands clasp tight round Elaine's limbs and bodily lift her, naked, to the night sky while Ivan, naked too like everyone else, leaps around dementedly filming the action. Then, in procession, the multitude advances towards the source of the thumping, growling music. It had been envisaged that we would repeat each sequence several times, but I'm beginning to see that this might not be exactly practical. The extras are joining in the spirit of the production with enthusiastic abandon. People are grooving wildly around the central mass of bodies bearing the giggling Elaine slowly and unsteadily into the wood.

We pad in rhythmic procession towards the sacrificial grove. The naked, painted bodies, caught in the stabs of laser beams Mikey has directed from his central command platform, look like a flickering fire of demonic forms. The feel of still warm earth on bare feet is massively primeval. When we get to the main circle of light, there is Nadine, regal as a carnival queen, her hair teased out in a huge Afro, a glittering, spangled cape round her shoulders, her lovely breasts and belly painted exquisitely by Cy into a pattern of curlicues and spirals that intertwine to lead to her tautly erect nipples. Each nipple is fitted with a special clamp that grips and extends it. They look like they're two inches long at least. The make-up makes Nadine's eyes glow like headlights in the dark. She stares wildly into the night, completely gone. It is an awesome sight. Like an LA gala screening of *The Rocky Horror Picture Show*. I'm both devastated by the amateurishness and impressed by the deeply tribal energy released. The effect is shockingly erotic. Maybe this thing is gonna work after all.

I notice Cy crashing around in the undergrowth. He stumbles towards the throng, camcorder on his right shoulder. A lithe young woman breaks away and sashays provocatively towards him, then embraces him. By the time he has disengaged, I notice his handsome dick is at least semi-erect. I wonder where that'll get parked tonight. I jog across to him and mutter sniffily, 'You're s'pposed to be working, not enjoying yourself.' He turns towards me and grins and I feel his erection brush my thigh. In spite of the fact I know he's deliberately teasing me, for a fleeting moment, I really feel like lying back on the earth, opening my legs and pulling him into me. I actually consider whether anyone would notice. Then I pull myself together and remind myself there is a job to be done here.

By now, Elaine has been thrust on to the platform of Cy's altar and bound to it with a handy supply of leather thongs. She is on the very edge of hysteria. Ivan is in real tight, getting close-ups of her face and her squirming torso. You'd really believe she was about to get sacrificed. I pray nobody has a sharp, pointy object about their person and gets carried away by the heat of the moment. Then I remember that everyone is stark-naked, so would have nowhere to secrete a sharp pointy object. Nowhere very comfortable, anyway. Nonetheless, I decide to call a time out and screech 'Cut!' at maximum volume. It takes about three or four interventions before everyone stops the dancing and regains their composure.

Water bottles are passed around and I release Elaine while Nadine rearranges her records. I tell Elaine to relax and stroke her gently, as you would a nervous animal, while I struggle with the knotted thongs. I remember how breathing up horses' nostrils calms them down and, without thinking, bend over her face. Elaine completely misunderstands and her hand comes round the back of my neck. Our lips collide for a few seconds before she releases me and looks up at me with her big, moonlike eyes. I am momentarily confused. It's like I'm face to face with Bambi again. For some reason, I whisper reassuringly, 'I'll look after you, don't worry.' She smiles and nods. Ivan calls out 'Ready for a take,' and we go again.

We take it back to Elaine's entrance to the glade. She smiles down at me reassuringly this time. I frown back. This'll totally fuck the continuity up. Last time we did it, she was kicking and screaming like there was no tomorrow. God knows how it'll cut. But Nadine has picked up on the change of ambience, too, like the great DJ she is. She is all closed-eyed and ice-maiden distant. She builds the music using a powerful, surging, bassline with snares kicking in to make a disjointed, very spare, very hardcore pulse. I recognise one of her best tunes, 'Keep It In (The Groove)'. I could do that, I think.

Elaine is laid, almost tenderly, on the altar. She looks up, wide-eyed and wondering, at Nadine, who stares back haughtily, the beautiful Witch Queen in *Snow White*. Several fit young men are gathered at the front, stroking Elaine, paying homage to nubility. I'm relieved at having that responsibility taken away from me at least. Nadine plays with the mood, sneaking jointlessly through her first mix. People move and wriggle to the beat. Ivan glides in, ghostlike, with the digital camera. I notice Cy balanced on a speaker cab to get a wide shot. Some of the extras are shouting and whistling now, asking Nad to give them something, like a pack of lost wolves howling to their leader. Nadine looks coolly through her lowered eyelashes, completely unmoved by the increasing crescendo of noise. I realise I'm holding my breath. Then, bam, she hits the stop button and the music bounces into reverse. Without missing a beat, she executes a perfectly judged cut straight into 'Plump Out The Nite'.

They do. Suddenly the glade is a mass of dancing bodies, arms raised to the stars, body parts bouncing in unison. Somewhere in the middle of all this is Ivan busy filming the bare feet stamping on the earth. Cy is crouched on the altar now, astride Elaine, his camcorder shoved in Nadine's face to get big close-ups. Then he springs into the midst of the dancing throng. I see Ivan's camcorder lifted high in the air to pan around the frenzied mass, then he emerges from the mass and looks at me, manic-eyed and yelling 'Big fucking, yes? I *tell* you so!' His body is covered in sweat and, with his deep chest and grizzled body hair, he looks like a latter-day centaur. He turns and heaves himself back into the throng, forcing his way to the front to get shots of Nadine, who has now thrown off her cape to crouch there, proud and naked, while madly spinning her discs, Nefertiti on speed. I shout in Nadine's ear that she is a goddess. She smiles a distant acknowledgement, then looks into the sweatily grooving crowd and throws some deep-down dirty bass into the mix.

I realise there's nothing for me to do now. If I were to call 'Cut', no one would take the slightest notice, even assuming that they heard me. Cy's body painting makes it look like a posse of skeletons having a rattling good time together. Primitive and pagan, exactly what we wanted. Hey, I've done my bit, so isn't it time for me to enjoy? That's what Ivan told me to do, just relax and let him do his stuff now. I think I'm gonna consider myself temporarily off duty. And I think my pill is kicking in now. So, being redundant, I jump into the throng myself and give it some best dance-hall moves, rolling my arse in pure Nadine style. This is fun. People are dancing in a tightly packed bunch, bodies jammed together, skin sliding on skin. Several of the guys are moving into a more responsive mode, shall we say, but nobody's minding much: the mood is sexy but distinctly unthreatening. People are not dancing singly or in pairs, but en masse, all up close and friendly. Smiles and stroking all round. A hand rests on my waist and a body leans into mine. Then a camcorder lens appears over my right shoulder. It's Ivan or Cy trying to steady their shot. Hey, that's OK, go for it, boys. We're all here to help each other out. It's about thirty seconds before I feel the semi-hard-on nestling between my buttocks.

Hang on, I've been here before, haven't I? I know from previous experience this sort of thing can only mean trouble and I really should stop it here and now. I mean, I'm the one supposed to be in control, aren't I?

But, as we move, the hard-on grows till it's rigid and taut between my sweaty, curvy cheeks. I can't stop imagining the plumped-up dick sliding there and I'm very aware of a growing feeling of slippiness radiating from my groin. Somehow, I just don't seem able to turn round and point out that all this is a little presumptuous, to say the least. Anyway, whose dick is it? It can only be one of two. I'm going to get so angry about this impertinence as soon as I can ignore the distraction of the ragingly taut cock sliding up and down the crack of my butt. Involuntarily, I push back against it. Shit, why did I do that? The body behind tightens against mine and immediately we're grooving as one to a very primal rhythm indeed. Ohmygod, too late to glance behind me and I'm far too terrified and distracted to turn round now.

The distraction is compounded by a yearning to curve my spine just a tad further while, at the same time, I'm trying to ignore an urgent desire to spread my feet to open my cheeks ever so slightly. Shit, the yearning is irresistible. A flex of my arse and, whoops, suddenly the swollen member has hit its groove more intrusively than ever. Knocking at the door, so as to speak. The angle of attack means it's outside rather than inside the dwelling, but the situation is about as intimate as I've ever been with anyone in public, recent performances notwithstanding. The tip has found the entrance and, eyes closed, I know if this carries on, I'll soon have to open up and pump down. I'm not even sure whose cock it is, I realise with a shock. With an even bigger shock, it dawns on me that I don't actually care. Shit, shit, shit, I must get a grip on myself, urgently. I know I really must pull away from this little tango now. It's getting more intimately purposeful by the second. With enormous willpower, I decide to make a break for it before it's too late.

I open my eyes again, determined to go into action, to find myself staring into the lens of Ivan's camcorder. So, if Ivan is filming me from the front, who is behind me? Only one person it can be. It's just at this point that Nadine switches into her *pièce de résistance*, 'Outlaws', the climax of the evening. The crowd surges forward and forces everyone tight up together. The cock slides easily between my slippy thighs till it's head is forcing my lips. We're almost coupled up. My reasonable voice is desperately hollering to be heard above the baying and whooping of the crowd. 'Never get your face on camera; leastways, not during sex!' I swear that I will eliminate every frame of this in the edit. I sneak a guilty glance in Elaine's direction. She's getting into her role now, flailing round like she's terrified. Hah, maybe she's seen us. My dirty unreasonable self is just loving the idea of her watching me with my juicy cunt being rubbed and virtually penetrated by her boyfriend's ragingly hard cock. My pill's coming on and I'm vaguely aware that there's something happening at the altar but I don't give a shit. I feel self-control self-slipping further away. If somebody doesn't do something soon, I will have to let this cock slide in right here and now, right in the middle of this mass of sweating thrusting bodies, right in front of Elaine, right in front of Nadine, right in front of Ivan. Ohmygod, you have completely lost it now, you have completely lost it, I can hear myself thinking. If something doesn't happen now, this second . . .

But it does. There's a sudden pop and the effect of time slowing down and we're all plunged into darkness and silence. No more lights, no more music. It's gone incredibly peaceful, quiet and dark. Pitch blackness in fact. I wonder what's happened to the power? Oh yeah, the power. Fuck!

10

Everything freezes, then the whistling starts. Fuck, if someone doesn't do something there'll be a riot. Fuck, I am the Designated Grown-Up. That someone's me, isn't it?

I do a quick recce. I can just make out the shadowy figure of Nad, guarding her decks. Cy has disappeared. Where the fuck is Ivan? Where the fuck are my clothes? I give up groping round in the dark when the dark in the shape of gurning naked people starts groping back and decide to head for the decks, where at least I'll have height advantage. Several close encounters of the intimate kind later, I am near enough to the decks to make out that the shadowy Nad figure is in fact Ivan filming the north London boys in what appears to be a Maori war chant thing in Russian. Sorta the Vulgar Boatmen on acid. I resolve to decrease my drug intake there and then. It is, however, an arresting sight. Ivan has got an impressively flat belly for a man his age. I wonder what state his arse is in. He obligingly turns around. I'm impressed. His butt may possibly be his best feature, still rounded and pert. I can see what Celia sees in him. Standing up on the stage orchestrating all of this mayhem, Ivan is in his element. He is a star.

Unfortunately, now that Ivan has pointed a camera at them the Edmonton gang seem to be have formed the impression that they too are stars and as such they want to perform. When they turn to face me I get the distinct impression that they intend to perform on me. One of them utters a guttural groan that sounds something like 'Oooomaaaan!?!'

They start lumbering towards me. I expect their knuckles are hurting, from all that scraping the ground. When they are almost upon me, they stop, uncertain what they should do next. During the pause, I remember that I am naked and probably reeking of sex, alone deep in a forest at night and surrounded by half a dozen naked Neanderthals. I should be terrified. But I'm fed up with this game. Where *has* everyone gone? I grab hold of the nearest ape and bellow into his face, 'The lights? What happened to the lights?' Fear creases his face. His cronies cringe away behind him. I hold firm to my captive baboon, who I get the distinct impression is tripping, and shake him. '*Where. Is. The. Light?*' He wobbles his head dolefully and starts shaking. It occurs to me that, at this very moment, he is probably deep in the throes of some transcendental, pagan, mystery-cult time-shift experience. Do I give a shit?

I don't. I'm tempted to tell him that Jesus loves him but I need to find out what the fuck is going on more than I need to fuck with his head. I point to the tree and say very slowly, 'There were lights in the trees. What has happened to them?'

Mistake. The whole troop looks agitatedly up into the branches. One of them starts wailing 'The light has gone, the light has gone.'

I change tack. 'This is a film shoot. There were lights. What happened?'

The faintest glimmer of comprehension appears behind his dilated pupils. He giggles. 'The sacrifice went mental and escaped and everyone, like ... *chased* after her. And she, like, climbed up a tree to get away? And there was a big sort of zhoom? And everything just kinda stopped ...'

Shit! I want to go home but I am gripped by something terrible. I believe it might be a sense of responsibility. I grit my teeth and force myself to say, 'Where is the sacrifice?' This is apparently a sufficiently inspirational statement for the ape to adopt me as his new leader and escort me to a bush. Inside I can just make out the terrified eyes of a cornered animal. An Elaine. I don't risk getting on all fours to investigate with monkey man and his troupe still in evidence, so I release him and instruct him and his pals to go over to the house and either find someplace to crash or fuck off back to Edmonton. I watch them lumber away, then squat down and call into the bush. 'Elaine, c'mon you can come out now!'

The bush begins to quiver and a whimper emanates from inside. 'You said you'd look after me.'

The bush is spikey. I am naked. What can I do? I go in. Elaine launches herself at me and wraps me with her bony limbs. She is gibbering, 'I want my mother.' She has lost it.

To humour her, I croon gently, 'OK, Elaine. I'll take you to your mother.'

She digs her nails into me and hisses, 'Brother!'

Owww! Fucking hell, enough of gentle.'Yeah, sure. Mother, brother, whatever. Now, come on.' By the time I manage to drag her out my body is lacerated and not just from the bush. Elaine's nails are long and she uses them to cling on to me until I am able to deliver her to the only person I still have any faith in: Dali.

When I peel her from me and attach her to him she calms down some, probably 'cos his suit gives better purchase than my skin. He looks anxiously at her and asks if we should find Cy. Excellent idea. I instruct Dali to take Elaine back to the stable block and sedate her with tarboush or something, while I in the meantime locate Cy.

I spot the slinky bitch on heat who was dancing and fooling with him at the start of the shoot. Her face is partially obscured by the curtain of black hair swishing round it but I know it's her. I'm figuring on asking her if she's seen Cy when her body starts jerking like a bullet-riddled corpse in a spaghetti western. It's only after several seconds that I realise there's another body coupled in firmly behind her. A vigorously thrusting, shoving muscular body that's pumping her into uncontrollable jerks and twitches of pleasure as she's taken standing in the middle of the dance floor. I'm temporarily overwhelmed by a clutching spasm of jealousy in my belly.

Even though it's dark, I know it's Cy. I don't so much smell him as feel him. It's like my body's fitted with censors that start zinging whenever he's in range and right now they're zinging at maximum velocity. I can't stop myself from watching. I am transfixed. My body is zinging and my head is scrambled with a medley of dodgy Radio 2 tunes: 'It Should Have Been Me', 'I Put a Spell on You', 'Your Cheatin' Heart'. Ohmygod, that's an Alison medley. What's possessed me?

What's possessed everybody else?

Something grabs my leg. I yelp and fall on to something soft and squishy and warm. The soft, squishy, warm thing envelopes me. I realise it is a naked human body, of indeterminate sex. In fact, more than one body, and these bodies are squirming and wriggling over and under each other. Hands run over me, stroking my belly, cupping my tits, exploring what orifices they can find. I feel a definite erection slide against my arse. A face appears from out of the mass and a mouth is clamped over mine. A tongue is forced into my mouth and I accept it. Someone slight, a girl maybe, clasps her legs around mine and begins grinding herself into my thigh. Hands grasp my hips and the cock slips into the cleft of my buttocks. The girl starts kissing my breasts. I am being attended to by at least three amorphous forms, maybe more, I can't tell. I feel myself slipping away, like I'm drowning in a sweating, heaving sea of warm skin. There are hands everywhere now, grasping, feeling, holding, stroking whatever they come into contact with. I just want to lose myself in this undulating mass of flesh. I just want to be touched. I've almost lost my sense of identity, like I've degenerated into primitive soma, part of one larger organism, no longer Zita any more.

The full moon comes out briefly from behind the clouds and I get a glimpse of the heaving heaps of polymorphous perversion strewn around the wood. It dawns on me: my first outing as a producer and I have managed to orchestrate an orgy. I'm surrounded by flesh sliding in and on and out of flesh. Fuck, what am I doing? Shit, what if Ivan says something to Celia? What if Paul hears about it? Worse, Saskia? Oh shitty shit. I force myself to disengage and wriggle and slide myself away.

In my solitary capacity of Designated Grown-Up, I am responsible for making sure that everything and everyone is safe and sound and delivered back to who or where it belongs. The realisation brings me back to reality. Marvellous. I get to be mum while everybody else, Cy included, gets to indulge in the best group grope since they cleaned up Hollywood. Fan-fucking-tastic. No wonder all of the producers I've ever encountered seem to have been perpetually irritated with the world.

I stagger back to the house. Ivan appears now clad in some kind of blanket affair that makes him look like a cross between a Roman emperor and Ghengis Khan. He envelopes me in a big sweaty bear hug and to my eternal shame I burst into tears. So embarrassing. Ivan doesn't act like I've just whimped out or anything. There's no 'There there, shoosh shoosh,' with Ivan. He bursts into tears himself, then hands me the inevitable bottle of Stolli, claps me on the back and declaims, 'Zita, I have to thank you for making me do this. I thank you for reminding me how much fun filmmaking is!' I take a slug of the vodka and after politely wiping the neck pass it back to Ivan, who takes another slug and sits down at the table in front of me. 'A producer who lives and loves for the production, a producer with real passion. Hah! This is a rare, rare thing.' Everything gets kind of blurry at this point. I am vaguely aware of an interlude of Russian folk song and then the bit where Ivan tells me that I will be the producer of his next great venture, the project that will put him back on the map. Reassert his talent, rub their faces in the dirt (critics), remind them (the industry) of his vision, show the emasculating bitch (?) who is a man. There's the bit where I agree to do it and shortly after that, I think, the bit where I decide to go outside for some fresh air and ... oh, yeah, the bit where I pass out.

11

A strange, earthy smell fills my nostrils. My mouth is clogged with dirt.

'Zita?'

All around me contorted faces call out my name.

'Zita!'

Shining, sweating bodies writhing and copulating while I watch.

'Zee-tah!'

All of them, screaming at me, asking me this, telling me to do that.

'Coo-ee. Are you listening?'

Listening to what? And why am I eating grass? I unscrew my eyes open. Nadine and Ivan are staring at me. The light is hurting my eyes. I've got a mouthful of grass. Ohhh, yeah, right. It's the post-production meeting, on the lawn at Tanglebush. And I must have fallen asleep again. Shit.

I spit most of the grass out and sit up. 'Yeah, I'm listening,' I say in a don't-be-so-fucking-stupid voice. It's a total lie. I'm actually suffering from post-shoot trauma, a serious dose of total nervous/physical exhaustion coupled with post-narcotic comedown and a dash of creative dread. Everything feels kinda flat. It's less that 48 hours since the shoot but it feels like a week. Tanglebush still looks like a festival site when everyone's gone home. There's loads to do and, of course, all of it is my responsibility.

Nadine looks smugly self-contained while Ivan bombards me with questions of the 'Have you

done . . . ?' variety. I bark back, 'Yes, I have done . . .'
and then I make a mental note to sort it a.s.a.p.,
despite the monumental hurdle of not having a
budget to pay for any of these things that need doing:
clearing litter/washing up/viewing rushes (they're
brilliant!)/booking the edit suite/ordering replacement
bog rolls/whatever. Do I get any thanks? Do I shite.
I'm sure producers shouldn't have to put up with this.
I add a note to make sure the BWM application gets
in the post the moment I get back to Camberwell,
which will be tomorrow at the latest, if I have anything to do with it.

'So?' goes Nadine.

I make a meal of spitting some more grass out of
my mouth, to buy time to guess what she might have
been talking about, then resort to forcing Nadine's
hand by replying, 'So what?'

Nadine lights a fag and looks bored. 'So, what have
you done about the edit suite?'

Aha, my one success. I smile smugly. 'Sorted.' And I
announce my latest coup. 'I've managed to sweet-talk
one of Paul's editor pals in a facilities house. As much
time as we need.' Nadine and Ivan do not look as
impressed as they ought. 'In Soho. For *free*,' I add.

Ivan grunts something that sounds like 'good' but
Nadine just picks tobacco from her tongue and says,
'What's the catch?'

Jesus, no wonder I didn't see this bitch for six
months. I calmy explain, 'There is no catch, Nadine.
We just get the downtime, that's all.'

Nadine goes, 'Downtime? Like, that'll mean, oh,
midnight to, say, six in the morning?'

It's my turn to do the so-ing. 'So-o?'

Nad rolls her eyes. 'So-o, Zita, when do I get to
work?'

I make a huge effort to keep my temper. When is

she supposed to work? What about me? I very politely point out to her that I have postponed securing myself some very lucrative *paid* work in order to produce her fucking promo. She purses her lips and equally politely informs me that somebody has to bring in some cash or we don't eat, never mind finish the project. I can't believe she's being so unprofessional. And this entire spat takes place in front of Ivan, who she seems to have forgotten has donated his services for free. Presumably in the belief that we are together enough to actually deliver.

Ivan clears his throat and says, 'You know what I think we need?'

Nad and I stop glowering at each other and look at him expectantly. At last, the great man offers his wisdom. Years of experience will be brought into play. 'I think we need a party,' he says.

A party? We've just had the party-to-end-all-fucking-parties and now he wants another one? He stands up and continues, 'A wrap party. Everyone has worked hard and now we should relax. To celebrate! We need a party for the crew. We need to get drunk together. I know about these things. Trust me, I am Russian.'

This last remark seems a tad pointless, Ivan's relationship with Stolly being well known.'You agree?' Nad and I are still giving each other the icy daggers but Ivan takes lack of response as an affirmative. 'Good. I have to go home now. You will sort it, Zita?' I'm about to ask Ivan if there is anything else I should be doing, like mowing the lawn or sending birthday cards to his relatives, when Nadine pipes up. 'Oh Ivan, you will be bringing Celia?'

'Celia does not go to these sort of parties,' he says heavily.

I'm thinking that this is just all too depressing

when I have my brilliant idea. 'Oh, why not?' I blurt out. 'You gotta bring Celia to our soirée, Ivan! We'd be very disappointed with you if you didn't.'

Nad snorts and then drawls, 'Yeah, it would be so lovely to see her. You must bring Celia, I absolutely insist.'

Ivan gives her a very strange look then says, 'Yes. Of course. I'll ask her. Thank you.' He arranges to meet me at the facilities house and gets off.

When he's gone, Nad sneers at me disbelievingly. 'Soirée? Is that what you and Paul get up to in Camberwell?'

I sneer back. 'Oh, you must bring Celia, Ivan, I absolutely insist!'

She curls her lip some more and reminds me that getting Celia on board would ensure the distribution of the finished piece. Duh! Like I don't know this. Like I also don't know that Celia Draycott moves in the same circles as Clare Dodderidge. (Big World Media. *My* brilliant new career. C'mon, keep up.) Like if I box clever at this soirée thing then pretty soon lots of positive stuff about me will be filtering through to Clare via Celia along that old meejah grapevine. Yeah, like none of the above has occurred to me. Double duh.

Obviously I don't say any of this to Nad. Instead I say very patiently, 'Which is why I called it a soirée, Nadine. Celia being a proper grown-up, sophisticated, *Camberwell* kinda person and all that.'

Nadine shrugs and goes, 'Fine, you're the expert on Camberwell. You deal with it.'

Which leaves me having a nightmare. Half my time is spent going cross-eyed in front of banks of video monitors at the edit suite, which incidentally, in the having-a-nightmare category deserves a whole subgenre all to itself. You think I'm exaggerating, don't you? Using a bit of hyperbole for effect. Well I'm not. OK, case this scenario.

It's the early hours of the morning. You're in an edit suite. A tiny/airless/windowless corridor of a room that's stuffed with monitors and VCRs and time-base correctors and such like. The thermometer's way up in the nineties. 'Cos of all the electronics, you're not allowed to smoke. You're sitting between a nice Danish editor chap, who is doing you an enormous favour because he is a friend of your boyfriend, and a formerly famous Russian film director.

So far, so good, eh?

OK. Suddenly the footage you're viewing starts feeling strangely familiar. Like you saw it in a dream or something. The camera is swooping through a crowd of naked, painted people. It's all body parts and writhing limbs and faces caught between agony and ecstasy.

So far, so what? you're probably thinking.

OK. So what if it's your face that fills the monitors? Your face, slick with sweat. Your hair hanging down in sweaty tendrils. Your mouth gaping open. Your eyes half closed in the throes of an ecstatic, orgasmic moment. 'Wow, Zita, you look totally cabbaged!' What if it's your boyfriend's friend who's about to see you more or less get mounted in the middle of a fucking orgy?

You hit the ALL-STOP button with a wallop, that's what! Lars stares at me with a why'd-ya-do-that? look. Ivan is leaning forward concentrating on the screen. 'This is very good, continue.' Lars presses PLAY.

'No, stop!'

Lars stops and leans back in his chair looking between me and Ivan. 'Do I stop or continue?' Before Ivan can answer, I suggest that Lars take a break while

Ivan and I discuss some creative points. Lars stands up and stretches. 'Sure, I need a coffee anyway.' When Lars is out of the room I say to Ivan, 'None of this stuff is to be used, OK?' Ivan hits PLAY and says, 'No, not OK, Zita. We will view it first and then I will decide if we use it.'

My head is lolling backwards, the sinews in my neck stretching. A camera lens (Cy's) is poking over my shoulder. Ivan's camera follows a line of sweat down my neck. A pulse jerks under the skin, sending the sweat on a different course. The camera runs down my body. A brown hand squeezes my tit. My nipple, swollen and almost purple, pokes out from between strong brown fingers. The camera pulls out to include my undulating waist. My body is arching rhythmically, my belly pushed out. My hand grasps the brown hand and guides it downwards over my stomach, down to my bush, pushing it into the nest of the curls. The camera goes back up to my belly, muscles shifting under the skin. The diamond in my belly-button flashes. Then my body is sort of bucked forward. The camera pulls back to my face. Ohmygod, I look like I'm coming! My face pants silently at me. Ohmygod, am I coming? Then blackness, where the lights went.

Ivan is already rewinding. Oh my fucking God. This is so embarrassing. What was I thinking? I nearly fucked Cy in the middle of a crowd of hundreds. Fuck. Now I know that I didn't actually fuck Cy but, as far as that footage is concerned, I might as well *have* done. Shit!

I need a fag. I tell Ivan that I need a break and wobble to my feet. He grunts and says, 'So do I.' Is he being funny? I shoot him a look but his face is all innocence. He follows me out to the little kitchen area, where we find Lars, who starts quizzing Ivan about *Eva Baby* and what it was like making films in commie

Russia. Ivan prattles on about Mosfilm and going to Cannes, and then he starts going on and on about being sent as a cultural ambassador to various Third World countries and how, best of all, he liked Cuba. By the time he hits the bit about how he was going to do his follow-up feature there, Lars is doing enough of the rapt-attentive stuff for the pair of us, so I tune out. Cuba makes me think of Paul and whether nearly fucking Cy counts as the same as fucking him. I'm gonna have to think this one through. First, I watched him fuck. Then I pissed over him. Then I wanked myself off thinking about him. Shit, that was all dangerously close to breaching the infidelity clause. Now this. I hadn't realised how close to coming I was. In fact, I'm not sure I didn't. I'm thinking how I'd better go and view those shots in private when Ivan's voice cuts back in. 'So, Zita, I will book for Havana, yes?'

I realise that Ivan is talking to me. Without even glancing at him, I mutter, 'Yeah, Ivan, whatever,' and head on back to the edit suite alone.

I study my face filling the monitor screens. Half a dozen Zitas pose naked before me, every one obviously in a state of arousal. My eyelids stutter down as I manipulate the jog/shuttle control, frame by frame. My mouth slips open and I can see my chest moving in and out in rapid, shallow pants. Eyes closed now, I throw my head back. Right in front of me, a girl is blatantly losing control. The moment is coming back to me now. I feel a tightening in my crotch and squirm against the editing chair. Shit, it's making me horny. But I can't tear my eyes away from the screens. I'm fascinated by how I look: dishevelled, sexual, worse than feral. Is that me? I can feel a pulsing in my cunt. I'm doubly shocked at myself: shocked at what's up on screen, shocked at the sensations the footage seems to be provoking in me. I seem to be losing all sense of modesty and control. This stuff is far too hot, there's no way we can use it.

'Hey, this is really something. I bet you're really excited, Zita, aren't you?' I hit ALL-STOP once again and flush beetroot. Did I do it in time before they came in?

'Oh, fantastically so,' I say airily, avoiding looking at Lars while I try to figure what he's burbling about.

Lars obligingly helps me out. 'Ivan Punin making another film, in Havana, and you his producer! You're going to be famous!'

I nod dumbly. Ivan drains his coffee mug and claps Lars around the shoulders. What are they on? They chunter away to each other while I surreptitiously sniff Ivan's mug for vodka. I'm going to be famous. Yeah, right.

12

So, I'm dividing my time between night shift at the edit suite, begging favours off everyone I know (well, mostly people Paul knows), and trying to organise this fucking soirée. Unless you count getting in litre bottles of plonk and a load of Waitrose dips as a soirée, I've never done one before. Jesus, in Shepherd's Bush it's considered sophisticated to offer your visitors Pringles, but this bash involves Celia and that's different. How would Saskia tackle it? Duh. She would get caterers in. If I had any money, I'd get caterers in, but herein lies yet another problem. I haven't got a budget. Yours truly will be footing the bill, which means it's gonna be a budget soirée.

I cheerily ask Nad if she wants to come and help me choose the food but Nad shakes her head. 'I don't *do* soirées, Zeet.'

And fuck you, too, I think, but don't say it. Instead I keep grinning. 'Nope, but I know a man who does!' Then I head off to talk to Cy.

C'mon, gimme a break. Time to get hold of Dali, that's all, and I know he's in the stables, engaged in a deep-and-meaningful with Cy. They've both got their backs to me, mumbling about Elaine (natch). I go to clear my throat but Cy does his eyes-in-the-back-of-his-head number and says in a mocking voice, 'Do you want something, Zita? I'm kinda busy.'

I can't help my stomach dropping like a falling elevator but I get a grip and cut to the chase, telling him about the soirée and that he's invited and so on.

If he's not *too* busy. 'And Elaine, of course,' I add dryly. Dali looks kinda startled but Cy just smiles beatifically at me and says, 'We'll try.' I smile beatifically back and say, 'Do.' Then I turn to Dali and ask for a word in his shell-like.

Not what I had in mind at all.

What I did have in mind was effortlessly organising something beautiful and sophisticated. At least Dali's up for helping me. He twirls his moustache and asks, 'What does beautiful and sophisticated mean to you, Zita?' As Me'Met's is the most sophisticated place I know (and Celia is probably a prime example of Me'Met's target clientele), I decide to do homage to Me'Met's. Dali claps his hands and goes off on one. 'Bedouin rugs, floor cushions, lanterns, couscous, olives. And tarboush. Everyone likes tarboush. And finger bowls with flower petals in.' Sounds right to me. Yeah, this soirée malarky's a piece of piss. Concentrate on the ambience. Celia works in film in *New York*, for Chrissake, so I doubt if she ever actually *eats* anything, anyway.

I spend most of wrap party day at Camberwell. The very first thing I do is post that damn CV. There, the die is cast. Off my conscience now. Dali is getting most of the stuff himself but has given me a wants list of extras, so I'm gonna borrow Paul's china/wine-glasses/throw from the bed/music ... I'm unsure about the music. I figure Celia likes classical but what about Nadine? Fuck it! Nadine will bitch no matter what I do. I throw in *The Greatest 80s Album in the Whole World Ever*. Oooh, and perhaps a few bottles from the bottom of Paul's wine bin as well. I stuff everything into the MGB and hightail it back to Tanglebush, popping two speed traps on Western Avenue en route. Dali and I dress the set (sorry, patio) till it looks something like the courtyard of an

Arabian brothel. Then, soirée sorted, time to think about me.

I have a bit of a fashion crisis. After several false starts, I decide to do what I do best. Urban babe, right? Last time Celia saw me, I was somewhat underdressed, so she needs to know that I *can* scrub up. I opt for the trusty little black number Paul bought me when we first started seeing each other. I was *so* impressed I couldn't speak. Paul looked embarrassed and said, 'It's from Joseph,' and I, being a smartarse, said something like, 'Gee, tell Joseph thanks!' Paul didn't get it and when I told Nad, she just said, 'Guy's had an irony bypass. Keep the frock and dump him.' Ah, Paul. My guilt muscle starts playing me up. I try to call him but can't get a connection (natch).

Consequently, I'm late for my own soirée. Is this cool or not? Doesn't seem to matter, as everyone looks pretty relaxed and, I'm glad to say, has made an effort in the dress department. In my absence, Dali has been emceeing and it goes without saying he is looking impeccable. Celia is doing blonde sophisticate in navy-blue palazzo pants, shirt and, I do believe, Jimmy Choo wedge-heel sandals. Nad, in a Bianca-Jagger-meets-Jackie-Brown white trouser suit, looks like her negative. Ivan, stretched out on the creaking house couch, has resurrected the black leather trouser/Hawaiian shirt ensemble and then there's Cy in classic bad-boy T-shirt and jeans. Annoyingly, he looks so beautiful, it hurts.

They've found the vino without my assistance (it has 'Rothschild' on the label, so, I reason, it can't be crap), and I need to play catch-up. As I gracefully position myself next to Celia, and opposite Cy, Madonna instructs me to get into the groove. I will. By the time Mikey, Stephen and partners arrive, everyone has loosened up and the vibe is nice and chilled.

Celia, in particular, is having a whale of a time. Dali is unbelievably skilful at manipulating people, drink and food. If a group looks like it's flagging, he dives in and swaps everyone around. And Tanglebush, lit by fairy lights and candles, drenched in incense and musk from the jasmine climbing over the French windows, is doing its best to be fabulous. My mate the owl hoots for added aural authenticity.

Stephen starts skinning up and I have an anxious moment when he offers it to Celia. But she smiles. 'God, it's been years,' she says, and, reclining over Paul's brown-leather floor cushions, takes a draw, then immediately lapses into a coughing fit. So uncool, but Nadine makes a big fuss of her, getting her drinks, patting her back. Ivan stares into his glass and, just as I think something's brewing, he starts talking wine.

'Lafite '88?' (Sniff, gargle, swallow.) 'Beginning to drink very well, I think. You are a connoisseur, Zita? So, your opinion please?'

I glug some back and say that, yes, I'm drinking very well too and everyone laughs. Even Cy grins. Ivan raises his glass in a toast, saying, 'To Cuba.'

Cuba? Please don't tell me he's serious about that. But, perfidious bitch that I am, I bounce the toast back: 'Cuba, *estupendo*!'

Ivan laughs. 'It will happen, Zita. Trust me.'

I'm laughing too. 'Yeah sure. Trust you, you're a director, right?'

Not a bad start, but I'm anxious to get the business over. I launch straight into what a genius-man-of-vision/creative force/generous-helper-of-new-raw-talent kinda guy Ivan is, my aim being to segue into Nad's vid, and arrange a time for Celia to come and check it out. Celia listens graciously and makes positive noises and then goes all jokey and says, 'It sounds fabulous. You know, I'm amazed. I really didn't think it would happen!' She takes another slurp of Paul's wine, splashing her enormously expensive shirt in the process. She doesn't seem to care. 'I assumed you were a pair of *Eva Baby* groupies.'

Nadine and I dart glances at each other. 'Of course, I realised how ridiculous that was immediately.' She drains her glass. 'I mean, attractive young women like you? Silly, with his . . .' Celia is windmilling her arms around in the air, searching for a word, before finishing on, '. . . circumstances.' She breaks into peels of laughter.

Ivan clears his throat and everyone looks at him. To my amazement, he is calm. 'Celia, perhaps you are unused to smoking pot.'

Celia wipes the back of her hand over her mouth and slurs, 'Plenty of things I'm unused to, Ivan. Doesn't mean I can't *indulge* once in a while.' With that, she turns to Cy. 'Now, I gather you're a painter. I am *so* interested in art.'

Cy, who has been watching the whole exchange with a wry, sleepy-eyed smile, leans forward and takes hold of Celia's hand, the one holding the joint. Nad does rolling-eye stuff towards Ivan, who is contemplating the bottom of his empty glass. Dali shimmies in to neatly block Ivan's line of vision while topping up his glass, declaiming, '*Eva Baby*, such a beautiful film.' This boy is a diamond. I, meanwhile, grandstand as Cy presses Celia's hand to his mouth, fixing her with his let's-get-naked-now eyes. It's only when he takes a toke with her palm pressed to his lips that her expression changes. I dunno what he's doing, but it certainly brings the colour to her cheeks. She lowers her eyes coquettishly. Oh bletch. Some creative mingling is called for.

Dali does a clever replenishing-the-olives man-oeuvre whereby he wriggles himself between Celia (who frankly is making an exhibition of herself) and Cy. Nadine seizes the opportunity and starts rabbiting at Celia, flattering her shamelessly. 'What is it exactly you do Celia?' Then, 'Oh [*gasp*], and you're *so* young too. [*gasp!*]' Then, slyly, 'Zita has ambitions in that direction, don't you, Zeet?'

I shrug bashfully but manage to mention casually that I am *thinking* of applying for floor manager on Big World's new kids' show.

Celia smiles noncommittally, and slurs, 'One *helluva* lot of people have applied for that post,' then goes back to having her ego massaged by Nad.

An hour later everyone's getting along just fine and dandy. Dali's giving Cy an Indian head massage. Not to be outdone, Ivan grabs one of my bare feet and begins demonstrating his reflexology technique. I'm trying to focus on what Celia said about *Massive* but the most distracting sensations are whooshing up my legs. Nad grins wickedly. 'Toe sucking is supposed to be very soothing,' she says. I make a half-arsed attempt to break free of Ivan's grasp just as the opening bars of 'Sex Machine' start pounding out. Nadine whoops and pulls Celia up to dance just as Ivan starts the amazingly creative tonguing. Ohmygod, he may as well be sucking my clit – I have got *the* most sensitive feet. And shit! What will Celia think?

Celia will probably think nothing. Nadine is spooned in behind her, hands on her waist, inciting her to shake her booty like a dancehall queen. I relax and watch Nad pull Celia on to her thigh, encouraging her to grind her nonexistent butt. Stephen and Mikey are enjoying the show, their girlfriends too engrossed in watching Dali trickle sesame oil over Cy's bare shoulders to care. Shit, everyone is way too stoned. Dali's healing hands start kneading Cy's beautiful golden skin. I fight the desire to moan. Ivan's attentions plus Cy's oil-drizzled torso are too much to bear. I mumble, 'More wine?' and stagger away to the kitchen to splash water over my face.

When I return, the mood has changed. Celia is flopped on the couch while Ivan is shouting, 'Celia, you have said enough,' followed by a silence that not even Dali can fill. Oh, shit, not the toe sucking? Then, a titter of mirth emerges from Celia. Within seconds, she is laughing uncontrollably.

Without a word, Ivan walks straight to their car, starts the engine and roars off. Celia is *so* pissed, she thinks this is so hilarious, she is hysterical. Between sobs of laughter, she blurts, 'Don't mind him. He's Russian y'know!' which segues into hiccups and ends with 'Oh dear, I feel sick.' Last I see of her, Nad is helping her through the French windows. A fucking disaster. I leave everyone else to realise the show is over and head back to the kitchen to start on the washing up. Ten minutes later, I realise I'm being watched. Cy is standing in the doorway with a pile of bowls.

It all starts very innocently. A splash of water hits me as he dumps the crocks in the sink. I splash him back (natch). Then he does this tidal wave that soaks me. Tee-fucking-hee. I grab him by his locks and try to force his head in the sink. Next, we're wrestling around in a major water fight. Cy has me pinned in a corner and I'm soaked head to toe. Cy is staring at me. I look down. The sheer material clings so intimately, I might as well be naked. I look back up. There's heavy-duty lust in his eyes. He moves in close so I'm trapped, me against him, belly to belly. Cy's mouth is right before my eyes. I watch, transfixed, as it moves to make words I know that clever girls do not listen to. His lower lip, roughened on the outside where he's gnawed it but smooth and crimson inside, pushes out to make the first syllable. 'You . . .' Lips part. 'Are . . .' Sharp, even teeth in view. 'Fucking . . .' Mouth purses. 'Gorge –' It's one of those I-know-exactly-what's-gonna-happen moments. I can't wait, I've got to jump before I fall. Impulsively, I grab his face in both hands and snog those luscious puckered lips. And zing go the strings of my cunt as Cy returns my kiss ferociously. Naturally, this is the point when Nadine enters.

Cy turns to her and, unbelievably, Nadine chins him. Cy just rubs his face and smirks, while she spits, 'Out of fucking bounds!' Jesus, what is going on? I grab my cigs, and stomp off to the woods, where I chain-smoke and cringe. What a fucking fiasco. When my fag packet is empty, I decide to sneak back to my room. I'm heading towards the house when, suddenly, I feel a hand over my mouth and I am being dragged backwards, away from the light and into the woods. I scream and struggle and try to hook my legs around my attacker but I can't. He/she hauls me into the bushes and dumps me on the ground. I take my chance. I spin round, kicking and flailing and then stop. Shit, it's Cy.

We sprawl there, chests heaving, glaring at each other. 'You know your problem, Zita?' he pants. I'm trying for a retort but Cy doesn't wait. 'You just can't be honest about what you want.' I shake my head. 'No?' he asks. What's the point of words on this crazy night? I wrestle my wet frock over my head and throw it away among the leaves. I kneel in the light of the rising moon filtering through the branches. I let Cy look at me. Then I crawl up to him and kiss him hard.

Cy kisses me back, down my throat, on to my breasts. The events of the night and the cooling wet fabric have left their tips so taut they're almost hurting. I reach round his head till my fingers entwine with his locks, then I pull him on to my tender, swollen nips, which he takes fiercely in his mouth, one at a time. Then he slides down my belly till his tongue is delving into the folds that wrap my clit. And I'm pulling at his hair and telling him breathlessly that I know what I want all right. Whereupon the bastard stops his licking, and stands up right in front of me.

He unzips his flies and pulls out his swollen, livid cock. He's so fucking animal, I want him to do whatever he wants to me. He obliges. He twists his hand in my hair, yanking my head back, and begins wiping the end of his cock around my mouth. I can feel pre-come smearing my lips. My cunt begins to ache. 'You're a dirty little tease, aren't you, Zita?' Cy's dick is forcing my lips apart. 'Lick it, Zita.' I close my eyes and run my tongue over the swollen glans. 'Lick it properly, Zita, like the hungry cunt you really are.' I begin lapping all the way along, tickling the underside, letting the tip of my tongue probe everywhere, down to the veiny base, into the golden hair round his balls. 'Now, in your mouth.' I part my lips and suck on Cy's cock till it swells to fill my mouth. 'Is this is what you wanted, Zita?' Cy's voice sounds distant. 'When you spied on me and Elaine?' He pulls his cock from my mouth and looks down on me. 'Tell me what you want, Zita.' I tell him what I've been desperate to say for weeks. Without taking my eyes off his gorgeous, golden cock, I whisper, 'I want you to fuck me.'

He pushes me round abruptly so that I am facing away from him on hands and knees. He splays my thighs and guides his cock into my cunt, mounting me from behind. At last, is all I can think, at fucking last, and I work backwards against his thrusts to take him slowly inside. His cock is so enormously, rigidly erect, it hurts. I wince thankfully as it forces up me to the hilt. Then he begins a vigorous heaving, and we're soon into hard fucking. I bounce against him, my eyes closed, my mouth a rictus grin, as I think of the dirty little fantasy I had the day I pissed on him and how now we're doing it and I drive back faster and harder as his hips push to meet mine till we're pounding into each other so wantonly that I lose my balance and we collapse together on to the dried-leaf-littered woodland floor, still desperately grinding. His hand reaches round to my mons and a finger touches my clit. Ohmygod, my clit. I alternately rub myself up against his clutching, working fingers, then back against his driving cock. It's so high up me that I'm being skewered. His cock swells so taut and big that I can feel it stretching me and I nearly cry out but I don't and he is pumping violently inside me just as a shuddering orgasm wells from my aching, overstimulated clit and fans out to engulf my whole jerking, shaking body.

Cy climbs off me and whispers, sarcastically, 'Don't forget to tell Paul how much you're missing him.' Then he walks away, leaving me face down in the dirt, trembling and sweating and totally confused. I don't like Cy. I'm not even sure I like myself. I don't know what game we're playing. But I do know I love being fucked like that. And I'm gonna have to do it again.

13

And the nightmare continues ...

I said that long, hot, summer nights in an over-heated edit suite form a horror subgenre of their own, didn't I? Well, in this particular episode Ivan's been sent out on a mission to buy ice cream, Lars is in another suite and I am alone with Nadine. This is the one night that she has deigned to put in an appear-ance, and, on the one night she deigns to put in an appearance, she chooses to go weird on me.

We're sitting in silence until some of the incrimi-nating footage of me and Cy comes up. It's only facial close-ups and we look so good (well, abso-fucking-lutely rampantly gorgeous, actually), I've let Ivan per-suade me to allow a split-second clip before it cuts to Nad. I'm picking up a not-happy vibe from her. Then she drawls, 'Who exactly were you trying to spite there, Zita? Me or Paul?'

Uh-oh! I choke on my coffee and buy enough time to try for righteous indignation. 'Excuse me?' Nad does some silent-and-meaningfuls at the monitor. Does she think I'm upstaging her or what? In case something *has* been said, I hedge my bets and mutter, 'It was Cy who came on to me, Nadine, and anyway I was just *acting*, for Chrissake.'

There's a bit of a hard-stare contest but Nad looks away first, which is the nearest she ever gets to backing down. I relax (a bit) but then Nad starts doing this big sista act. She goes all home-girly and even starts wagging a finger at me. She calls me naïve (again), and makes some uncalled-for remarks about Cy, then, for her big finish, kisses her teeth and says, 'I thought you had a little more self-respect than Elaine.' Then it's all pursed lips and folded arms and tense silence.

I can't muster a suitably feisty riposte. So, in lieu of one, I resort to changing the point of attack and harrumph indignantly. 'So when did you become such a big fan of Paul, Nadine?' She starts playing with her nails and doesn't answer (a good sign). I take the opportunity to grumble on more. 'If I was interested in fucking Cy, I would have the honesty to say so, which wouldn't happen anyway as I wouldn't fuck him if he was the last man on fucking earth.' (So I'm lying. I'm a producer. It's in the job spec, OK?) I can see the corner of Nadine's mouth trying to twitch into a smile but I'm pissed off with her now, so I continue, 'And since when exactly did who I fuck, or not fuck, become such a big deal to you?'

Her nascent smile evaporates. 'Oh, it's no big deal, Zita. It's merely that, *exactly* the moment you start screwing someone, I don't see you again for six months. Not until that person drops you, of course.' Once again, I'm all out of witty retorts. Partly because she is completely out of order. Partly because I've got an irritable feeling that, despite the total unfairness of the allegation, somewhere in there lies a grain of truth. I open my mouth to protest but she's on a roll. 'You're doing it again, Zita. What's sad is that you are so fucking self-obsessed, you can't see it.'

I don't dignify that one with an answer beyond a snort. An expressive snort that says: Me, self-obsessed? I, who am working for free/gratis/at great personal cost even, for this other person's benefit, is self-obsessed? Puh-lease.

Nad ignores my expressive snort and does one back

but she adds words to hers. 'You can't see it, can you?' I'm, like, 'See what?' and she snaps, 'For God's sake, Zita, you are so fucking naïve. Man, you can't even lie well. Everyone knows you fucked Cy, Zita. *Everyone*.'

Shit. I open my mouth to protest but nothing comes out. Fuck. Everyone knows? Nadine tosses her locks. 'I take it you're gonna have the honesty to tell Paul about it?' She asks, adding some 'Hmmn, hmmn?'s for good measure. The best I can manage is, 'And are you gonna have the honesty to admit you're just a jealous bitch?' Then it's face-off time. Flashing eyes, straining neck muscles, and I'm thinking this is it, this is the end of our friendship, but Nad looks away again and when she looks back her expression has changed.

Nadine is beginning to scare me. Her eyes have gone glittery and she looks almost wild. She raises her hand so fast that I flinch, but she doesn't hit me. Instead she drags the point of one of her nails down the side of my cheek along my mouth and down my neck. She smiles a wounded-tiger smile at me. 'Zita, I told you. We're friends. When I said it, I meant it.' I nod uncomfortably with Nad's nail digging into my collarbone. She bends her head in close to mine and I can feel her breath on the side of my neck. I watch our reflection in the monitor, superimposed over Nad's face from the shoot. My reflected face, pale and worried, carnival-queen Nadine up on screen, real Nad's forehead pressed into my hair. I can just make out her voice softly murmuring, 'I meant it.' Sweat trickles along my jawline. I put a hand up and my fingers are wet. Not sweat, tears.

It's official, I'm scared. Nadine is crying. Nadine never cries. I don't know what to do. I pat and there-there her while she nuzzles her wet face into my neck. After thirty seconds of this, Nadine pulls herself away and stands defiantly in front of me. She wipes her eyes with the back of her hand, and smiles a little shamefacedly. 'OK, I'm a fool.' She sniffs, then turns on her big, let-the-sun-shine-in grin. The big brown eyes are luminous with unshed tears. She purses her lips determinedly and nods to herself, then she sighs heavily. 'I'm a fool.' I'm caught completely off guard. It's very hard to resist Nad when she's this rakishly disarming. I take her hands and pull her on to my lap, so that she is sitting astride me in the wide, heavily padded editor's swivel chair. I'm not big, but Nad floats on me, as light as a feather. I stroke her hair and say, 'I know.' I haven't got a clue what I know or why, really, it just seems the right thing to say.

Nadine holds my face delicately in her hands. 'Do you?' she asks. Then, she bends forward and kisses me lightly on the lips. Nadine is a very good kisser. She gently tugs at my lips and bites my lower lip teasingly. Then she backs off and laughs at herself. 'I really am such a fool,' she says, and kisses me again. More passionately, this time. She lifts my hair, kisses me round my neck, till she's at the nape. She licks and nips and nibbles me there, knowing this is my secret spot. I told her about it years ago. The one place guaranteed to get me into a trance. My face is buried in her bony cleavage and my nostrils are full of the warm, aromatic Nadine smell that is unique to her. One of the things I really like about her physically is that she always has this clean, comforting, musky scent about her that's nice to be up close to.

Next thing, Nadine is untying her halter-neck top and her tiny bosoms jump free, the tips bobbing around by my mouth. Her purply-black nipples are almost bigger than her tits. Nad pauses, then hesitantly begins stroking one along my lips. I'm strangely curious about how it would taste. Somehow, my lips part and the nip pushes, or is sucked, I can't tell, inside. The flavour of her skin, like bitter chocolate, coats my tongue. She puts her arms round my head and cradles me to her. Her nip grows tauter and longer and she begins rocking on my lap. Then, her other hand takes mine and pulls it slowly down towards her groin. Her vinyl miniskirt has ridden up, so my fingers go straight into her bush. I automatically flex my hand and a nail snags on one of Nad's thick hairs. I feel it snap as Nad pushes my hand further till my fingers find her swollen pussy lips. I'm shocked and try to pull away, but Nadine grips my hand fiercely.

'Come on, Zita, please,' she pleads. 'It's my turn. I'm so fucking horny. Do me. Please.' She cups her hand over mine, interlacing our combined fingers, then, rocking her hips back and forth violently, she rubs her pussy fiercely against my imprisoned fist. I'm not really in a position to object. Nadine might be famously skinny but she's fit, and she's got an armlock on my head, her tit stuffed into my mouth and her knees wrapped firmly round my thighs. Part of me wants to push her away and scream and spit her out of my mouth. But, despite the fact that this is all a bit of a cheek, it's also weirdly exciting. Nadine losing control is a totally new sensation. She's always the one who is cool, calm and collected. And, after seeing myself on screen, it's kind of interesting watching another woman lose it.

Anyway, there's no way I can stop things 'cos they're being forced on me (none of this is my fault, OK?). I grip Nad's teat delicately with my teeth and nip. Nadine moans and fumbles with my hand, separating a couple of my fingers, then pushes them up her. Immediately, the muscles of her cunt grip on me tightly. She starts drawing her breath in harsh gasps and bouncing herself against my hand while teasing her breast in and out of my mouth. My free hand unwittingly slips round her slinky hips and cups the muscular dome of her tight, muscular arse. Her skin is sheened with sweat but cool as satin. Nadine is frigging her clit with all her might, repeatedly and hoarsely muttering, 'Oh Zeet, please,' like a mantra. She's whipping her nips in and out of my teeth and I'm biting them angrily now, no pretence at delicacy. If she wants it rough ... My free hand is fingering her arsehole, slippy with her juice, and suddenly I've got fingers up inside her back and front and she's howling and crying and moaning and yelling and I can feel the muscles pulsing as Nadine arches and comes like a wildcat tearing at its prey.

'Jesus, Nadine,' I hiss. 'You could have been more discreet, made less noise. Lars is in the next room.'

Nadine refastens her halter-top and winks at me. 'You just don't know how to let go, girlfriend.' Then she jumps off my knee and goes, 'Fag break?' like nothing has happened.

I'm confused again. 'Nadine?' I ask. 'Didn't I tell you I'm not a lesbian?'

She evil-eyes me for a second, then laughs. 'Zita, you crack me up.'

My sense of righteous indignation is genuine now. 'You think it's funny, Nadine?'

Nad goes hand-on-hip cocky 'What's the big deal, Zeet?'

I'm verging on irate. 'You just made me ...'

Nad puts her finger right between my eyes. 'Zita, I didn't make you do anything.'

I remove her finger and pout. 'Yes, you did.'

Nadine throws her hands in the air. 'You are so fucking repressed. Can't you just admit you liked it?'

'That's not the point,' I snap. (I mean, I didn't.) 'You fucking took advantage, Nadine.'

That shuts her up for a second, then she goes,

'You're having a laugh, aren't you? I took advantage of you? You're one selfish, self-centred bitch, Zita. You know that?'

I've gotta hear this. I give her a *do* tell look and she says, 'I thought that maybe you fucked me 'cos you liked me, Zita, but oh no. It was all just to get back at Paul, wasn't it?'

My turn to laugh now. 'Oh, dead giveaway, Nad,' I sneer. 'I'm right. You're jealous.'

She rolls her eyes, 'As if . . .'

'As if you'd take Paul's side for any other reason. Just have the honesty to admit it,' I interrupt.

Then she hits right below the belt. 'I take it you've had the honesty to tell Paul you've been fucking me *and* Cy then?'

She must realise that she's gone too far 'cos she does this stupid lezbefriends thing and tries to kiss me. I'm having none of it. I turn my head and snarl, 'Fuck off, Nad. I'm only helping you with this fucking project 'cos I feel sorry for you, but as soon as it's over we're finished.'

She kinda recoils, then says in this icy voice, 'I don't need your fucking help, Zita. The project's over. We're finished now.' Then she does this big nose-in-the-air Ms Ting exit.

Fuck! I don't know what to do. I wait for Ivan and tell him (a version of) what happened. I think he'll go mental but he just shrugs his shoulders. 'It's no matter.' It's *no fucking matter*. It mightn't be to him but I've worked my fucking tits off on this and I've told everyone I'm doing it. And oh fuck: I've put it on my CV.

Ivan hands me a Magnum and says, 'This is Nadine's baby, no?' he said. 'We will leave the finished cut to Nadine and she will take it to Celia and Celia will help her. Trust me, I know. I'm a director. I have had my babies too.' I stare glumly at the screen while Ivan chunters on. 'Besides. We are going to Cuba.'

Cuba? Is he insane? I'm gonna fuck him off but then, once I've thought about it, the possibility of time out from Tanglebush, from Nadine and Cy and Elaine – especially Nadine – kind of grows on me. Fuck it, I'll go to Cuba.

The moment I get my ticket from Ivan, I tell Paul. He nearly wets himself. Paul, being a film snob, has heard of *Eva Baby*, of course. I hear his excitement mounting till it boils over with a 'God, we're going to have to get together, babe, aren't we?' Hey, now we're a *real* meejah couple. You know the type: jetting to exotic locations, snatching brief interludes of passion in the middle of projects. Then I realise he means himself and Ivan. I put him right on that one p.d.q. If there's any getting together to be got, it will be with his Official Girlfriend, natch. Nonetheless, he remains distinctly upbeat and impressed until I mentioned we're flying out Cubana, the national airline of, you got it, Cuba. 'Oh, *ultra*-low budget, huh?' he sneers, reverting to his usual, cynical tone. I don't understand until I board the Illyushin, the jet that time and technology forgot. God, I fucking hate it when Paul's right.

But at least he is on my side, I think, as the Illyushin eases its way down the Miami seaboard towards Havana. Well, he is for the moment. Nadine's sarcastic words are ringing in my ears: 'I take it you've had the honesty . . .', blah, blah . . .' Bollocks. What should I do? I consider my options:

1. Don't tell Paul and hope he never finds out. But what about fly-in-the-ointment Nadine? OK, she *hates* Paul, but, after her recent performance, who knows . . . ?

2. Tell Paul and beg his forgiveness. Nah, begging's not an option.
3. Don't tell Paul and, *if* he finds out, insist that I was gonna tell him but I didn't wanna hurt him. Hmmm, cheesy.
4. Stop worrying and, if the worst happens, deny everything and tell Paul he shouldn't listen to rumour.

That one'll have to do. Shit, since I moved to Tangle-bush, I seem to have completely tangled up my head. The thing with Nadine, the thing with Cy. Why is it, whenever I think of Cy, I get this alarming flutter in my belly? He seems to have invaded my senses. I can't work out what the rules are to this game we're playing. Or who's winning. I'm not sure I can say, hand on heart, it's me.

By the time we arrive at Jose Marti, I am not one whit the wiser. But, now, I don't actually care. I walk out on to an old-fashioned set of aeroplane steps and sniff the balmy, night-scented air. I'm in Cuba! Only one week maybe, but hey, I am here, in fucking Cuba! Land of white sandy beaches, sugar cane, salsa, Havana Libres and louche men in crumpled white suits.

It's so me.

14

I gather we are staying in the Old Town so I have romantic visions of balconies and marble foyers and those big, torpidly rotating ceiling fans. And I am *so* looking forward to a shower and air-con. Our cab pulls up in Calle Industria. Industry Street. The neighbourhood ambience feels remarkably similar to Shepherd's Bush, right down to the crumbling stucco. Before us is an archway, big enough to drive a bus through. Ivan pushes at the ornate, rusted gate and we step into a courtyard. I look up through tiers of wrought-iron balconies supported by a combination of rusty scaffolding, wooden buttresses and string to dancing lines of washing decorating the atrium like flags.

'Ivan, what kind of a hotel is this?' I demand. We have climbed three storeys without a reception desk in sight. There's a multitude of marble (of the chipped variety), a barking dog (huge) and a gaggle (more accurately, a giggle) of children.

'We are renting an apartment,' he informs me. With that, a woman (foxy, long of limb, high of cheekbone) opens a battered louvred door and shepherds us into a large, airy, high-ceilinged room.

I sly-eye her as she slinks around the apartment showing us the amenities. No glamorous ceiling fan and no air-con but there are huge shuttered windows that open on to an external balcony. Bathroom facilities are on a par with Tanglebush: a hosepipe affair in a cupboard in lieu of a shower. My standards of faded grandeur are now pretty high, but this is right up there. There's just one thing I have to sort. 'Ivan?' I ask. 'Where do you and the fox sleep?'

His quizzical look confirms my suspicion that I'm about to be privy to another Alison scenario. You know, sleepless nights listening to the ol' give-it-to-me-Big-Boy stuff? Perhaps this time in Spanish. The fox answers for him. 'You have a problem?'

I shrug. 'Um, just wondering where you sleep.'

She gives me a hard stare. There's enough of the tough ragga chick about her to make me disinclined to pick a fight. Then a knowing smile slashes her face wide open. 'I sleep at my mother's, OK?' I'm wondering how fluent her English is, in case she's understood what I've said. She has.

Ivan switches to Spanish and by the way Ms Fox is laughing I know that he's flirting with her. Enough of this. I decide to move things along by interrupting. 'Ivan, I wanna drink.'

He says haughtily, 'Of course. I was asking Yolande where we should go.'

She interrupts, 'El Lido. *Enfrente de la casa.* Maybe I go there later too.' Then, I swear, she winks at me. It's like the coolest, toughest girl in school has just taken a shine to you. I feel weirdly pleased. I know that's really sad, but I'm low in the gal-pal stakes at the moment, remember.

My new pal, Yolande, gets off, leaving Ivan and me to sort the domestics. The apartment has only one bedroom, which makes things easy-peasy. I get the bed, he gets the couch. To pre-empt any potentially embarrassing seduction scenes, I spell out to him that I am here to work and will under no circumstances be allowing him into my bed. His drawl is unnecessarily derisory. 'So, Zita, you believe I wish to fuck you?'

Ahhh ... Rule 202: never accuse someone of wanting to screw you unless you have the evidence. I brazen it out, 'I didn't say that, I said –'

Ivan solemnly takes my hand in his. 'Zita, baby. I swear that I will not try to enter your bed. Or otherwise ravage you.' Is he taking the piss or what? He's bugging me now. Besides which, why doesn't he want to ravage me?

'Oh, I'm not worried Ivan,' I purr. 'I'm here to work, so there won't be any time for ravaging. And I have met your wife, remember.'

Ivan's smile freezes on his face. 'Zita, forget about Celia. She forgot about me a long time ago. And don't worry about work, either. There will be plenty.'

For a brief moment, Ivan looks angry and for some reason I feel guilty. All I wanted was to get a few things straight. Let him know that I am not the original good time to be had by all. I am a respectable media freelancer with a live-in boyfriend to whom I am faithful. Normally.

'Look, Ivan. About Nadine's shoot –' I begin, but he holds up a hand to stop me.

'Yes, I know. You worked very hard and I did not say thank you and you did not make money. But now I say it. Thank you. You did good work. This is why I ask you to come with me, not to sleep with you. You will make a great producer, I know.'

Hmmn, soft soap or what? So, why doesn't he want to ravage me, then? I don't have long to ponder, though, because he continues, 'And I think you should relax here in Havana. Your boyfriend will be fucking with the continuity girl, or somebody, so you should have a good time too.'

I glower at him. What does he know about Paul? What does he know about Paul's shoot? I come back immediately. 'It's a documentary, Ivan. They don't have continuity supervisors on a doc. And, if they did, I am sure that everyone would be behaving impeccably professionally.'

He looks at me, runs his hands through his hair and utters a dismissively Russian grunt. 'Yah, yah, Zita. We are ready to go?'

We're round the corner from the Floridita, the bar Hemingway frequented on his Havana sojourns. This is more like it. This is the Cuba I expected: louche, glam, decadent. It's just so me. I wish I'd changed now. That black Joseph dress would look great here. Ivan orders daiquiris while I arrange myself decorously on the bar stool playing Betty Bacall to his Bogie. There's a long mirror behind the bar, which I watch me and Ivan in. Me sipping daiquiris in the Floridita with a famous Russian film director. How cool is that? Hah, if Paul and Saskia could see me now. Ivan is telling me about the project but I keep drifting off. C'mon, I'm exhausted, gimme a break! By the time I tune back in, Ivan has segued into a rant about prewar Germany, so I guess I didn't miss much.

After a couple more daiquiris, Ivan starts getting antsy. He mutters something about not finding Lola in here and suggests we go the Lido. I smirk at him. 'Looking for Lola', eh? That's like dirty Russian slang for something to shag, as in 'Yolande'. We head back to Calle Industria, where Ivan immediately enters the crumbling building opposite our apartment. I guess he doesn't know Havana as well as he pretends, because there's no sign of a bar. 'Ivan, where are we going?' I ask.

Ivan points to a staircase even more decrepit than the one at Yolande's gaff and says, 'The roof, Zita, the roof.'

My mouth dries instantly but Ivan is already climbing the spiral stairs. With no real alternative, I follow, eyes shut, pressing myself against the wall. Then I feel a light breeze and I open them again. I'm on the roof. Whoosh. A rush runs through my body – an ears-pounding, palms-sweating, legs-shaking, eyeballs-spinning rush. Did I tell you I'm scared of heights? Terror-struck is more accurate. It's a purely rational terror. I know, if I get too close to the edge, I'll have to surrender to the inevitable. I'm no Alison. I wouldn't fall: I'd jump.

Then I hear voices. Beyond a little structure that houses ducts and pipework, I see a pool of light. Then, a burst of music of the high-tenor-voices-and-strummed-guitar variety, and then laughter. I steel myself and walk round some ducting to be faced with a coconut-matting beach shack and a selection of rickety chairs. A flickering neon sign (original fifties) announces Bar Lido – an empty Bar Lido, apart from three blokes singing to each other and a very dapper hundred-year-old barman-dude wearing a Panama and smoking the biggest fuck-off cigar ever seen. Cool. But wait, how cool is this? Panama doffs his hat at Ivan and me and says something like 'Bebay?' Sweet, the old guy is flirting with me. I dimple at him, settle myself at the bar and check the bar menu. I can have anything I want, as long as it has rum in it. Oh well, when in Havana . . . I order a *mojito* and right on cue, *el grupo* launch into their rather mournful version of (you guessed it) 'Guantanamera'.

It doesn't take so long before I'm feeling mellow. As soon as I finish one cocktail, Panama calls me Bebay, I twinkle and he gives me another. I point my stool so I can look out over the city (keeping well clear of the edge) and relax a bit as the bar fills up with assorted types. OK, this is Havana. It would be nice to share this with Paul but he'd probably get sniffy. He cannot distinguish between shabby chic and squalor. More of a Floridita guy, I guess. I'm shaken from my reverie by a commotion. Yolande has arrived, and everyone knows it. She's changed into something more funky for the evening: a cropped T-shirt with the Cuban star slap-bang over her titties and baggy cotton trousers worn so low that you wonder if gravity is perhaps not as strong in Cuba as on the rest of the planet. Anyhow, it fully exploits her unreasonably slinky hips. Her hair is severely cropped to her skull but she's got the sculptured features to carry it.

''Ola, Comrade Yolande,' Ivan says, grinning drunkenly at her.

She grins back, flashing her gold tooth, and slinks over to us saying in her husky voice, 'In Cuba, you say *compañeros*,' before casually planting a kiss on each of my cheeks. For some unfathomable reason I go shy and blush. She's simultaneously irresistibly animated and cool, a jazz-chick. Even when, next minute, she's leading the community singing.

Two hours, three more *mojitos* and another daiquiri later, I am no longer shy. I am singing, full belt into the beautiful starry night, 'Cunt in the mirror...' I have Ivan draped about me and amused/bemused messages being telegraphed to me from Yolande. Ivan orders yet another round of drinks '*Por mis compañeros*', then launches into one of his long-distance rants about the beauty of Cuba (everybody smiling in agreement), the beauty of women (everybody smiles even more), the beauty of Cuban women in particular (everybody smiles again, particularly at Yolande). Then he slides back into his prewar-Germany spiel. I'm lost. Maybe it's political, I dunno. After twenty minutes of this, I'm too tired, and way too drunk, to follow anything of what is going on, so I bid my goodnights to my new-found pals in the band and my boyfriend behind the bar and my new girlfriend

Yolande, before I stumble across Calle Industria to our apartment, pausing only to kiss the woofy dog that lives on the landing, and collapse into my beautiful, big, soft antique bed.

'Wooaaahhooh!'

I am face down, naked and squirming, slowly pushing my cunt into something warm and slippy. I know I'm face down because, when my eyelids dragged apart, the lashes stuttered across the pillowcase like velvet dragging over concrete. I worm my head under the pillow and try to will away the wakefulness sneaking up on me.

'Ahoooh.' I am being unwarrantedly hauled back into consciousness. I don't want to go there. I'm anxious to return to the land of warm and slippy. Somewhere, somehow, I'd been trussed up in a shack or a wooden cabin, or something like that. My bare arse was flagrantly offering itself to the world. A dark figure – no, *figures* ... Dark, handsome, male figures, were stroking and smoothing the peachy cheeks of my arse. Their hands were going everywhere, everywhere private, and I couldn't stop them. They were entitled, I was chosen. The figures were planning to take advantage of my position. I was dimly aware that the first hard cock was just about to present itself at the entrance to my slippy hole, when I'd been so rudely woken.

'*Wooaaaaa!*' The sound fills my head. It's Alison. Fuck it, ignore her, she's dead. Breathe. In, out, in, out. I start drifting, sinking further back, vaguely aware that my hips are moving in sync with my breathing. Moving against my hand, which seems to have found its way down there too. In, out, in, out. My mons is following the same solid rhythm as it rubs against my hand. My fingers have parted the hairs to explore my mushy groove. They've found my clit, and it's plump and available. I spread my thighs and push down firmer, harder.

'Ooooohah!' Alison lets rip another howl. Duh, it's not Alison come back to haunt me: it's that fucking big smelly dog that lives out on the landing. Whatever it is, it's fucking determined. I roll over on to my back and lie for a moment absent-mindedly twirling pubic hair round my fingers. It's like being in a float tank, listening to whale music or something. I reach out to the side and I feel the dusty slats of the wooden window shutter. Shit, I'm awake now. I sit upright and put my feet on the cool tiles of the floor. Inching my way along my bed, I advance into the fuzzy blackness, arms stretched out, sleepwalker style. I pause in the arch that frames the entrance to my sleeping alcove. The shutters are ajar in the main room and I realise that I must have been asleep longer than I thought because a soft, milky morning light is washing in to illuminate the room very dimly.

I sniff the air. The room smells like a fish factory. I'm about to go and open the windows because I don't want Ivan making any saucy comments when he gets back, when another howl fills the space. I look to the couch and realise that Ivan is, in fact, back and has his face buried between the splayed thighs of an impressively supple Yolande. I press myself back into the shadows. I should make my way back into my little den but my legs won't take me. Ivan sits back on his haunches and lifts Yolande up by the waist so her arse is supported by his chest and her pussy is directly in front of his mouth. Her lithe, neat legs are splayed either side of his head, her slim ankles dangling in space, her toes curled and pointing to opposite corners of the room.

She moans something huskily in Spanish that ends

with '*compañero*'. Ivan laughs and stretches an arm down the side of the couch, and when he comes up again he has a bottle in his hand. I watch with a mixture of horror and fascination as the neck of the bottle hovers over Yolande's exposed cunt. He says something to her in his own language. I've never heard him speak Russian before. His voice sounds thick, dirty, guttural. Russian seems an appropriate voice for dirty sex. The bottle gets ever closer to Yolande's vulnerable hole and I hold my breath as Ivan gently rubs its neck along her slit. Unconsciously, my hand closes over my own pussy and I stifle a groan. It is very wet.

Yolande moans some more and her legs tense and her ankles interlock behind Ivan's head. I can see her head thrown back on the couch, her eyelids open but her eyes rolled right back in their sockets, just the whites showing. I can see that she is completely lost in the grip of sensation, panting now, beyond even the ability to howl. She begins to lift her crotch rhythmically upwards to the bottle neck, desperately inviting Ivan to do something more to her with it. Anything he wants. She is lost in sex.

Then, he tilts the bottle and Yolande and I gasp simultaneously as the liquid splashes down and sluices over the groove of her open cunt. The sweet smell of rum fills the room. My clit tingles at the thought of the hot burning alcohol as Yolande's gasps becomes a long anguished cry, drowning my own muffled cries. Ivan clamps his mouth over Yolande's pussy and laps greedily. Unlike the sensual, lingering kisses he was giving it before, now he's rough and harsh and aggressive. Yolande is pushing her groin fiercely upwards into Ivan's face, crying and whimpering. I squeeze my lips together, trapping my clit between them, but it's not enough. I begin rubbing and fondling the swollen labia against the fat, hungry bud, faster and harder, in time with Yolande's own desperate thrashings. My head is filled with images of Cy fucking Elaine, Cy fucking me, me pissing in Cy's mouth. Did I dream that? Whatever, difference here is Ivan seems pretty focused on giving Yolande a good time. My legs begin to buckle just as Ivan pulls Yolande on to his cock and she lets out a long, wavering, high-pitched scream and Ivan pitches and yaws into her spreadeagled cunt, pumping into her.

The panting in the room slowly subsides till it merges with the distant grumble of the waking city. As silently as I can, I slip away to my room.

15

I'm hot. I'm sweaty. I'm extremely irritated.

I tossed and turned for the rest of the night and lack of sleep is not helping a cataclysmic, welcome-to-Cuba hangover. I am covered in mosquito bites. I am destroyed from flying four thousand miles in a corned-beef can with a sex beast who I'm not sure I want to be in the same city with let alone sharing a room with for a week. I am phoning Paul from the balcony (the only place I can get a signal) to organise time out with my boyfriend before the Beast, who is hosing himself down in the cupboard that does for a shower, reveals to me how much of last night he can remember. I am trying to ignore the four-storey drop into the busy street below. And now, Paul, my boyfriend, thinks he can get away with, 'Darlin', I really do *want* to see you but there's no way Saskia'll give me time off from the shoot to get to Havana and back.' It's all tight shooting schedule, blah, opposite end of island, blah. Blah, blah, blah. As you can imagine, this less than enthusiastic response to my suggestion that we meet up for R+R leaves me feeling immensely underwhelmed.

Paul's prevarication is fuelling my suspicions about him and Saskia again. But I am not jealous. As I said, I am irritated. Because, even if he has been fucking that woman, now the Official Girlfriend is on the scene, the only civilised course of action would be to drop his location entertainment instantaneously and give the Official Girlfriend (i.e. me) the fucking of a lifetime so as not to arouse my suspicions. And frankly I could do with some serious fucking. Some neuron or other in my brain fires up and I get a confusing image of Ivan that morphs into Cy in my head. Oh, bollocks. This is all Paul's fault and I can't even tell him. I mean, if he hadn't left me without so much as a farewell orgasm, then I would not be in the state I am now. I would not have been lured to Tanglebush, would not have fucked Nad, or Cy, and last night would not have happened. Not that anything did, beyond my having to witness Ivan's novel way of mixing cocktails.

Oh, I don't want to go back there. Especially while I'm talking to Paul. Concentrate. OK, the reason I'm not jealous (apart from the untenable pot/kettle situation I find myself in) is that I don't really think that Paul has been fucking Saskia. Now that I'm away from Tanglebush, I can think straight. I know what Paul's like. If something isn't in his schedule, it don't happen. We're talking Mr Organised, remember. He's almost certainly being weird about meeting me because it isn't mapped out in his week-to-view. Tuesday, shoot exteriors; Wednesday, fuck Zita. I just have to persuade him to find a window that's all.

'OK then, I'll come and see *you*,' I say reasonably. I don't really have a clue where he is but, since I know Cuba is an island, it can't take me that long to get to him.

He laughs and I experience a twinge. I've forgotten how sexy Paul's laugh can be. 'Zita,' he says, 'get real. Aren't you supposed to be working too?'

Maybe it's the vast amount of antihistamines I've consumed but I feel completely calm. I get real, and propose a compromise. 'We can meet halfway.'

There's a pause and then Paul says, 'Well, where did you have in mind?'

Bollocks! I don't have anywhere in mind. I stall for time, drawling, 'Ermm . . .' down the phone while Paul starts making 'Gotta go' noises. My brain seizes up completely. Then my mobile is snatched away. I spin round to catch it, stumble and panic as the drop looms before me. My legs begin to wobble. Shit, I think I'm going to faint till Ivan puts his arm around my waist to steady me with his free hand. I hear him rasp into the receiver, 'Paul? Hallo. This is Ivan Punin ... Yes, hello ... Zita will meet you at Lake Hannabanilla on Wednesday. I can only afford to let her go for maximum one night, so you be there, huh?'

I don't fucking believe this. I grab the phone back off him and hear Paul simpering, 'Mr Punin? A-mazing! Y'know, I really thought *Eva Baby* was the film of the eighties. Ermm [clears throat], Ivan, it would be great to meet up with you if you could spare the –'

I cut him off mid-fawn and say curtly, 'Paul, don't gush. So, you *can* get away from the shoot, then? Are we gonna do this Hava Banana thing or what?'

His stunned silence appeases me somewhat. I've never heard Paul wrong-footed before. It's a good sound. He mumbles, 'Yeah ... Wednesday? Yeah, I could do that.'

'Fine. Wednesday it is,' I snarl, closing the conversation abruptly.

Ivan is still propping me up, with an arm cosily round my waist (in a brotherly way, OK?). Now what? Do I go for the jet lag + antihistamine + alcohol I-can't-remember-anything gambit? A 'Last night, I had the strangest dream' kinda thang? Instead, I say, a tad huskily, 'Do you think we should, um, talk ... about the project now?' and disengage. Ivan nods. 'Yes. We will do it over breakfast. We go to the Lido.'

The rooftop bar seems to double as a cafeteria as well. We have omelette (big luxury, apparently) while Ivan explains, 'I have to see Yolande, to pay her money.' My God, he's honest, I think. Ivan must have seen my jaw bounce off the table top, because he adds, 'For our stay. I give her dollars for the room. She is the, what is it? Daughter of the sister of an old friend.'

'Niece,' I say but he's already off on one of his rants.

'The story is perfect for Cuba. The bourgeois school-teacher Rath will become a repressive CDR function-ary, Señor Roja. Lola will still be Lola, naturally, and the nightclub will stay also, but I think we change the name. The plot is a metaphor for the conflict between fading, ageing communism and sexy but savage capi-talism. My interpretation is good, eh?'

Hallo? Am I missing something here? Ivan beams at me expectantly, obviously looking for praise, and, loath as I am to disappoint, I cannot help myself.

'What are you talking about?'

'Zita,' he says, 'I thought you understood? Did I not explained myself correctly last night? *The Red Angel*? Why we are here? Our project, the film we are going to make, remake, in Fidel's Cuba? We are going to remake *The Blue Angel*. Remember?'

'Ivan, you mean *The Blue Angel*, as in 1930? As in Marlene Deitrich?'

'Why, you don't like it?' asks Ivan, looking hurt. Now, maybe I laid on the incredulousness a bit too strongly. But, you see, that's a classic film. An old film, but an incredible, beautiful one. It's the film that *made* Marlene Dietrich – the one where she sits on the bar stool, smoking the cigarette in the holder, dressed in the man's coat and top hat and showing those incred-ibly long, long legs. And just oozing stylish, sophisti-cated, luminous, dominatrix sexuality.

I start backtracking. 'No, no, Ivan. It's a brilliant concept and everything,' I blurt. 'And it's brave, the way it pits you against the original director ... what's his name?'

'Von Sternberg,' says Ivan. 'You mean, because he is forgotten now, too?'

Oh, Jeez, I'm digging a deep hole here. I smile very, very positively. 'I mean, it's a challenge, that's all.'

It is. Very brave. It's the film that *nobody's* dared to remake because where do you find someone sufficiently strong, and erotic, and talented, to play the irresistible Lola? You have to find a second Marlene Deitrich. Here is your basic problem. All of a sudden, previous conversations drop into place. I ask Ivan outright how we're gonna do it.

'Zita, when I make my first film ... You know, *Eva Baby*, that you say you've seen but I think you haven't?' I blush. Ivan continues, 'In that film, I use only amateurs. Real people. I want raw life, I want the audience to feel it's real. So, here we do the same thing. If we cannot find Lola here, we cannot find her anywhere, because Cuban women are the sexiest in the world.' Hang on, I think, we've done this bit already and the audience isn't here any more. So we've flown four thousand miles to find our Lola, i.e. to cast some local exotic for the lead in a film about what Ivan calls 'the sleaziest nightclub in screen history', (i.e. the Blue Angel). He continues, 'You will say nothing about this to your boyfriend.'

Well, that suits me fine, 'cos I'm gonna be too busy fucking Paul senseless to talk about work, anyway. I can't believe this. Me taking time out from my hectic workload as super-producer-woman to rendezvous with my gorgeous camera op boyfriend in a mountain retreat in Cuba? Shit, I'm even impressing myself here. And I'm glad I hired the jeep. It was rather more expensive than anything else on offer from the hire company but I look so fabulous in it, I could not resist. 'Charge it!' said Ivan, so I did.

I drive down the Malecon, the main drag of Havana (one side faded, crumbling, ice-cream-coloured colonial buildings; the other, Caribbean breakers crashing over the sea wall, sending sea spray spinning across the road). I avoid the motor scooters and the rickshaws and the Chinese flying pigeon bicycles with entire families balanced on them and check out the fishermen and the rubber-ring guys and the couples and the dealers and the whores and the secret agents.

When I've been up and down the Malecon four or five times and the locals are starting to recognise me, I decide I'll try going through the tunnel. Well, in the absence of any kind of road sign, it might just get me out of Havana. I need to cover as much ground as possible before it gets dark. Cuba doesn't do lights or road markings and all the road signs are of the *Revolucion o Muerte* variety. The roads were built by the Americans before Fidel and his comrades, sorry *compañeros*, got going and they're big, wide, fuck-off roads, though not exactly well maintained. The rest of the traffic seems to be impossibly romantic cowboy-looking types on horses, bicycles, herds of cows/goats, the odd truck ram-jam full of people and a few other regular tourist cars. But, hey, not many lone gals in jeeps. Is this cool or what?

At Santa Clara, I head off for the mountains. The road becomes a dirt track and I'm glad of the four-wheel-drive. It's very hot, and very green. I'm beginning to wonder if I'm going in the right direction as there is absolutely nothing that looks like a hotel. I trundle through a little settlement, nothing but three or four whitewashed huts overgrown by some big purple flowering bush, a few kids playing baseball in the dust and a couple of cowboy-looking dudes escorting a train of mules. I stop the jeep to let the lead cowboy go by, mostly so I can get a good look at him.

I can't see his face 'cos he's wearing a wide-brimmed hat but, as he trots by, he nods down at me and I squint up. I don't see the gnarled, bristled walnut face I expect but a smooth, unlined, boyish one. High, wide and handsome, I think the expression is. I smile vibrantly and, bless him, he blushes. Hey, I made a cowboy blush! I wait until his mate bringing up the rear goes by and go for the double. 'Hanna Vanilla?' I call out hopefully. He looks down and nearly falls of his horse. I'm wearing my leopardskin bikini top, so maybe my cleavage was a distraction. I try again. This time, I'm rewarded with a shy, sweet smile from a pleasant-featured twenty-year-old. He nods and gesticulates up the dirt road and further into the bush.

Almost disappointedly, I watch them pick their way up a narrow trail into the hills, their backs swaying lazily against the motion of their horses. Wow, these guys make Cy look camp. I wiggle a bit in the seat. Mmmn, that was a pleasant aperitif. Am I going to be glad to see Paul. I drive onwards, every so often getting a view of the mountains tops. A distant cloud of red dust hangs among the intense green, moving slowly ever upwards. I'm sure that's my cowboys. Every time I see that dust cloud, I get a little twinge. I needn't have worried about missing the hotel, though. It is huge – Russian brutalism, I think, is the architectural style – and it is apparently devoid of other guests. I have come to the *Mary Celeste* of hotels.

Once I've got to my room, I get my kit off and drape myself across a chair on the verandah that overlooks the lake. It's just getting dark and there are fireflies zipping round like tiny balls of neon. The whine of mosquitos sends me back into the room and I wash a handful of antihistamines down with a mouthful of rum.

I lie on the bed and decide to rub some lotion into

my skin. I have made up a concoction of insect repellent and moisturiser. I rub it into my breasts, my tummy, my hips, my thighs. I daren't go anywhere near my fanny 'cos, once I start there, I doubt I'll be able to stop. I make do with spreading my legs wider and wider and tracing a pattern on the inside of my thighs. I'm hot and tired from the drive and deliciously woozy. Perhaps the anti-histamines *and* the rum were a silly idea. I drift into a half-trance, absent-mindedly tickling the skin between my cunt and my arsehole. A collage of images flickers across my brain: Cy's swollen cock filling Elaine's mouth, stretching her lips; Ivan's face buried in Yolande's cunt, her head thrown back violently on the couch; Nadine's curly head bobbing between my own thighs as I lie in the sunshine at Tanglebush. I'm lazily running my fingers up and down and around my slit, vaguely conscious of a key turning in a lock somewhere else, somewhere deep in the hotel.

It's all like a dream, a very enjoyable dream. My fingers have found my clit now and I'm afraid they're not going to part company for a little while. I'm not sure what's really happening, apart from an increasingly luxurious feeling of wellbeing fanning out from my pussy. I sigh and relax even deeper into the sensations that the tip of my finger is producing on the nub of my clit. My pretty, pink, plumped-out clit. She's so wonderfully good to me. I've found exactly the right spot now, exactly the right amount of pressure, exactly the right speed. I don't move except to vibrate my fingertip. Not even when I vaguely hear the voices, not even when I hear a door open. I spread my thighs wider and continue to stroke the length of my cunt as the voices drift into the room. It's the two figures from my dream from the other night, I know.

They've come back to finish the job they were so rudely prevented from completing.

They are clearing their throats and someone is saying 'Gracias.' How polite, to say thank you for the little show I'm giving them. Then someone gets on the bed besides me. 'Dirty girl!' the someone's voice rasps in my ear. 'Dirty little slut, wanking herself for everyone to see.' I keep my eyes tight closed. It's nice having an audience. I like the idea of their watching me pleasure myself. I'm getting flashes of the fireflies behind my closed eyelids. As I knew, once I hit my groove, no way would I be able to stop. My knees curl up and open as I rub increasingly feverishly. 'Dirty whore,' says the husky, familiar voice and my hand is grabbed and yanked away. I groan and arch my back but my eyes stay tight shut. Suddenly, something plump and firm is driven unceremoniously into my cunt, right in deep. How good of the figures to finish their work. They have merged into the two young horseback *campesinos* I met earlier. I wonder which one has just mounted me. He is driving against me harder and faster now. I can hear his panting in my ear. He knows my name, 'cos he's calling me Zita. I reach one hand behind my knee and pull my legs as far back as I can to get maximum depth, while the other returns to wanking my clit. I rub myself mercilessly while the body on top of me thumps itself against me violently. There'll be nothing left for the other *campesino*, I'm afraid, 'cos I'm gonna come now. I've got to come now, my clit is desperate to throb, I can't possible wait any longer for release. '*Wooaaaa!*' The sound fills my head. Oh, God, I could outgroan Alison any day. It's a long one: 'Wooaaahhooh!' The sound continues in a long, drawn-out fade as the churning, clutching, pulsing pleasure in my groin slowly begins to subside. Good job that *campesino* has come, too, I think, and I manage to murmur a *'Gracias'* to him before I drift speedily away to complete unconsciousness.

16

'What?' I demand, a little too sharply, and look up argumentatively into the smiling eyes of the young waiter. Cute, if you ignore the bad haircut and puppy fat. 'The *señorita* is ready for another drink?' he repeats politely. I swirl the remains of my rum round the ice and drain the glass far too rapidly so that the dark liquid spills on to my chin and down my neck. I duck my jaw in (not the most flattering of angles, I belatedly realise) and check out what kind of a mess I have made. A rivulet of rum trickles between my tits. I click my tongue in annoyance at the complete waste of a naturally seductive moment. Boy Waiter is appreciating it, certainly, but what about my boyfriend Paul?

Boyfriend Paul, who should be sitting opposite me with his tongue hanging out at the spectacle, is on the phone to Saskia, his slut-bitch producer, instead. I'm tempted to phone Ivan in retaliation but I know that he'll just say something sarcastic. So I take the matter out on Boy Waiter. I bang my empty glass on the table clumsily. 'I have said yes already.' Boy tears his eyes from my cleavage, lifts my glass on to his tray, and snakes off towards the bar. I've gone native and am wearing another frock purloined from Nadine, which I assume she acquired during some brief flirtation with salsa. It's hot, it's pink, it's short, it's swirly. It's that kind of a frock.

The last 24 hours have been like a honeymoon: i.e. too good to last. After the stupendously whorish, if semi-conscious, wank-fuck-fest with Paul, I dozed off and woke up hours later in a big crumpled bed, alone. The bed felt wrong but I could still smell Paul's peppery sweat on the scratchy sheets. So my head told me that I was in London. I felt disorientated and, weirdly bereft (of what I didn't know) and buried my face in the pillow breathing in Paul's odour. Paul's in Cuba, you're in Camberwell, I told myself miserably.

Yeah, and those whooping screeching birds are just feral parakeets, my smartarse self told me right back.

OK, then, Tanglebush, said depressive me.

Uh uh, cleverclogs me corrected myself. Way too hot for Tanglebush. Then someone had rolled me on to my back. 'Cy, why are we doing this?' I sighed.

'Sigh, I'm going to fuck you. Clear throat. Zita, why are you giving stage directions?' Paul's voice, Paul's smell. I sat bolt upright, nutting him in the process.

'Ow! Fucking hell, Zita!' Paul, whom I'd travelled four thousand miles to see, and then some, was sitting on the end of the bed holding his nose, his eyes full of unshed tears. Thank Christ I didn't call him Ivan!

But I got away with it and, as I said, the rest of the day has been like a honeymoon: too busy fucking to talk. I've kept Paul sufficiently employed with his own tongue to prevent him reflecting on my own earlier slip. Which is good, because there's not much to say anyway and, like I said, it solves the problem of my calling him Cy or Ivan, or his calling me Saskia. Though life would be a lot easier if he would. Why? Because then I could be elegantly hurt, that's why. I'm now convinced that he's fucking Saskia, by the way, and not just 'cos I'm feeling guilty about Cy, either. I'm convinced but I can't do anything about it because I haven't any proof. Damn. How *did* we get that monogamy clause in our relationship? I really don't care that he's fucking Saskia and I want to be able to be all cool and worldly and tell him so. 'Darling I don't mind you fucking Saskia but it's terribly bad form to call her when you've just climbed out of bed stinking of me.'

Which was the first thing he did the moment he ran out of spunk and we stopped fucking. Which, incidentally, I didn't say anything bitchy about at all. Nope, I just concentrated on being the cooler half of a glitzy media couple and bit my tongue. Which is getting kind of sore from having my teeth firmly clamped into it. Which brings us right back to what he's doing right now. Phoning Saskia, I mean.

When Paul eventually rejoins me at the table, boy waiter has replenished my glass three times and I can no longer focus on which Paul to pout at. 'Sorry 'bout that darlin',' he says, taking my drink and finishing it. 'You know how it is.'

'Yeah, know how it ish,' I slur, 'and how ish Shashy?'

Paul shrugs and waves for more drinks without answering. Hah! Too uncomfortable to talk about her, eh? My tongue, now it's freed itself from being pinioned between my teeth, is suddenly all loose and flappy. 'You know, Ivan said you wouldn't be able to see me 'cos you'd be too busy fucking the continuity girl.'

Paul sits back in his chair and smiles at me. 'You know, Saskia said you engineered this whole trip just because you were jealous.' My intake of breath is so sharp and sudden that I develop hiccups. Paul laughs and leans forwards and kisses me on the end of my nose. 'Of course, I said that was impossible.'

I try to recapture the honeymoon feeling and go for a seductive smile that's somewhat marred by my hiccupping. 'And why is it so impossible?'

Our drinks have arrived now and Paul does some business with the swizzle stick like a bad actor before replying. 'C'mon, Zita, you can't even engineer finding yourself someplace to live, never mind a trip across the Atlantic.'

I down my drink to stop the hiccups, wipe my mouth with the back of my hand and say, 'So how do you think I got here then?'

Paul smiles in a totally condescending manner and says, 'Zita, you are so naïve.' That familiar sinking elevator returns and not in a nice way.

'In what way am I naïve?' The waiter is hovering with a menu and Paul doesn't answer me. Instead he takes the menu and starts reading it. I snatch it from him and snarl, 'For Chrissake, Paul, there's only gonna be one thing on it!' I turn to the waiter and snap, 'We'll have the rice and – What's the matter?'

Paul's experience of Cuba, it turns out, is somewhat different from mine. Unlike me, he is staying in a proper hotel – one with a regular bathroom and a restaurant that has food and everything. And he's the one supposedly making the hard-edged, true-to-life documentary. I feel hugely superior. When I tell him how I am living and what it is like in Cuba for the real Cubans, Paul starts laughing.

'What's so funny?' I ask beginning to giggle myself.

Paul takes hold of my hand 'Zita, you are naïve because you can't see that Ivan's project is the pipe dream of a failed director going through the motions of pretending he's still in the business.' My giggle sticks in my chest. Suddenly I feel stone-cold sober. This from the man who'd been panting breathlessly down the phone how *Eva Baby* was the film of the eighties only days before? 'Oh, Mr Punin, it would be *so* great to meet up if you could only spare the time . . .'

I can't believe Paul is being such a two-faced cunt. Paul's not like that. Not my Paul. I mean part of the reason I like him is that he's managed to stay clean of the same meejar twat symptoms he is even now currently displaying. He doesn't sound like Paul. He sounds like Saskia. I begin to squirm. I know that his opinion of Ivan is completely wrong but I can't explain why. My cheeks throb red, as my emotions veer from head-under-a-blanket embarrassment that maybe Paul is right, to insulted rage that I am, in Paul's opinion, a complete airhead for believing in Ivan. My confusion isn't helped by Paul smiling at me the whole time, his sexy let's-go-upstairs-and-get-your-knickers-off smile. My lovely, successful-media-couple fantasy bubble doesn't so much pop as develop a slow puncture. I wriggle in my chair, uncomfortably feeling very much the old me. The one who can't even organise someplace to live.

'Anyway, how come you met him?' Paul asks.

I swipe his glass from him and take a sip. It tastes sweet and cloying. 'Oh, when I was out with Nadine.'

Paul rolls his eyes theatrically. 'I might have known she'd be involved in there, somewhere. I hope you didn't let her into my flat.'

The last of the air escapes from my bubble and it hangs between us like a flaccid dick. 'Neither use nor ornament,' I sigh sadly to myself.

Paul's turn to snap: 'What?'

I down the rest of his drink. 'Nadine's not been near your flat, Paul, and neither have I much,' I say matter of factly. Paul has a wobbly-eyebrow look all over his face now. 'I, in fact, have not been in it once in the past six weeks,' I continue. 'I've moved in with Nadine.'

Paul tuts loudly.

'That is so typical of you, Zita. You are so fucking flakey. If I'd known you *were* going to move out, I could have arranged for someone else to flatsit.'

My turn to be incredulous. I've just more or less told him that I've been sleeping with a woman and all he can think about is fucking domestic security. I cannot help myself. 'Paul,' I say earnestly in my best British B-movie-heroine voice, circa 1940, 'I've left you. I'm living with another woman.'

Paul's eyes roll so far back into his head that he looks like he's possessed. When they roll back down again he has swapped his incredulous face for an even more unattractive one. The one my old headmistress used to wear: the face of a disapproving nun. My turn to giggle. 'Oooh, you're shocked!'

Paul actually slams his fist on the table. 'Oh, grow up, Zita!'

I've never seen him so annoyed. I lean back in my chair letting my (well, Nadine's) already short skirt ride high up my thighs. 'You must be shocked. Otherwise you wouldn't be so angry,' I slur triumphantly.

Paul leans forwards and says very slowly, 'Zita. I'm angry because you've been wasting your time hanging round with losers like Nadine and this ... this Ivan character, instead of getting Big World sorted.'

The unexpected appearance of my old head nun brings out the schoolgirl in me. I tilt my chair back and begin to rock on its back two legs. 'Have found work.'

Paul groans and rubs his eyes. 'Look, Zita, I admire your gumption at wangling a free holiday but stop kidding yourself that what your doing is working.'

In the absence of gum to pop in an insolent manner, I curl my lip. 'Whaddya think I'm doing now, then?'

Paul leans back and sighs. 'You're making a fool of

yourself and, by the way, that reflects very badly on me.'

I let my chair right itself and I fall forwards on to the table. 'How, exactly?'

Paul shakes his head. 'God, Zita. Ivan's known as "I-vos" in the industry. Sassy knows his wife. She says that the poor cow probably subbed his project to get him off her back.'

Oh ho. Sassy says, does she? I was right. He is fucking her. Which is a handy revelation because my head is reeling and I'm too pissed to play any card other than the righteous-indignation one. 'And how much is Sassy subbing you? For you to get her on to hers?'

Paul slaps the table again but this time he's laughing and shaking his head and muttering to himself in the manner of someone usually referred to as being-cared-for-in-the-community. Not the reaction I hoped for.

'Well?' I ask, hating the way my voice sounds. But, once you've shown your hand, you've got to stick with it.

Paul does a bit more chuckling and takes hold of my hands in his. 'Sorry Zita,' he says between laughs. This is better. Boy Waiter, who had retreated to a respectful distance, steps up to our table again and starts collecting tableware. I'm all set to let the subject drop when Paul says to himself, 'I dunno, she gets me every time.'

I can't leave it now. I mean, *she* gets him *every time*? 'What do you mean?' I ask him.

'Doesn't matter, nothing, private joke,' he says in an I'm-changing-the-subject-now manner. *Private* joke?

'Private with whom, exactly?' I hiss. Boy Waiter abandons his pretence of not listening and stands arms folded next to me looking expectantly at Paul. Paul takes one of my cigs. Paul doesn't smoke. This is bad.

'Zita, it's not important.' Pause to choke on ciggy. 'But I'll tell you because you're making such a big deal of it.' Continue in choked voice. 'Saskia bet me that you would accuse me of fucking her. And I just lost.' Stubs out ciggy.

I feel sick. Really. An I'm-gonna-throw-right-now sick, not the metaphorical parrot sort. So my exit from the restaurant is kinda drama-queeny. First, I hurtle straight into Boy Waiter, toppling him over and landing with my cleavage in his face. Next, I crawl my way up and over his prostrate body, concentrating intently on avoiding vomiting over the lad and ignoring the fact my right tit has popped out. Finally, I stagger to my feet and sprint from the room in a hand-clasped-over-mouth, eyes-watering, white-as-a-sheet way. No doubt it'll be added to the legend of the drunken slut-wanker of Room 303. I can only hope the hotel staff are charitable and assume that Paul had just told me he was fucking my mother, or father. Or something. So much for acting elegantly hurt, huh?

17

I was hurt, though. Paul had broken a fundamental rule. The deeply important don't-have-private-jokes-with-women-other than-your-girlfriend rule. After I'd dragged myself over Boy Waiter, I'd bolted for my room and crawled into bed carefully arranging myself on the very, very edge of my side. I fell into unconsciousness before Paul appeared and when I woke, I was still in the same position. I wouldn't have minded if Paul was likewise clinging to his side of the bed but he wasn't. He'd taken advantage of the extra bed space and was sprawled untidily across it, snoring gently. I decided to go for a swim and clear my head for the argument I intended to have with him when he surfaced. But, once I was up, I had a far better idea. I wrote the note out three times, careful to get the handwriting just right. Not too scrawly (in case he thought I was upset) and not to neat (ditto). 'Didn't want to wake you. Got to get back to work. Speak to you soon. Zita. X.'

'Ow shit!' A particularly deep rut shakes me out of my hung-over postmortem of the night before. I tighten my hold on the jeep's steering wheel and change down yet another gear as the wheels lose traction yet again. I'm sure the road wasn't as bad as this yesterday. Sure, my mental energies would be better spent driving rather than angsting about the things Paul said but they insist on floating through my brain. What if Saskia's right about Ivan? What if I am making a fool of myself? 'What if I'm lost?' I say out loud as the jeep judders and lurches along the increasingly pitted track.

There is nothing that remotely gives me an indication of where I am. Everywhere is greenery, of the spiky, lush or straightforwardly exotic variety. I get a sinking feeling in my groin but I'm not going to panic. Yet. Do you make deals with yourself? I do all the time. This one goes: if I turn back, then Paul's right; but, if I can find a way out of this mess, then fuck him, I'm right. So I drive confidently onwards. An hour later the countryside is getting wilder, my tongue is cemented to the roof of my mouth and I can barely see for the sweat pouring from my brow. I've got three mouthfuls of water left, I'm managing about five miles an hour and the fuel indicator is wobbling ever nearer to E.

Another thirty minutes and the jeep crashes into a particularly deep rut. In my effort to haul out, I rev the engine frantically, churning up a great cloud of red earth. Then, unexpectedly, the tyres bite and the jeep shoots out of the hole. I, like an idiot, cling grimly to the steering wheel while keeping my foot clamped on the gas pedal. The jeep roars along like a rocket in a sandstorm. Suddenly, ahead of me, I see a figure astride a horse. At least, I think I do. A pale rider on a pale horse. The rider's hand is gesturing at me. Ohmygod, Death!

I throw on the anchors and the engine stalls. Silence. Through the shimmering dust, the spectre advances towards me. I fight a portentous sense of doom and tell myself not to be absurd. This is not an Ingmar Bergman film. As the dust settles, I hear a whinny and realise that there are, in fact, two horses and two riders. Two recognisably cowboy riders! My heart soars. It's an omen, I'm right. Ivan's right. Paul and Saskia can go fuck themselves, or each other, I don't give a flying.

The cowboys walk their horses towards me and I stand on my seat so that I'm level with them. One of them starts pointing down the road and jabbering in Spanish. I shrug and show them my empty water bottle and point to my mouth. The cowboys talk Spanish to each other and then one of them kind of turns his horse around and reverses it towards the jeep until it's parked level with me. More gesticulation indicates he wants me to get on the back of his horse. OK, let me recap here. I'm in the middle of the mountains, I'm lost and miles from anywhere, I'm a woman alone and a cowboy asks me to climb up on his horse. What do I do? Duh! I climb up on his horse, of course.

I've never ridden equine pillion before so I'm kinda surprised to find myself about a mile off the ground. Horses are so fucking big, aren't they? Fortunately, my cowboy, who is called Changui or something like that, has a waist as slim as his shoulders are broad and it's a good job he doesn't have an ounce of fat on him, I'm telling ya, 'cos I've wrapped myself around him *very* tight. I do this, because, no sooner am I wriggled in behind than he walks his horse down a cliff face. I do not exaggerate. Off the dirt road and right over the edge of a deep, deep ravine. I am certainly going to die.

While Roberto, the other cowboy, is slashing right and left with his machete to clear a path, Changui's horse puts its front legs out straight and pointy, and kinda folds its back ones up beneath itself, so the bit where I am (the back-seat bit) is way up in the air. When horses slither down mountains, do you know what they do with their rumps? They wiggle them, that's what they do. And me, stuck on the end and pressed groin-to-bum with Changui, I'm being wiggled too. To avoid looking down the ravine and into the face of certain death, I close my eyes and start laughing semi hysterically. 'You're gonna die, Zita!' I can't help it. I'm going to be die at the hands of the boys in the bush and perversely it just brings back memories.

The Boyz'n the Bush, Pete and Zack, who shared the house in Shepherd's Bush. Always waving their razors at me, just 'cos I'd used them on my legs. Oh, bollocks, why am I thinking of Pete and Zack? Fuck, when, if, I ever get off this horse Changui is going to have a heart-shaped indentation in his back where my beating organ has been hammering against him. I concentrate on the feel of Changui's neat arse switching rhythmically from side to side with the sway of his horse. Oh, yeah. Something else about horses. Besides their strangely pleasant, musty, animal smell, they're fucking wide beasts. So wide, my legs are doing the splits. Between my nipples pressed into Changui's muscular back, my clit squashed and rocked against the saddle and my heart thumping in my chest, I no longer know whether I'm coming or going.

How fucking ironic. Sex and death. I am about to die and my last thoughts will be of Pete and Zack. Jesus, oh yes, they'd love it. Their kind of thang. Endless hours spent getting off their heads and having wrecked conversations about shit like this. Did when I lived with them, anyway. Ten most embarrassing moments to recollect on your deathbed. 'You have to fuck a Spice Girl or die, so which one d'ya fuck?' That kinda stuff.

We're back from a night's raving, still buzzing, and we've crashed out in Zack's room 'cos he always has some blow to wind down with. Zack takes a big lungful of spliff. 'Pre- or post-Ginger?' he splutters.

I snatch the spliff from him and take a drag before

he makes the end all soggy. 'Stupid question. You'd fuck any of 'em, if you had the chance,' I taunt.

Zack throws his works at me. 'No, I wouldn't, and if you're gonna hog that, roll another!'

I never roll joints if I can help it so I pass the skins and tobacco on to Pete and insist, 'Yes, you would, you fucking liar, you'd fuck anything.'

Pete stops flicking through Zack's CD collection and starts fumbling with the ciggy papers. 'I wouldn't fuck Sporty,' he says earnestly.

Zack snatches the spliff back from me and takes a deep drag. 'Does that mean you would fuck Posh?'

Before he can answer a low moan seems to emanate from the fireplace. We all look at it then each other, then Zack starts giggling. 'OK. You have to fuck Sporty Spice, or Alison, or die. Which one?'

I'm not having this. I mean, I feel obliged to show some sisterly solidarity with Alison and besides, if I don't keep the boys in their place, they'll start getting uppity. 'Oh, fuck off, Zack. You'd love to fuck Alison. I can see your hard-on from here.'

Pete starts giggling hysterically. 'Ahh, Ahh, Alisoooon!'

Zack lifts the cushion he's placed over his crotch and throws it at Pete and I see that he really has got an erection. This is too good a chance to let go. 'Aagh, Zack's got a stiffy' (c'mon, I've done two pills and smoked a load of skunk, this is as adult as I'm gonna get, believe me).

Pete, who is giggling hysterically by now, blurts, 'It's not Alison he wants to fuck. It's you.'

I look at him, open-mouthed. Zack shrugs at me, then says to Pete. 'So? You said you fancy the little prick tease too.'

This I am not expecting. I mean I know they fancy me. I'm a girl (I meant it when I said they'd fuck anything) but aren't I supposed to be an honoury boy in this situation? I'm somewhat lost for words. Pete finishes rolling his joint, takes a drag and passes it to me. 'OK, Zita. Your turn. You have to fuck Zack, or me, or die. What'll it be?'

'What makes you think I want to fuck either of you two wankers?' I say sour-facedly.

Zack takes the spliff off me and says with a beatific smile, 'You'd want to fuck me 'cos I've got a nice knob. It's seriously handsome.'

Pete sits up and says indignantly, 'My cock's incredibly better-looking than yours.'

'Sez who?' sneers Zack.

When I've stopped laughing, I pick myself up off the floor and say, 'You wanna beauty contest then?' The boys look at me hopefully.

'And you'll fuck the winner?' asks Zack.

I have no intention of fucking either of them but the potential for blackmail that this scenario offers is just too good to let go. I smile enigmatically and Zack scrambles to his knees, unbuttons his flies and whips his cock out. It is kinda handsome. For a skinny lad, he's very meaty, and impressively swollen for someone who's done a pill. Not to be outdone, Pete drops his kecks and steps out of them. He's got his back to me so I get an eyeful of his fine hard buttocks. I'm kind of distracted by how the hair on the inside of his thighs grows in little clumpy swirls, so, when he spins round and I am eye to eye with his stiffy, I do actually gasp.

'Aaaaaaghhh!'

Eyes wide open, I cling to Changui and try to weld myself to his back. Changui's horse has just leaped down the last few metres of ravine to reach the bed of the gully. Roberto is yelling and pointing at something with his machete. *'Mira, señorita, mira!'* Oh, hang on. What kind of a cowboy offers you a mirror when you've just plunged head first over a cliff? I knew they were too good-looking to be straight. I push my dust-coated sunglasses on top of my head to make out what Roberto is proudly gesticulating at. *'Mira! Mira!'* I peer up the steep-sided valley. There's no fucking mirror, just a broken bridge. A bridge, a broken bridge. A broken bridge I was about to rocket right over. Duh! The Angel of Death did stop me from driving over the broken bridge. These two cowboys have saved my life!

Roberto starts patting his horse's rump and beckoning me. Aha. I'm getting quite good at this sign language. He wants me to swap horses. As they have just saved my life, I reckon I can presume that they don't intend to take it away from me now and, truth is, this is beginning to feel like an adventure. I'm having fun. Which is why, instead of saying thank you kind cowboy please point me back to the Hotel Hannabanilla, I swap horses and cling tightly on to Roberto as we climb up the other side of the cliff/valley thing.

Roberto is chunkier than Changui. Not fat, just more solidly built. Changui has a slim waist and a long back. Roberto is short and thickset. My arms don't go right around his waist like they did with Changui. Now, I know that you're gonna mock me about this, but I can't help wondering if their cocks are similarly proportioned.

Zack's and Pete's are kinda opposite to their outside appearance. Pete's a little neat-looking guy with delicate features. His knob is on the short side, too, but it's anything but delicate. More Cumberland sausage than chipolata. Zack is thin and tall and speccy and I'd assumed he'd have one of those pencil knobs, but, like

I said, he's meaty. He holds on to it by its base and points it at me. Pete immediately protests, 'Cheat! He's wanking to make his bigger.'

Zack continues stroking his cock. 'It's an erect-knob beauty contest.' I notice his voice has a catch in it.

'So, it's a wanking competition?' Pete demands, his fist already clamped around his stubby dick.

Alison lets out another low, desperate moan and both the boys' members stiffen. Their ends fill right out – Zack's a deep bluey purple and Pete's a fetching raspberry pink. Now, here's the problematic part. These boys are just mates, I've just started seeing Paul and I'm certainly not looking for any distractions, but my nips are at attention under the thin material of my T-shirt.

Sweat is running down between my tits and I'm sticking to Roberto's back. His shirt is soaked. Where Changui will have a heart-shaped indention in his back, Roberto will have two sweaty holes bored into him. The swaying of the horse, the heat, my hangover all combine together. When we finally arrive outside a ramshackle cabin I'm emotionally and physically exhausted and decidely woozy. Changui swings himself off his horse and raises his arms to help me down from Roberto's. My sweat-slicked body runs the length of his, the material of my T snagging and almost riding over my tits. Not that it matters much. The sweat has rendered it almost transparent and my dark puckered nipples are extremely prominent.

'*Gracias, compañero*,' I say, recklessly attempting Spanish. Changui smiles and dabs the sweat from my face and half leads, half carries me through the door of the cabin. Inside it is dark and cool and smells of tobacco. Not stale burned tobacco, but the sweet fresh smell of tobacco leaf. I'm so glad to be out of the sun.

'*Café?*' he asks. Even I know what this means. I nod. He settles me down on a blanket covered divan affair and I sink back exhausted and watch him and Roberto do complicated stuff with coffee pots and stoves through half closed eyes. When the coffee comes it's thick textured and dark. Roberto sloshes in a shot of rum. As I sip the hot sweet liquid, a shudder runs through my body and I close my eyes thankfully and relax as the rush spreads outwards from my tummy.

My nipples have remained embarrassingly erect. I guess the chafing has made them like this. A flush has crept up my body and I'm incredibly hot.

I feel like I'm getting another rush from my pill. I notice that both Pete's and Zack's eyes are fixated on my nipples, which are very hard and full. When I've done a pill, my tits seem to become ultrasensitive and this can send out all the wrong signals. I pluck at my T-shirt to cool myself some more. A low guttural moan fills the room. I think Alison must be going for it now. 'C'mon, Zita,' Zack says hoarsely. 'Show us your tits.' Automatically, I lift up my T-shirt to expose my tight, rigidly hard nips. They're so big, I'm pleased and amazed and excited by them. Zack's and Pete's breath is starting to come more harshly and their hands start moving faster. Is this a beauty contest or a race?

Zack and Pete move closer to where I am kneeling on the floor. Alison's moans get more and more frequent, more and more urgent. I watch in fascination as the boys' balls tighten as their hands begin to blur. I look down at the two boys' cocks as they pull furiously on themselves as my beautiful nips stand proud and pertly ready to receive. Zack is holding his cock delicately between his fingers, pulling the skin back in short jerks towards the base. It is straining upwards towards me. Pete has his grasped more firmly in his fist. I notice that there's a bead of moisture at the tip. Zack lets out a hushed moan and moves so the tip of his prick is sliding over my left nipple. Pete's cock is just touching my right. Then Zack's cock swells up and he gasps and stops pulling. Half a second later, his prick suddenly jerks and starts shooting come all over my breast and up to my neck. Immediately, Pete cries out and his cock starts pumping in his grasp, spilling creamy sperm down over my chest. I gasp myself as Pete's come mingles with Zack's and rolls down and over my blazing hot nipples.

18

Hot burning nipples? Oww! *Owww!* I sit bolt upright
pulling my steaming, sodden T-shirt away from
myself. I've spilled hot rummy coffee all over my
chest. Roberto throws a cloth to Changui, who dances
around, making ineffectual dabbing motions. As his
fingers brush against my tummy, my skin tingles and
fizzes like a sparkler. I experience a flash of heat in my
groin so intense that I look down to make sure that I
haven't spilled more hot liquid there. I look back up
into twin pairs of brown eyes ping-ponging between
my tits and my crotch. Changui, the lean cowboy,
coughs, then removes his shirt and offers it me, giving
me a rather fetching view of his torso and fine set of
pecs. Incongruously, around his muscular neck is a
delicate string of red and white beads, pretty against
his skin, which is as dark as the coffee stain on my
now useless T. He and Roberto gentlemanly turn
away. Changui's naked back is even more hot-flush-
inducing than his front. A perfect wedge shape. I have
to physically restrain myself from reaching out and
tracing my fingers down each bump of his spine.

I try to whip my T-shirt over my head but unfortunately it's so damp, it clings to my skin. I end up
bobbing and weaving around with the material
ruched round my shoulders so that, when the cowboys
turn back, assuming I'm done, they get a fine and
prolonged view of my sticky tits. In desperation, I haul
extra hard and the material rips and I'm standing
there in front of them, topless. We all freeze and I

know it's one of those shared Alison intimacies: each and every one of us is thinking of fucking.

'Whooah!' I say. 'Whooahwhat's that thing over there?' I blurt, attempting to disguise a decidedly Alisonesque moan by pointing to what looks like Action Man in a red and white cloak, with a full sized smouldering cigar wedged between his outstretched legs and a tumbler of rum beside him. When the boys turn to see what I mean, I slip into Changui's shirt, tying the tails in a knot under my tits in order to show off my neat belly. '*Esto es la orisha*, Chango,' says Roberto. '*Santo*?' he adds when he sees my incomprehension.

'Oh, saint?' I reply. The boys nod vigorously.

'Saint Chango,' they confirm and then start conversing rapidly in a combination of sign language, Spanish and broken English.

After half an hour of this, plus a few more rums, I have a headache, but I have learned that:

1. The boys are into Santería
2. Santería is like a combined version of African religion and Catholicism
3. It's big on saints (the *orishas*), which is why it's called Sant-ería
4. Action Man represents Chango, the Santeran ruler of thunder.

The boys seem pleased I listened to all this. Then they tell me that there's going to be a *bembe* that night, which is like a service. It appears that unlike Catholic saints, *orishas* are up for a good time (the local equivalent of sex and drugs and rock 'n' roll, as far as I can gather). In fact the whole thing sounds more like going clubbing than going to mass. I wanna go. Roberto warns me that the ceremony will go on all night and into the next morning. I'm right up for this and tell the boys I ain't gonna take no for an answer. The boys shrug and start getting ready for the hop. Cool, huh?

We tramp through the forest under a full moon to a large, open house. There's a real buzz going on, with loads of people in colourful clothing milling round. Roberto communicates to me that everyone has dressed in their *orisha*'s colours. People are sitting around chatting and laughing and nobody gives me any weird vibes. There is an altar in what I guess is the ceremonial area and what looks like a big soup tureen in front of the images. People have brought offerings of pots of rice and fruits and vegetables. Whatever they can, I guess. I lay down a $20 bill, which is all I have on me, but it seems to go down well.

A man makes a signal and everyone shuts up. Changui whispers, '*El Babalawo!*' very respectfully in my ear. The priest, I guess. He holds up a container of some brew, spills it about a bit and does some chanting. Then he offers it round for people to have a swig. Everyone does and, as I've paid my $20, I guess I'm entitled to a swig too. It's sweet and *very* strong. While I'm trying not to cough and splutter the *Babalawo* draws patterns on the floor, then does some more chanting and lights a load of candles. Then the drumming begins.

It's really loud and powerful. You know when you stand near the speakers in a club and the bass fills the pit of your stomach and vibrates through your whole body? Exactly like that. And really good, too, like breakbeats in dance music, getting faster and faster. My whole body is full of the sound of the drums and soon I'm shaking and shuddering to the music. It's like the rhythms go round in circles, circling inside my body. My skin is a drum and my hair is like lightning and the drum is thunder. I can see the coral moon staring through the roof like a wide round mirror. She has an amber stare that dissolves my body. I am tied to her by limpid skeins of gold. And the taboos that hold people down are dissolved by this stare of the moon, calling her own to her circle. *Yeye dari yeyeo*. Then someone is blowing in my ear and someone else is rubbing the palms of my hands. There's a vibe like when someone has too big a rush when they've done too many pills and everyone else looks after them, bringing them down. I can't believe it when the boys tell me it's all over. Fuck knows what was in that brew but I've lost four hours. I feel like I've done a pill. You know, one minute you're checking your coat in the cloakroom, then you have a bit of a dance and before you know it, it's five in the morning and time to go home.

We walk back together in silence, Changui leading the way along the dark track. I'm buzzing but in a strangely calm way. I can feel everything that's going on around me through my skin. It's very, very still and incredibly warm. I realise that I am soaked. My body is running with moisture and the air is burning as it goes into my lungs. Roberto's hair is sparkling with thousands of water droplets, like a halo. A rumble of thunder makes us all jump and laugh, then the rain comes. There is no point in trying to stay out of it and I don't want to, anyway. Changui's cotton shirt is drenched and clings to me so, spontaneously, I take it off. Then I slip out of my shorts and stand naked in the tropical rain. It feels incredible on my skin. I lift my arms up to the downpour. The boys just stand and look at me, understandingly. I rub my hands over my body and openly caress myself – my tits, my tummy, my bush – and laugh. My body feels great, my breasts are full and my nipples, as you'd expect, rock hard. I'm moist and wet between my legs. I draw my breasts up to their points and pull the nipples firmly out so they're stretched and look the boys in the eyes, grinning. I know my gorgeous nips have seduced the boys with their stiffness. They're seducing me now. I'm as horny as hell. I'm a fucking she-devil, whore, seductress, a rutting wild cat. I don't know what happened at that *bembe* but I could eat men alive tonight. I need them, now. Good job there are two fine specimens to hand.

I reach out for Changui but he steps out of my grasp, fiddling with the beads round his neck. I know he wants me because his hard-on is practically ripping through his sodden trousers, but I'm in no mood for coaxing. Roberto is not so reticent. He rips off his clothes and pulls me to him, squeezing my tits and digging his fingers into my buttocks. His hand spans my two holes, his fingers searching each one. I stand legs akimbo to allow him maximum access till we tumble on to the soft rain-soaked earth. Then, wordlessly, I push him down on his back and sit astride him, grabbing hungrily for his cock. As soon as I find it, I guide it straight into my cunt and swallow it whole. Then I ride him slowly, voluptuously, lifting my hips up and round in an arc, grinding myself on to him. I reach back and shove two fingers up into myself to help fill the hole.

Me and Roberto bang silently, urgently, against each other. I drag my eyes open to look up at Changui. He's standing before me naked in the rain, his hard-on right out in front of him, watching me fuck Roberto, wonderingly. I reach out and take his cock in my hand and pull him fiercely towards me. Then I take Changui's cock in my mouth and I finger myself hard while Roberto thrusts himself up into me. But there's not enough to fill me. I pull Changui out of my mouth and almost drag him down to his knees. Then, still holding his fat cock, I lead him round behind me. I lie flat on Roberto's body so my arse is spread and my half-filled cunt exposed. Changui knows what to do. He mounts me too, placing his cock at the entrance of my pussy. Then he pushes, relentlessly, forcing his dick in next to Roberto's. My hole is unbelievably stretched till it hurts. I bare my teeth in a murderous grimace but it's what I want, what I need. Simultaneously, they pound me and we fuck in the mud, with me biting and scratching like a jaguar. Changui has one hand round my tits and Roberto is suckling on the other, my nip drawn out by his lips. I shake and pull my tit, tempting him to nip her and hold her prisoner between his teeth, and he does. Changui's playing with the other nipple, pulling her out exactly like I did to myself in front of the two boys only minutes before. I want Changui to pinch her hard now, and he does, fiercely. His other hand is down between the cleft of my cheeks, fingering my arsehole. My own fingers are on my clit. All bases are covered. The boys are devoted to satisfying my needs, I don't have to ask for anything. There is complete silence but for our panting and grunting as we heave our bodies against each other, animals copulating in the night. I can feel their huge cocks pushing and sliding inside me, stretching my cunt to the limit. It's the most a marvellous, satisfying, fulfilling sex I've ever had. I need two men to satisfy me. It's incredible to be taken like this but, weirdly, I'm in control. Of them at least. I'm losing control of myself. Completely. I'm gone. I'm wild. I'm Alison on heat. I need to be fucked. Fuck me, you bastards, fuck me. I come, yowling and screeching like a banshee in the night. I don't know or care about the boys. It's my cunt that's queen tonight.

* * *

I wake up next day in their little hut sandwiched between them. A cream-cheese-on-rye sandwich. Me soft and white, the boys hard and brown. I yawn and sit up and immediately scream. The *Babalawo* from last night is standing in the doorway. My scream wakes the boys up and they sit up too. They shush me, nothing to fear. He's come to see me. He's come all this way to give me a necklace. Maybe he feels like I paid too much for the party or something. The necklace is made of coral and amber beads, pink and gold. It's really pretty, similar in style to Changui's.

The priest goes into solemn mode and chants a bit and gives me some kind of a blessing, which is cool, even though I can't understand what he's saying. It's something to do with how I was dancing last night. I guess they were just really surprised that a white girl could dance at all. Whatever, the boys seem to be really impressed and tell me that a great honour has been bestowed upon me. When the *Babalawo* has gone, the boys take me back to my jeep and escort me back to the junction where I took the wrong turning. They give me a massive sack of mangoes as a present. The Habaneros will enjoy them if I don't. I drive back to Havana feeling so confident and purposeful. I know now how I did the right thing by following my instincts. It's gonna be so easy to prove Paul wrong.

19

I've explained to you that I'm scared of heights, haven't I? About my terrible anxiety rush? The whooshy, blood-hammering-in-the-ears, sweaty-palms, trembly-legs, eyeballs-spinning rush. That one? Well, I've got it now. The closer I get to Havana, the stronger it grows. Maybe it's a side effect of all those antihistamines. Or maybe the stuff I was slipped at the *bembe* contained some weird psychoactive, and this is the comedown. Whatever, all I know is I'm driving to Havana with little to show for a three-day recce except a somewhat bruised fanny, a sack of exotic fruit and this impending sense of doom.

After I've dropped off the jeep, I drag my sack of mangoes the three blocks to the apartment with an old skool tune buzzing round my head, 'Don't-push-me-cos-I'm-close-to-the-ey-edge'. It makes me think of Nad and that makes me feel more panicky, so I try to blot it out by rehearsing a witty and amusing ten-good-reasons-I'm-a-day-late speech. It's shite. I'm kinda hoping that Ivan will have found our Lola and will be so overcome with optimism and excitement that he won't notice a teensy problem like I've done fuck-all for three days. That he'll be so quivering with artistic enthusiasm, I can just jump in and be swept along beside him in a swirling flow of creativity.

This unlikely fantasy bolsters me enough to fuel my bursting into the apartment with a shit-eating grin all across my face. Ivan is slumped over the couch with a half-empty bottle of vodka in front of him and a glass in his hand. (That bottle *is* half empty, not half full, believe.) 'Looking for Lola?' I quip. Now, I had aimed for chirpy sass, but I miss totally and my sad attempt at repartee tumbles out as a mocking, accusatory sneer. Ivan knocks back his drink. 'I thought we could do it, Zita. I thought my old friends, my *compañeros*, would help me.' He smiles and wipes his hand across his face 'But no one has time to see a has-been.'

So much for the big creative buzz. Seems Ivan has been in this black mood all day, drinking and not getting drunk. That nagging voice is back, the one that says, 'You're just playing at making a film ... The director's a loser ... Blah, blah, blah.' The one that says, 'OK, so you blagged a holiday, now forget all about this producer malarky and go home to Camberwell and grab that job on *Massive*.' Jeez, what am I doing? I'm 26, I'm homeless but for Paul, friendless but for Nadine and, unless I get my finger out, jobless but for Ivan. Two of them aren't speaking to me and one of them's a mad Russian drunk. Fucking brilliant. This is such a fucking cliché, I can't bare it. No, no, no. Paul cannot be right. I won't let him.

Think, I scream to myself, think. In the words of the song, 'I'm-try-ing-not-to-lose-my-head.' A little voice whispers in my ear: hang in there, you'll be fine, as long as you don't look down ...

'Come on, Ivan.' I wheedle 'We *can* do this. Trust me, I'm a producer!'

Ivan laughs. A hollow mirthless laugh. 'So, Zita. You found Lola, then, in Hananbanilla?' Ivan raises his glass to me, adding morosely, '*Dosvadanya*, Zita. There will be no film.'

I'm not having that, I think. How dare Ivan morph into a drunken, depressed, has-been? (I ignore my own guilt about not being around to motivate him while I've been away on an extended shagging break.) I *know* this film will work. I *know* Ivan's the one to make it work. OK, OK. As producer, I have to exude confidence and energy, perk everyone up and generate more faith than the whole of the Vatican. I go straight into one. 'Ivan, you're not gonna find Lola sitting on your arse and getting pissed.' I insist that we decamp to the Floridita for some less melancholy inspiration.

We arrange ourselves in a line on stools at the bar. The bartender deposits daiquiris in front of us while I take in the polished mahogany sweep of the bar, the dicky-bowed barmen and the smiling, fashionably dressed punters all thinking they're drinking a toast to Hemingway's ghost. It occurs to me that the Floridita is about as far up its own arse as Me'Met's. I can't believe I thought this place was cool. It is not Cuba. Unless Lola is a thirtysomething tourist (plenty of them here), there's no way we're gonna find her in this dollar trap.

I look down, take a deep breath and go for it. 'I-van,' I say sweetly, 'run your casting theory past me again. Y'know, the one about only using real people.' Ivan stiffens but I continue. 'The one about gritty raw life and the audience believing the characters are true.' He turns a laser of Slavic anger right into my eyes. I've provoked him now. However, the row that follows is a venomously quiet English row. Woah right there. The drunken, depressive Slav has left me to play the uptight English ice maiden. That Celia's role, isn't it, not mine? I decide I'm not playing this game any more and close the issue (for the time being) by flouncing out.

I flounce straight back to the apartment and into the shower. I imagine all the nicknames Saskia will be coming up with for me. Luckily my mum had the foresight to give me a darn near unpunable name. As I cool down, I remember Rule for Survival No. 73. Just do it. Who says I have to be a failure? It's fuck-the-lot-of-them time. I resolve that I can and will find Lola all by myself. I change into the pink dress 'cos, if I do have to go down as a failure, I'm damn well going down as a shit-hot-looking one. As an afterthought, I add my new necklace. It goes prettily with the dress and it reminds me I have a secret. Then, all frocked up, I hit the streets.

And walk right into the reality check. I mean, this is a strange city and I don't know anywhere except the tourist haunts. Shit. Now what? Across the road, the neon sign of the Lido blinks welcomingly. Why does the only decent bar I know have to be on the roof of a crumbling building? I grit my teeth. It will have to do.

I'm gratified by the long louche whistle of appreciation as I sashay up to Panama's little beach hut bar. A hundred and ten he may be, but the old dude's still got an eye for the laydeez. I slide on to a stool and he fixes me a *mojito*. (After the climb up the stairs I need it.) The house band strikes up a soulful, melancholic little sol number. By the second *mojito*, I'm on autopilot. I just need to talk and Panama's a great listener. My troubles just tumble out of me. I don't care he can't understand a thing I say. He keeps nodding and looking wise and kind and replenishing my drink. I tell him about our search for Lola but pretty soon I've segued into Cy/Paul/the *bembe* stuff/Nadine/the trouble with Ivan. 'Where's Ivan?' The voice comes from somewhere over my left shoulder.

Sitting at the stool behind me is Yolande. Hey, my tough gal pal! Except, wow! She's all frocked up in an extravagantly dressy, full skirted red and gold number with her head wrapped in a high, dramatic turban to match. She's also acquired a serious collection of jewellery: a mass of brassy bracelets and some earrings that put the dingle back into dangle. 'Where's Ivan?' she asks again.

I shrug my shoulders. 'Gone.'

She frowns a bit and then asks, 'Gone where?'

Hang on. Why's she talking about Ivan? What about *me*? I thought she was *my* friend. Then the memory of Ivan lapping rum from her cunt invades my brain. I slurp the remainder of my drink and slur, 'Down a drain? Back to England? Into the hereafter? Fucked if I know.'

She gives me a full-on hard stare. I return it. Bad move. Even frocked up she looks hard. But she turns away and starts babbling on to Panama in Spanish. Which is totally rude. They keep glancing at me. A dead giveaway. I just know they're talking about me. I can feel the anger starting to bubble up from the pit of my stomach. She produces a little cigar and asks, 'Do you have fire?' Do I have what? Is she being funny? I look up into her insolent gaze and, for a moment, she reminds of someone. That heavy-lidded, sultry look is so coolly familiar. It bugs me. I know I've just seen the answer to something or other but the question has escaped before I can hold on to it. She smiles at me, flashing her gold tooth, and waves her cigar under my nose. Fire? Yeah, too right I have fire. I fumble round in my bag and pull out my lighter. I deliberately set it to flame-thrower mode so when I spin the wheel a four-inch flame nearly takes her eyebrows off. Yolande just laughs and bends her head to the flame. Then she says, 'We dance?'

We fall immediately into a somewhat clumsy rumba. Clumsy only on my part, that is, 'cos Yolande is incredibly good, confidently taking the man's part and moving me round the floor. I realise everyone in the bar is watching us. Watching me, actually. I'm glad I wore Nad's pink dress. Each wild turn reveals flashes of my thighs, which are looking slim and brown after three days driving a jeep in shorts on top of my Tanglebush tan. Hey, did I put any knickers on? Hey, I don't care. I like the idea of the guys in the bar catching sneaky glimpses of my hard, tight arse. I dance harder and faster, working myself into a lather of sweat and excitement, as my dress swirls and snakes and spins round my hips. The material whipping across my buttocks and the air rushing through my pubes. On a particularly extravagant twirl, my arm flies out sideways and I accidentally smack Yolande.

She grabs hold of my arm and flicks me so that I spin into her but doesn't catch me, instead lets me slam into a table full of drinks. It topples, sending me and the drinks crashing to the floor. I land upside down on the floor, with my skirts over my face. Now, all I can hear is Yolande's heavy chuckling laughter. Even the band has stopped playing. Yup, I am knickerless. I close my eyes. When I open them again Yolande is squatting down in front of me, still laughing. 'I am sorry, Zita, I play too rough, huh?'

She helps me to my feet and, while I'm still trying to figure out what the fuck is going on, says 'Are you ready? Come, we are late.' I look at her blankly. She clicks her tongue, very Nadine-esque. I get that whooshy feeling again and my fingers start worrying my necklace. Am I ready for what? I'm about to protest when I think, Fuck it. What have I got to lose? 'Yeah,' I reply, 'I'm ready.'

At last, I get to ride in the mythic dream machine of my imagined Cuba. A huge, sky-blue, bulbous-nosed, chrome-striped, leather-seated fifties gangstamobile. It burns oil and chunters and clanks like a steam engine but, God, does it have style. By the bucket load. Yolande drives, one arm out of the window, the tip of her cigar glowing in the breeze, the other on the wheel. After what seems like hours, we arrive at yet another of the run-down, ramshackle colonial buildings that Havana specialises in, and are courteously ushered through a door in a bricked-up archway and into a courtyard that is thronged with people. Half the women seem to be frocked up similar to, but nowhere near as dramatically as, Yolande. I see there are chalk marks on the floor and little piles of foodstuffs and some drummers in the corner. I know where I am. It's another *bembe*, except this one seems more formal, more organised, like a rave or something. There must be over a hundred people here, maybe more. There's a real sense of expectation in the air. And, somehow, our arrival has provoked it. Several people raise their eyebrows at me. Some speak to Yolande, about me I guess, but she is playing taciturn 'cos she doesn't reply. I look up at the night sky, the stars that seem so much brighter than in England. A voice murmurs in my ear. 'La Regla Lucumi. As old as people. For those who wish to control their destiny, Zita.' I glance sideways. Yolande is next to me but her lips aren't moving.

Then the drumming starts. The majority of people retire to the walls around the open room and I follow them, but Yolande stays where she is, at the centre of the space. People are shuffling along to the beat and chanting quietly. Soon, I too am moving with the beat. Yolande takes a swig from a bottle and begins to dance in a dramatic frock-swirling and sweeping motion. Everyone is watching, expectantly. Then she begins pacing around the room, talking to people in a strange dialect. A voice cries out, '*Yeye dari yeyeo*, she has come,' and, behind us, others in the crowd take up the same call. Yolande halts, as haughty and poised as a Nubian queen acknowledging her subjects.

The drumming picks up, heavy and dirty and familiar. Yolande's body has begun to undulate under the fullness of her skirts. She hardly appears to be moving but the ripples shaking through the fabric increase in violence until she appears to be cloaked in nothing but a fine orange mist. It's an incredible sight. An image of the sea spray crashing over the Malecon caught in sunlight. Despite the drumming building to a driving crescendo, I know the room is hushed, the onlookers transfixed by Yolande's energised body. Slowly, the dance becomes increasingly violent till her whole body is vibrating, from her fingertips to her feet. Abruptly, she pulls off her headdress and hurls it away. Then, she begins tearing at the fabric of her dress. She claws and rips at the bodice till her dress hangs open and her breasts are exposed, her dark skin glazed and satiny in the starlight. She holds her hands above her head, lifting her breasts so that their areolae point upwards, and begins shaking again. Her jewellery shimmies and clinks and spins points of light around the room. I watch them rush across the ceiling and down the walls. Yolande rents at her dress again, tearing away the material fiercely and shaking and shimmying like she's possessed. It's pure sex. Suddenly, she is right in front of me. Her heavy, hooded eyes slowly open, looking impassively into mine but not seeing me. The bodice of her dress is hanging in tatters round her waist. Then her lips purse and I am drenched in something wet and sticky. My head is spinning. Yolande *is* possessed, I realise. She's seeing *for* me. She is my mirror.

I'm trapped in the headlight glare of that wide, fixed gaze. My own hips are moving in response, like when you wake from a horny dream, grinding your cunt into nothingness. She is showing me something. In her eyes, I watch myself dancing at the country *bembe*. I see myself ripping my own clothes away. I drop till I'm in a limbo position, the sweat running off my straining abs. I see the muscles of my inner thighs shine and gleam, my mons thrust flagrantly forward, the cleft of dark hair leading down to the globes of my hard buttock, my groin pulsating, my naked shoulders almost brushing the floor, my nostrils flaring. I spin on to my knees, push them apart and arch my back so that my plump, dark vulva is presented, available for everyone. I am just aware of the hush of admiration, the faintly audible, collective intake of breath from the surrounding devotees, then '*Yeye dari yeyeo.*' I feel the cocks entering me as I'm taken, repeatedly, each man respectfully waiting his turn, his duty. Now, I know that this is what happened in the lost hours out in the mountains, possessed by the music, entranced and united with the spirits. Freely, unhesitatingly offering myself in a liberation of the soul. My God, I did that?

I'm not aware of much else very clearly from this point, although I am conscious of Yolande's luminous eyes locked into mine. I'm thinking how commanding she looks. How her performance permeates every corner of the room, holding everyone transfixed. How she radiates some deep, indefinable sense of power. And I'm wondering if Yolande is as turned on by her own animal energy as I am. There's this feeling, rising through my body, the trembling building from my feet, up my legs, till it reaches my fanny and then radiates out over my entire body. I think I'm orgasming in public, or perhaps Yolande is – I'm not sure who. Then I'm collapsing in a heap on the dusty floor. And, somehow, I realise that I've just found my Lola.

20

Everything has slowed down. Each time I blink, a black curtain closes. There must be things going on around me but all I can see is Yolande. She is covered in a fine golden mist. She is standing, head raised and eyes closed, while around us the dancing builds, wilder and more frantic. She is the centre, of everything. People are stroking her. A man is on his knees, kissing her feet. The violent spasms that racked her body have subsided. Then a voice enters my head. 'She is your sister. Take care of your sister.' It's like I've just woken up from sleepwalking or something. I shake myself and everything comes into focus. My cheeks are wet. I touch my face and lick my finger. It tastes sweet. A heavy alcoholic sweetness. Yolande is wrapped in the remains of her turban and dress and I am in my limp pink frock, holding her hand, like we are a couple of seven-year-olds about to go trick-or-treating. The drumming is an intense, pulsing throb, a million miles away. As neighbourhood hops go, this one is certainly hard-core. I'm having trouble keeping my head from spinning. Maybe we ought to leave.

Somehow, we end up back at the apartment. Was it Yolande who led me or did I lead Yolande? The apartment is Ivanless, so we flop down on the couch, Ivan's bed. A freeze frame of him drinking rum from Yolande's cunt flashes in my head again. Yolande looks into my eyes and I get a strong feeling that she is watching the same movie. My mouth is dry and I have to clear my throat before asking, 'Are you OK?'

Yolande stretches backwards over the arm of the couch and shakes her body like a cat does on landing from a big jump. 'Yes.' The turban material has fallen open to reveal a long slit of dark skin. I tilt my head as my eyes run down the length of the slit and then realise what I'm doing. I look away quickly and seeing the sack of mangoes poking out from under the couch pretend that I was looking for them. I reach down and pull a couple out, offering one to Yolande. Yolande holds it under her nose, then uncurls herself from the couch and walks over to the little kitchen, returning with a small knife. The headdress has slipped off, so she is only wearing the flounced skirt, remnants of her fancy dress. Her long chocolatey nipples are exposed. I wonder briefly if they taste like Nadine's, then shake my head violently trying to dislodge the thought. For the first time, I notice she is wearing a necklace very like mine. Yolande folds herself down on to the couch next to me and curls her lips back to sink her teeth into the exposed pink flesh of the sliced fruit. 'Did you find what you are looking for?' she asks before her mouth closes over the fruit. What does she mean?

I follow a trickle of juice as it runs from her lips down the curve of her breast to her nipple. 'You want to eat?' she asks. My eyes flick back up to meet hers. She has cut a slice of mango and is offering it to me, held on the knife. I tentatively press my lips to the blade, very aware that Yolande is holding a very sharp knife against the slit of my mouth. I take the mango between my teeth and flick it into my mouth with my tongue. Yolande's tongue flicks out and I realise that she is mirroring me. The atmosphere is charged.

To break the tension, I gabble, 'Yolande, back there. What happened? Why did they shout those words? What made you rip your clothes and go like that?'

'Like what?' she asks.

I close my eyes. An image of her bucking naked body flashes in my head. 'Um, wild. I guess.' I open my eyes again. 'And looking at me. Like you're looking at me now.' I add. I didn't mean to add the last bit but the words just slipped out.

Yolande raises her eyebrows at me. 'My spirit is Osún. My *orisha*. She entered me. They shout "*Yeye dari yeyeo*, she has come," because she has.'

I ponder this one and say, 'You mean, like, you were taken over by something else. You were possessed. Weren't you frightened?'

'To be mounted by my *orisha*? Were you?' she asks with a throaty, husky laugh, and I blush. Then she adds, 'Osún is wisdom, the wisdom of beauty, of knowing who you are. I let go, I am free.'

I'm trying not to blink. Trying to stop the slide-show images that flash inside my head each time I do. I stare fixedly at Yolande. 'How can you be free if something else, someone else, is telling you what to do?'

Yolande stares back. 'Nothing tells me what to do, Zita. Osún is in me. I am Osún.'

My eyes are watering. I have to blink. I see a crowd of hungry faces. I see me lying on my back, legs apart. I open my eyes on twin Zitas reflected in Yolande's black eyes. 'As she is in you.' Whooosh. I see myself stretched out on the hard earth floor at the *bembe*. Men and women surround my writhing body, stroking me, kissing me, fucking me. Yolande's voice cuts into my thoughts.

'You have done nothing wrong, Zita.' She smiles. 'You have a gift. Osún helped release that gift. Now you are free.'

I feel myself slipping into that pitch-black gaze of hers. Shit. She's hypnotising me. I'm shaking. I go to push my hair out of my eyes and realise that it is disgustingly sticky. I am covered in a mixture of mango juice and the stuff Yolande sprayed over me. She presses her face into my hair and sniffs. '*Aguadiente* ... I sprayed you a lot, huh?' She gets to her feet and pads across towards the room, shedding the remains of her bulky skirts so she is naked. Then she turns to face me and I look down, but not quick enough for her to notice that I was studying her slinky hips and full breasts. 'You like to look, huh?' I nod. I can't speak because of a dryness in my throat. 'It's OK. I like to look, too.' Yolande runs a hand over her body, watching me through half-closed eyes. 'So give me something to see.'

I'm in so much hurry, I fumble the zip at the back of the dress but Yolande tuts and spins me round, her long nails just scoring my back as she gently eases the zip down. When they reach the base of my spine, I feel my arse flex indecently and push out towards her. I'm very aware I'm willing those sharp nails to just keep going into the cleft of my buttocks, but Yolande merely slips the spaghetti straps over my shoulders and lets the dress fall around my feet. Then she scoops it up and methodically lays it on the table, smoothing out the wrinkles.

Then she turns back to face me. 'Come here,' she commands, and I do. She reaches out and her fingers trace up my chest before closing lightly round my necklace. 'You know this *ileke* is for those chosen by Osún?' She unfastens first mine and then her own, and holds them together in front of my face. 'So, we are sisters,' she says, and then lays our sister necklaces respectfully on Nadine's dress. 'Zita, you know you must not wear it when you shower or have sex?' I can feel the blood pounding in my ears, like the surf along the Malecon. 'Are we going to erm ... shower?'

Her musky smell fills the close and airless space. I am overwhelmingly conscious of her presence. I can feel sweat prickling over my body. She traces a bead down to my nipple, where it is poised in a glistening droplet. She lifts it with her finger, then rubs it on to one of her own, which hardens. Then Yolande takes my hand and traces my fingertip along the stretched and puckered nip. It blossoms more as I touch but I pull away. She touches my chin, lifting my head until our eyes are level, and looks deep into mine. 'Why are you afraid?'

'I'm not. I don't understand what you mean,' I stutter but she adds, 'You are frightened to let yourself go. You are frightened of falling. Jump. Osún will catch you!'

Then she takes my hand and leads me, naked, out on to the balcony. We are standing four floors above the silent Calle Industria, with a good deal of Havana's Old Town spread before us. I close my eyes and brace myself, gripping the wrought-iron railings with passion. My belly does a flip, which ends in a quiver somewhere behind my clit. I'm just conscious of Yolande taking my face in her hands and tipping my mouth up to meet hers, then kissing me roughly, biting my lips. Her kisses drop to my neck and she nips the soft flesh above my collarbone and round on to my neck. Her kisses run down my tits to my bursting nipples, then on to my belly until she is kneeling before me. My head is exploding. What if people look from across the street? What if Ivan come's in? Where *is* Ivan? Why can I taste salt? What if I slip and fall?

Tingles trail across my skin where Yolande's tongue has been. I let my head loll back and tighten my grip on the railings and pray Yolande will go lower. Mercifully, her fingers probe the start of my cleft while her tongue explores my sopping wetness. I run my own tongue around my lips as the salt taste increases and a warm wetness fills my mouth. Yolande is stretching the hood back from my clit with her mercilessly sharp fingernails to allow the point of her tongue to work over the swelling and along the grooves either side. I'm slipping, slipping ... An intense fire is building in my cunt. It radiates outwards, upwards through my body until it reaches my throat, and I open my mouth. I let go of the railings and my hands flutter in space. I'm nearly falling. Part of me wants to fall. Part of me is full of a hysterical terror. My fingers flex convulsively, scrabbling for something to hold on to, and my nails embed themselves in Yolande's cropped scalp. My knees sag and part and I pull her face hungrily on to my sopping cunt. Her lips clamp hard over my clit and she sucks. There's a rumbling sound, a deep, wild, reckless roar, like in the Tube when a train's coming. It surrounds me. Oh, Osún, I'm falling now.

My ears are ringing with the echo. Yolande unclamps my fingers and stands up. Her face is dark and beautiful. She will look incredible on film. 'Lola,' I whisper to her. Yolande leads me back into the apartment to where our necklaces lie. She refastens hers and hands me mine and Nadine's dress. 'You can have it if you want,' I blurt. It seems appropriate.

'Thank you.' She smiles and steps into the dress. I run the zip up her strong muscular back. The dress is indecently short on her, the skirt barely covering her buttocks. She struts round the room on her long, lithe legs, looking amazing. Then she rummages in a dresser and comes out with a scrunched-up piece of material. 'For you?' she says, uncertainly. It is a T-shirt, emblazoned with the Cuban star. Cool. I pull it over my head. Yolande folds herself down on to the bed and lights a small cigar. 'Lola...' she says thoughtfully to herself, savouring the sound. 'Why do you say that?'

I take a deep breath. 'Because I think you might be the Lola me and Ivan came to Cuba to find.'

She blows a smoke ring and fixes me with her Medusa eyes and asks suspiciously, 'What does this mean, I am your Lola?' I explain it all to her. Yolande stares at me for a little while and then says, 'Yes, we can do it, you and me, with Osún's help.' Simple as that. I look into Lola's beautiful black eyes and laugh. It's amazing. How come we never saw that our Lola was right in front of us in the first place? It doesn't matter, we've found her now.

I wake up entwined with Yolande on my bed. There's somebody in the room. I stiffen. It's Ivan. Ivan's back and he's smiling. I drift off back to sleep, safe in the knowledge that everything's going to work out just fine. Jump, and Osún will catch you. We can't fail.

21

Paul has a real whopper of a hard-on, a massive, shiny erection sticking right out in front of him. Big and firm and plump and silky-looking. The end is a ripe plum, ready to eat. I wanna eat it with my cunt. Right now. My cunt's so fucking hot. 'Cos I want some dick. Paul is advancing on me. Ohhh yes, yes, good boy. In, now. Shit, he stops and just rubs his own dick, a huge grin plastered over his face. 'I'm going to fuck Saskia,' he says. Bastard. *My* cunt wants some attention. Someone to touch it. God, *I've* got to touch it, then. Can't move. I'm trapped. Bastardfuckingwanker, he's gaffered me down again.

I can't move. My wrists are fastened to my ankles and I feel damp and sticky like I'm wearing tights on a hot day. (Tights on my tits? Duh! it's a body stocking, stupid, hole over my cunt so Paul can get access to my wet slit.) My tongue is trapped. Something over my mouth. Gaffer tape? Paul and his fucking gaffer tape. 'Nnghhmm.' I struggle and strain to move my hand. My fingers just reach my fanny lips. They're all swollen. Hot. I'm pushing my hips out and I can just finger myself. Then, I wrestle hard and everything shifts. My ankles are still tied but my hand is on my pussy. I'm wide open, I'm split in two from my clit to my arsehole. My cunt is hot and naked. (Hey, my pubes have gone. When did I do that?) I finger myself blissfully and smirk at Paul that I've manage to unzip myself. I look down at his cock.

Only it's not his cock. Unless he's grown a foreskin.

It's Cy's lovely cock: brown, dark and phat. Paul has mounted Saskia on her knees from behind. His hands have reached round and are pulling on her nipples as he rams her hard. She is braying like a donkey, spreading her cunt to take him right in. Paul turns to me and says, 'You shouldn't have lied to me, Zita.' I don't care, my cunt doesn't care. My cunt is horny. My cunt is not being a good-girl cunt tonight. My cunt wants dick. Cy has a lovely dick. I splay my pussy lips invitingly. Ohhh, my cunt is so hot it's steaming. Need something cold. Mmmmn, that's better. Wet running over my clit trickling down to my arsehole. Cy is rubbing an ice cube on my clit. God, that's good, but it's melting faster than he can rub. More ice cubes. He rubs harder, pushing them against my cunt. I wanna tell him to push them in, deeper. *'Push them inside, you bastard,'* I wanna scream but I still can't speak. Mouth is too dry, I can't breathe. Too hot. Thump, thump, thump. Jesus, if that's my heart, I'm going to die. Thump, thump, thump. Cy is ramming ice cubes into my gaping hole but they keep melting. At last my mouth is free. 'Fucking faster,' I scream. *'Faster, now!'*

'Ahhh . . .'

Thump.

Rrrrrip.

'Fuck!'

I try to sit up but find that I really can't move. It's dark. Hot and dark. I'm covered in sweat. My hand is squished over my groin and my legs are trapped and tangled in something. What time is it? Five thirty a.m. by the light of the luminous dial. Shouldn't that be the silvery moon? Or a runcible spoon? What the fuck is a runcible spoon anyway?

Thump, thump, *thump.* And what's with that fucking thumping? I release the comforting grip on my cunt and grope around in the dark for a light switch.

My pupils contract so fast in the blinding white light that my eyeballs creak. I unscrew my eyes enough to squint through one. Reality crashes down around me. I'm wrapped in Paul's sheet. Sorry, ex-sheet. There's a three-foot tear in it. Bollocks. Thud. Shit! And the City-bitch-girl that lives upstairs is banging on the ceiling. Ohmygod, have I been shouting in my sleep? Doubtlessly, there'll be complaints from the residents' association.

'I was having a nightmare for fuck's sake,' I mutter to myself as I extricate myself from the soggy tangle of 100 per cent Egyptian cotton and swing my legs on to the floor. This is so not good. I've been back from Cuba 48 hours and I don't think I've had any proper sleep yet. Why didn't Paul buy a more expensive flat? One with air-con. Clomp, clomp, clomp. Sounds like City-bitch-girl is going for a piss now. One with floors not made of tissue fucking paper. Chunder, clunk, rumble. Nope, she's having a shower. Pointless trying to sleep now. I need a drink.

I pad off to the kitchen and peer into the Smeg, savouring the blast of cold air. I lean my forehead against a shelf and watch the temperature on the fridge thermometer rise steadily from Paul's optimum three degrees centigrade and daydream about removing all of the shelves and climbing on in there. Nope, better not. Like I told Nadine, fridge abuse is against house rules. I close the door and remove the letter from behind the fridge magnets. Which, incidentally, contrary to Nadine's snotty opinion, are entirely acceptable if used in an ironic manner. Like Nadine's got her finger on the pulse? Like Nadine's been offered a job by Big World Media? I take my letter from the envelope.

At first I thought it was some kind of final demand, sorta formal and contractual, and there was way too much to read in my post-flight daze. The important bit was scrawled on the bottom. 'Re *Massive*: Love to have you on board. Call in and arrange start date. Clare D.' I fan myself with the envelope. I haven't made that call yet. I have a choice to make first. *Massive* or *Red Angel*? I can't do both.

Oh fuck. Who am I kidding? There is no choice. I have to take *Massive*. I feel relief already. Ivan's a pro, he'll understand. Tomorrow. I'll phone everyone tomorrow. Right now I need a fag. I grab some duty-frees and walk into the living room. Everything is tinged orange by the sulphurous glow of the street lights spilling in through the floor-to-ceiling glass doors that open on to the balcony. Shit, the blinds! They've been open all this time. Fucking Nadine. I close the blinds guiltily and look back into the living room. Furnishings won't get noticeably faded in a few weeks, surely? Paul needn't know a thing and it'll be all Nadine's fault if he does. Bitch is always trying to ruin my love life.

I slide the glass door open enough so my toes are just on the very edge of the balcony, no further. It's not much cooler out here but at least I can have a fag without triggering the smoke alarm. As you've probably gathered, I've moved back into Paul's. I came straight here from the airport. Back to life. Back to reality and reality was sitting there on the mat in the shape of the letter from Clare. I haven't been near Tanglebush at all. I'm gonna have to go there at some point to collect my stuff. But not yet. Don't want to see Nadine. We're finished, by the way. After that stunt she pulled over the promo, I don't care if I never see her again.

And Cy. I don't want him thinking that there's anything going on between us. We had a fuck, that's all, and now it's over, gone, finito. Yes, he's easy on the eye but so is Paul and he'll be back soon and it's time to knuckle down and get on with my life for real. It was always going to happen. Tanglebush is OK if you wanna be a feral slacker but I mean, Nadine and Cy are not going anywhere, are they? They're flaky, unambitious, irresponsible. I mean that whole slacker thing is just *so* twentieth century. Yeah. Tanglebush suits their lifestyle.

I blow a plume of smoke at the fume-clogged London dawn. All around me cars honk and fart and squeal. Sirens wail and alarms scream. Dogs bark and people sweat and swear and sweat and laugh and sweat. Summer in the city, huh? Tanglebush will be quiet and sweet-smelling. If I was in Tanglebush, I could just walk outside naked and roll in the grass to cool off. Roll around naked with Cy in the grass. 'No!' I'm not going there. That's behind me. A holiday experience, like Cuba, that's all. No one need ever know, not anyone that matters anyway. 'Cy. Fuh!' What will I get out of a relationship with Cy apart from really good sex? A reputation like Alison's, that's what. And who wants to be famous for coming like a shithouse door? Nope, not me. I won't be going anywhere with Cy. Nope. I'm a 26-year-old professional media woman. My future lies with Paul.

Shit, at 26, I've got to what Alison was still aspiring to at 38. I'm not going to end up like Alison. She could have been really successful if she'd just got her shit together. No, seriously. She had ability and everything but she just let her life get out of hand, I guess. Let things get out of control. And right here, right now, I'm taking control. I *am* gonna sort things out with Paul. We can make a go of this relationship. I know we can. Wait till he hears I've got the job. I can see it now.

Paul is smiling up at me. His great big shit-eating

grin is jumping around a bit 'cos I'm blinking back tears. He's standing up, whistling through his fingers. Applause is ringing in my ears. I look abso-fucking-lutely amazing, by the way, in a rubber, zip-fronted, fanny-skimming frock. Totally Barbarella. Liz Hurley? Eat your heart out, girl. Where is she, anyway? You can't have an awards ceremony without Liz. Ah, yes, there she is, blowing kisses at me. I'm making my speech but I can't hear what I'm saying. I can see my lips moving but it's like someone turned the sound down. Damn. I want to hear who I thank.

My mouth looks different. Collagen, I guess. I'm holding up my BAFTA now and gesturing for Paul to come and join me. Is that done? Feels a bit game-showy. Do I give a fuck? Hey, do I shite? I'm the brightest rising young star in television fucking history. Paul's by my side now. A bit behind me, actually. And we are so glamorous ... so impossibly beautiful ... so successful. My hair's all blonde and tousely. When did I do that? Hang on – the sound's coming back. '...And I'd like to thank...' My voice sounds funny. Why do I sound like Princess Anne? No, not her: someone else. Saskia. Why am I talking like Saskia. Fuck. I *am* Saskia. That's not me. That is Saskia. Saskia's the hottest star in the film firmament, not me. Saskia's being snuggled by Paul, not me. Saskia's getting kisses blown to her by Liz Hurley, not me.

'*No!*'

'Don't do it if you don't want to, babe!'

What? I open my eyes. I'm peering down over the balcony rail at a gurning string of home-bound club-bers. 'I'll come up if you're lonely,' yells a lad. Oh, fuck, and I'm naked. I'll have to go in now or they'll think I'm encouraging them. I can't bring myself to leave them with the last word. Don't want people saying that I'm slow-witted or anything when I'm famous.

What is it Paul always says? 'Be pleasant to the little people, they'll be your audience one day.' I stick my tits out while making a shushing gesture at the oiks, then smile benevolently and point to my wrist. '*Six o'clock, darling!*' Fuck. There will be complaints, I know it. I sneak back into the flat and decide to start with the making-myself-really-famous-and-successful plan straightaway. It's gotta be me, not Saskia, up on that podium with Paul. Lists. Lists are good. I'll list all my ideas for *Massive*. Pen paper. Notebook will be better. More professional. Paul keeps a supply of really neat leather-bound notebooks in the drawer of his desk. V. neat. V. stylish. V. successful media exec. V. Me.

While I'm rootling round in Paul's drawers I find some loose photos. Very un-Paul. He stores all of his photos in a series of colour-coded metal boxes. These are some photo-booth pictures. Probably from when he was getting his passport renewed from Cuba. I'm not surprised he rejected these: he looks like a twat in them. He's got a really stupid smile on his face. I rummage round some more and pull out a second strip, which are even more un-Paul. In these ones he's sharing the booth with Saskia in a very juvenile manner. I know what's happened. He's gone to have his passport photo taken and she's been arsing round shoving her head into frame. Shoving her tits into frame. God, Paul hates stuff like that. I'm just wondering why Saskia was with Paul when he was getting his passport photo taken when the phone rings.

'Zita. This is Ivan.' Figures. 'I'm phoning to ask you if you still want the attic room at Tanglebush.'

?

'Nadine said I had to ask you.'

?!?

'Zita, are you still there?'

I manage to speak at last. 'Ivan, I'm not being funny, but why has Nadine asked you to phone me at six in the morning?'

'I'm sorry, I didn't think. I'm phoning you because . . .' There is a strange tremble in his voice. I'm getting one of those whooshy, tingly feelings. This isn't good. Ivan picks up again. 'To let you know that I've left Celia and I need somewhere to live. And Nadine says I can have your old room at Tanglebush. If you don't want it.'

I make a stunned grunting noise that is vaguely affirmative. There's an even longer pause. Ivan says, eventually, 'I'm here now. What do I do about your things?'

'Yeah, sure, Ivan,' I go, 'I'll come and collect them.'

'We need to talk, anyway,' he adds.

We sure do. 'This afternoon, I'll come to you.'

No point in going to bed now. I make coffee and boot the computer. I'll do my list on the PC. Six hours later and I've practically written a report. I switch to Outlook Express and type in:

Back home. Everything fine except the flat ransacked and the car destroyed in ram-raid misadventure. JOKE!!! Seriously, everything is fine. Got job at Big World. Miss you loads. ZITA XXX.

My finger hovers over the mouse. Is this OK? It doesn't feel right, somehow. I stare at what I've written. Would Paul think it was childish? Would Celia write something like that? I don't think so. Why has Ivan left Celia, by the way? She's not an uptight ice maiden bitch at all. I got her completely wrong. She's cool. She put a good word in for me, ya know? Clare told me. Oh, please keep up. Clare Dodderidge. BWM's meejah-woman supremo. *That* Clare. I phoned her at 7.30 this morning to accept the job. I knew she'd be impressed by my early-bird tactics. She said she was looking forward to having me on the team, that she'd heard so many positive things about me from Celia Draycott. Now, is she a Top Gal or what?

Anyway. My message telling Paul the good news. Would Saskia write something like that? The cursor blinks perkily in front of me and I think of the passport photos. Yeah, Saskia probably would. But would Paul think it funny if I sent it? Fuck, why is everything so complicated? Is it normal to have to think really hard about how to word emails to your boyfriend? I delete everything apart from 'Back home' and spin round on Paul's ergonomically designed office chair, worrying. I don't know why I'm so down. Maybe I'm premenstrual. Maybe it's jet lag. I should be happy. I've returned from an all-expenses trip to the Caribbean, visiting my gorgeous and successful boyfriend at the same time, before returning to our fabulously chic pad in the heart of groovy downtown London (well, DesRes in the suburbs). I've been offered a *fantastic* job and said gorgeous and successful boyfriend will soon be home.

Home! That's the problem. Apart from the suitcase spilling dirty underwear all over the laminated wood floor, I don't think that there's anything of me here. Most (OK, all) of my stuff being of the second-hand-funky variety, Paul decided it did not fit his decor concept for the flat. Consequently, it wasn't allowed out of the packing cases when I moved in. I need to make this place more *homey*. More *moi*. I'll retrieve my stuff from Tanglebush and set to making a more Zita-shaped impression on this place. My heart flutters a bit at the thought of Tanglebush. A few loose ends there . . . Telling Ivan, avoiding Nadine, Elaine, Cy. Shit. Those ends aren't so much loose as being whipped around in a hurricane.

I spin the stool back to face the screen and notice that I've got mail. Surprise, it's from Paul.

Z. Shoot wrapping early. Flight ES404, arrives 13.40 LHR 19/07. Be in. Need to see you.

Five days' time! And, hey, *needs* to see me, huh? No sex for ten weeks but a casual fling with his right hand? (Oh, and one night's compassionate leave in Hannabanilla.) I bet he does. I picture a fit, tanned Paul, naked, lonely and very, very horny. A monster erection desperate for relief. (Definitely circumcised: I'm not letting Cy sneak into this fantasy.) He looks at my photo, propped up by his hotel bed, and sighs. Then he slowly kneels on the mattress, fluffs up a pillow or two and mounts them rather sadly. His tight buttocks clench and unclench rhythmically as they force his cock up and down the smooth cotton pillow slip. His eyes close and his hands grip the mattress as he starts to build a faster rhythm. He is imagining me, succulent and available, the moist grip of my pussy, the tightness at the entrance, my legs wrapped round his back, my nipples stiff between his fingers. His hands reach round as he mentally cups my arse and he draws the pillow in tighter to his groin. Soon, he is panting and pumping furiously into it, driving himself into the mattress, beads of sweat glistening on his shapely, muscular back. 'Zita,' he moans as his body arches and he spills seed over the surrogate me. Poor boy, he must be getting pretty desperate for the real thing by now. Yup, OK, I could be in for that, I think. I type in the reply. 'I'll be here, never fear. You bring the gaffer, I'll bring the champagne. Can't wait. Love Z.' I hit SEND, before I waver again and grab the keys to the MGB. Time to tie up those flagrantly loose ends before my loverman gets home.

22

I take my time driving out of London on the A40. It's so hot that all of the cars are bending and shimmering in the heat haze. I think of *Crash*, the movie – where the guy kills a woman's husband in a car crash that she survives and they have a desperate, sexual affair that involves doing it in crashed cars and what have you. The story was really set here. It should have been shot in Perivale, not LA, honest. Thinking about the film evokes a panicky feeling of similarity in my belly. Everything feels really strange. That time only two months ago when Nadine drove me out to Tangle-bush, the first time, it felt like we were making a getaway. You know, in the cowboy flicks, the way the baddy-heroes always have a secret hideaway behind a waterfall, in a canyon, or something? Well, that's what Tanglebush felt like to me. Now it feels more like *High Noon*. The closer I get, the flippier my stomach feels.

I nearly miss the driveway. It's only been a couple of weeks but the bushes seem bushier, massively overgrown. I put my foot down and bring the MGB to a skidding halt on the balding gravel in front of the house. As the dust and grit settles, I casually push my sunglasses on top of my head and take a look around me. Not a soul in sight. I replace my shades so I can stare into the windows a bit without anyone inside knowing exactly where I'm looking. The windows stare straight back. Tanglebush looks completely deserted. I experience an unreasonable feeling that the house is sulking at me.

I climb out somewhat stiff-legged. I feel unnaturally self-conscious. I head on up to the front door with my head held high and my nose in the air and my belly pulled in, my head running through possible attitudes I can strike if faced with Nadine. I'm so jittery I don't get beyond a rather theatrical flounce that I know Nadine will find something really cutting to say about – and she's so much better at dissing than I am. I'll never win if we get into a bitching session. Shit, I'll just have to make my flounce as dignified as possible.

I push the door open and step into the entrance hall. I needn't have worried, the house is silent. Simple rule of thumb. No music = no Nadine. I relax a little and begin climbing the dusty wooden staircase. I pause on the first landing and look back. My feet have left a trail of prints in the dust. These stairs hardly ever get used, there being another staircase at the back of the house that leads straight down to the kitchen. I feel sad when I realise that the first night Nadine brought me here, when she led me up this staircase, she really wanted me to be impressed.

The higher I climb, the sadder I feel. It's not supposed to be like this. Fuck, I am so sentimental it's untrue. I've got a beautiful flat in Camberwell. Why am I being all nostalgic for this dump? I pause outside DON'T GO THERE and agree fervently with the sentiment. Too fucking right. I take a deep breath and carry on climbing the narrow staircase that leads up to my bedroom. Ivan's bedroom. Whatever. I don't care who knows I'm here now. I pause outside my door, Ivan's door, and shout, 'Ivan? Are you in there?'

I've decided to be grown up about the whole thing and tell him straight. I take a deep breath and just blurt it out: 'Ivan. Sorry, but got to pull out of *Red Angel*. New job. Pressure of work. Good luck with the project and everything. Make sure I get invited to the premiere!' He just nods and asks me if this job is what I want. Like, duh-uh.

I laugh and say, 'Ivan, it's kiddie-prime-time broadcast TV. I'll be working under a really well-respected person in the industry. It's my big break!'

He nods some more and says, 'Congratulations.' What a pro. I nearly say how grateful I am for Celia's putting in a good word but manage to bite my tongue in time and substitute my little speech about how, even if we aren't collaborators any more, we must still be friends. I'm congratulating myself on how well I've handled things and waiting for Ivan to come out with the 'Of course, Zita, we must' bit. But he doesn't. He's extremely polite. But ... He totally does my head in, like he's trying to do my head in by being cold and distant. This is uncool and unfair. I was going to discuss Celia with him but if he's gonna be like this ...

He insists on carrying my stuff down to the car while I pack it all in. I get the distinct impression he wants rid of me. I retrieve most of the things that I borrowed from Paul for the dinner party, apart from the rather nice leather floor cushion. I seem to remember that Cy took somewhat of a shine to that. I wait until Ivan has gone back into the house before starting the MGB up. Instead of driving back to the road, I drive round to the stable block, tucking the car in round the side, well out of sight. I'm only retrieving Paul's floor cushion but I don't want to provide any weapons for the gossips, ya know? People who might want to pull me down now I'm on the verge of success. Jealous people like Nadine and, I'm sorry to say, Ivan.

I don't pussyfoot around making my entrance into the stables. The MGB is so noisy that anyone inside is going to know that they've got visitors. I yank the door open and step inside, as usual completely blinded by the change in light. So I can't see anything but I can smell Cy. I know he's in here somewhere. My heart starts pounding in my chest. 'Oh, you're back.' Cy's voice wafts down from high up in the rafters. I jump and locate him doing a sort of tightrope balancing act along a roof beam and, you guessed it, he's naked. I feel muscles tighten. No, not because of what you're thinking. It's this height thing. It really is! It extends to other people being in high-up precarious positions, too. I kind of draw a pattern in the dusty floor with my toe to avoid having to watch Cy swinging himself about above me.

'Yeah, I'm back,' I drawl as nonchalantly as possible before glancing up to where Cy is adjusting the knots that secure some kind of sculpture to the beams.

'So, what do you want?' he drawls right back at me.

I feel a flash of anger. I go for withering uninterest. 'My leather floor cushion, actually.'

Cy makes a kind of snorting noise and jumps. I suppress a scream as he lands with a dull thump next to me.

His sweet musky scent fills my nostrils and he is way too close, way too naked. I clear my throat and step back. 'Cy, what the fuck is that?' I ask, aware of the slight wobble in my voice. Cy smiles and starts pulling on a rope, lowering his sculpture from the roof before knotting the rope round a stanchion. Cy is behind me now.

'Do you like it?' I feel dizzy. Cy is so close that I can feel his breath on the back of my neck. 'I got the idea from the shoot. The sacrifice.' I shrug and Cy spoons in behind me, walking me towards the dangling collection of metal and leather and rope. 'You can help me try it out if you like.'

Yeah, right. I go for urbane, controlled superwoman

(your basic Celia) and laugh, 'Hahhahhah,' before purring, 'Now what makes me think that this trying out is going to involve sex?'

OK, this is the point where I tell him to fuck off and give me my floor cushion, right? Well, yeah, in theory. If I was thinking clearly. If I hadn't been upset by Ivan's unnecessary self-pity. Actually, this is the point where I undo my *ileke* and put it someplace safe. This *is* relevant, just bear with me, OK? You see, those passport photos of Paul and Saskia have been bothering me. The way I see it is that Paul has been fucking Saskia. It's the only answer. Those photos may have looked innocent enough on the surface but it's the innocence that does it. Overpally intimacy is a dead giveaway. Remember in Hanabanilla when he let slip that private joke thing he had going with her? Same deal. So, seeing as he's been fucking Saskia, I figure that I'm due a bit of strange myself. I'm not saying that I'm going to fuck Cy. Well actually I am. It's the only answer. The only way to tie up my loose ends with Cy is to fuck him. Closure, right?

Now I can't move. I'm trapped, suspended from the roof beams in the stables. Fastened sort of half upside down into Cy's sculpture. My shoulders are supported by a harness of leather and rope and my head is dangling inches from the floor, my hair brushing the dusty boards. At least I imagine that my hair is brushing the floorboards. I'm wearing a blindfold. There are leather cuffs around my ankles, which in turn are fastened to a metal bar, which keeps my legs spread apart. My knees are bent over another bar and my wrists are somehow tied behind my back to my ankles. The muscles of my inner thighs are stretched so they ache. I'm being split in two, my cunt a red slash, gaping wide open between my splayed thighs. Unzipped from my clit to my arsehole.

I feel wet. Something is trickling between my lips, pooling in my arsehole before running round to my back and dripping to the floor. I shudder. Something tugs at my fanny hair and my lips part. Short rhythmic strokes along my mons while my fanny lips are moved this way and that. My lips are being held almost perfunctorily, like I'm being inspected, but y'know what? I like it. Then there's some stretching and scratching along the smooth skin between my thighs and my cunt. I am being shaved. Made bare. Or is it laid bare? I mumble and am rewarded with a stinging slap across my arse. 'Ow!' Another smack and Cy's voice, 'Quiet Zita. Not a word.'

I am not having Cy tell me what to do 'Cy...' I don't get any more words out. Cy's cock is rammed into my mouth. He thrusts it deep, banging against my throat. It tastes bitter.

'Not a word, Zita.' My cunt feels cold. Like someone is blowing across it. I'm being dried and powdered. Or oiled, I can't tell. A hand is running over my lips, which feel very naked and plumped out. It feels dirty, like playing hospitals as a little girl, and my clit begins to swell. I know it's peeking out between my lips. The hand briefly flicks it, then stops. Oh, that's what I need, I want to tell Cy. Touch it, lick it, bite it, go on. But I can't speak. My mouth is full of cock. I suck on it hungrily and am rewarded by a tender kiss on my exposed clit. Then he stops. Fuck, it needs more than that. I'm half crazy with arousal now. I try to thrust forward with my hips but the restraint is so tight, I can't move. This is making me angry.

I suck harder and Cy's ripe cock swells in my mouth. Now, his mouth is clamped around my cunt. He is biting me, holding my clit between his teeth and gently rolling it around. I do the same to his cock. It stiffens more, if that is possible, until I am gagging on it. Something presses against my arse. At first I tense. It can't be Cy. He has only one cock and I know where that is. My buttocks are pulled apart and fingers circle my hole. I feel my muscles relax and a finger slides inside me. 'Go on, fuck her hard.' Cy's voice sounds thick. There is a pause then the finger is slipped out and begins to guide something else into my hole. Fuck, and I thought Cy was big. At first it hurts and I try to expel it, but just succeed in swallowing it deeper. I've been well lubed. I gasp, making a half-choked whimpering sound. Cy's hand reaches for my nipple and he tweeks it. 'Come on, Zita!' His fingers close around my nipple in a hard pinch. 'You're a horny cunt and you know you want it.' He releases my nipple and the pain is replaced by a warm tingly feeling. Then he buries his face in my cunt. His teeth close on my clit and I manage a throaty moan of appreciation. The other cock is pushing deeper in. The cock at one end is beginning to merge with the cock at the other. I slurp greedily on Cy's, tonguing and nibbling him frantically till his come hits my throat in waves. I swallow every last drop, drinking it down hungrily as the other cock rams between my spread buttocks. I don't know who it is. I don't care. Cy's right. I feel so fucking dirty. Tell them to fuck me harder, I wanna scream. They do, while Cy sucks me, till I shout, I yell, I explode.

I am wakened by low-angle sunlight on my face. I'm sprawled across Cy's mattress on the hayloft sleeping platform. He is curled up in a ball, breathing deeply. I fumble around for clothes and dress quickly, quietly, careful not to disturb Cy. On my way out, I retrieve my *ileke* from the nail it dangles from. For some reason, it makes me feel guilty but something makes me I resist the desire to hurl it into the bushes.

My legs feel shaky but I get to the car all right. I

lower myself into the bucket seat and wince slightly. I feel a blush start on my chest but I suppress it. The *ileke* is in the palm of my hand. 'I've done nothing wrong,' I hiss at it and start the engine up. With a bit of luck I'll be back in London before the commuter traffic builds.

23

OK. I think I'll have him on his back, staked out like a captured cowboy in a western. Or bent over a barrel with his wonderful peachy arse exposed to me? Mmmn. I like this. I circle him, my killer heels clicking. I look abso-fucking-lutely amazing. I am tall and tanned and lean and lovely. Shit, that doesn't help. I've got 'The Girl from Ipanema' running round my head now. Anyway, I look fabulous. From the tips of my Manolo's (it's my fantasy, so indulge me) to the big, swollen end of my strap-on. Cy's eyes plead with me to be gentle as he struggles against the gag. No, lose the gag. I spit on my fingers and slowly begin circling his neat bud of an arsehole. He lets out a low moan and I begin working my fingers in and out. He groans some more and I stop and he calls me a bitch. I bring the leather switch I'm holding in my other hand down in a stinging slap across his buttocks 'No!' I snarl, 'you're the bitch and you want me to fuck you.' He groans and I slap him again harder. 'Go on, bitch,' I command, 'say it!' He shakes his head and I begin working my fingers in and out of his tight little arse again at the same time as I strafe his buttocks with the switch.

'Fuck me!' he groans.

'Not good enough,' I say and pull my fingers from his hole, leaving his sphincter contracting against nothing

'Fuck me like a bitch,' he whispers and I thrust my strap-on into his arse up to the hilt.

No-no-no-no, let's rewind to the staked-cowboy scenario. OK, Cy's dick is swollen and purple, cruelly encircled by the cockring at its base. I squat down and blow a kiss at the end. It twitches and, as Cy gasps, I push my pussy into his mouth, brushing my lips backwards and forwards over his hungry tongue. Imprisoned in the cockring, his dick twitches and leaps like a caged salmon. I bend my head, extending my tongue to lick the single bead of pre-come that glistens on the end. Cy lets out a muffled groan and I push my cunt harder in to his face, smothering him. I hold his cock in between my teeth, nipping the full length of the shaft. Cy begins to buck his hips under me and I stand up. 'Please don't stop!' begs Cy. I change my position so I am straddling him and slowly lower myself on to his engorged cock. I allow just the tip to enter into my cunt and Cy's bucking becomes manic.

No, back to the bit where I'm straddling his face. He's begging me with his tongue hanging out. Annoyingly, an image of him spitting water down my throat keeps superimposing itself. I look into his lovely face and force it to be lying underneath me again. Cy's mouth is open and he's waggling his tongue at me. Bastard is laughing at me! Maybe I need to fuck his arse some more. Tempting, but no, I have a better idea. I release my cunt muscles and send a shower of piss gushing into his mouth. He gags and splutters and laps it all up and I laugh. 'There's a good boy. You drink it all up and you might get your reward.'

'What reward is this?'

I shake the last drops of pee on to his outstretched tongue and slowly begin to lower myself down.

'Zita?'

My cunt is going to swallow him whole.

'Zita are you feeling well?'

Shit! I'm wedged at chest height between the edge

of a table and my chair. Half a dozen faces stare at me. Ohmygod, my first BWM production meeting and I end up under the table (literally). And, ohmygoda-gain, I'm wet. Please don't say I've wet myself in front of Clare Dodderidge. I wriggle myself vaguely upright. Clare looks expectantly at me over the top of her scary grown-up specs. 'Um, yes.' OK, good news is I've tipped a bottle of Evian in my lap. 'I'm fine, thanks.' What the fuck were we talking about? 'Um ... Irreverence. We need lots of irreverence on *Massive*.' Bad news is that my legendary ability to think on my feet has deserted me. Clare's giving me a don't-bullshit-me-girly, look. Shit, I'll have to go for honesty. 'Clare ... I ...'

OK, so I ditch the honesty gambit and throw a faint. I get away with a jet-lag/working-all-night/heat-wave thing. Well I'm not gonna tell her that I'm passing out because I haven't slept for nearly three days because I've been too busy fucking, am I? Oh, behave. It's not Channel 5, y'know. No. I give it my best brave-little-soldier, show-must-go-on act, then come over all woozy before I actually say anything. She buys it. I think. Well she gets her driver to take me home, anyway.

As soon as he's gone I sneak round to the garage. I've got some urgent business to attend to. See, I've decided that there's no point in pretending any longer. OK, Cy isn't a great respecter of women and probably not the nicest boy on the planet but he has to be in the running for the sexiest. Great body, beautiful face, loads of sex appeal and a filthy, dirty mind. As Paul has had ten weeks of screwing Saskia (oh, c'mon, get real), I'm entitled to same with Cy, don't you agree? I need to do this so it's only fair to get it out of my system. Nadine was right about one thing: a girl's gotta be what she's gotta be. Except I've got, at most, five days. So, I have a lot of ground to make up.

I point the MGB westwards and hit the throttle. It knows the way itself. I've got only one aim: get to Tanglebush as fast as possible, rip my clothes off and get stuck into another six hours or so of orgasmic research till, eventually, I crawl out of Cy's bed reeking of sex.

Most of the creativity has come from Cy so far, but I intend to change all that. I'm getting competitive. Which, I guess, is the new me. I've spent most of the day plotting an alternative scenario (witness the Evian Incident). I have been playing some delicious reruns of my rather primitive wallow in the mud with Roberto and Changui in my head. There are a number of combinations it would be *very* interesting to explore. I've got it into my head I'd like to try some reverse casting with the truss game. I also want another guest appearance by the mystery cock. There was something totally wanton about being taken and not knowing who by. I told Cy I want the other one there today. Told him he was gonna have to share me again. Shit, my loose ends are flapping again. I fully intend to make the most of the few remaining days before Paul returns and I know all this must end.

A big splot of rain hits the windscreen, just as I press down hard on the accelerator. The sky has gone all black and threatening and it's very, very close. I'm just wearing a white cotton sun dress (v. virginal!) and some Chloé perfume. When I arrive at Tanglebush, there's a first rumble of thunder. I park in my usual place and swing on into the stable block. First surprise, Cy ain't there. Second surprise, Elaine is.

Elaine is draped over Cy's old couch naked, of course, and in a noticeably available fashion, to be honest. And she's watching me carefully but emotionlessly. This girl is weird. There's something about her that brings out the bad side of me. Actually, she disgusts me, with her mindless passivity, her fucking Bambiness. I just want to bully her. I saunter over to her and stand above her.

'What're you doing here?' I ask.

She looks at me quite cooly. 'You wanted me here,' she replies and settles back in the couch, even more provocatively than before.

My brain is whirring. Cy knew I was gonna be here around 3.30 and he's been as hot for these sessions as me. So where is he? I think I'm twigging his plan. Cy has arranged for Elaine to be here because he wants some action between me and her. I feel a flush of anger. Hey, this was supposed to be *my* day, not his. Or maybe Elaine's heard about me and Cy (does that mean Nadine knows?) and she's come here with some weird plan to muscle in on our sex games. 'Cos of the Red Dress incident, she no doubt assumes I'm bi. Elaine seems to be getting a bit cocky about things but I don't think it's backed with any real confidence. I can play-act, too.

I haul my dress over my head and pose before her naked. Might as well get straight to the point. 'OK, are you gonna do me, or me you?' I ask.

'I thought I was gonna do you,' she replies cooly.

OK, let's keep going. 'You want to fuck me?' I check.

'You want me to fuck you?' she replies, unfazed. The girl is getting annoying. Where's Cy got to? Probably up in the rafters, watching all this. It's some kinda pre-fuck floor show for him. Perhaps he's got a bit jaded after three days of almost continuous sex. Maybe his tanks have got a bit drained, and he needs some stimulation. Maybe it's some kinda sex-bluff scenario, and, when I pull out, he'll come swinging down, laughing and claiming I'm a prude and he's won on points or something. Well, screw him. We'll see who cracks first.

I sit on the couch, then swing myself alongside Elaine. 'So, for some reason, you think I want you to fuck me, Elaine. Is that right?' I purr, using my very best heavy-lidded, sultry look for good measure. She shifts her weight slightly so her shin is hooked behind one of my thighs and rolls me closer towards her. Then her eyes droop and she moves in to kiss me. She kisses rather well and the kiss is accompanied by one hand gently but firmly clasping my pussy and squeezing while the other reaches round my waist and holds me tight. To my annoyance, I yield. I'd completely forgotten to allow for the fact that I'd spent the entire day in a state of growing sexual tension and that my normal defences are in a rather disorganised state. OK, if this is Cy's idea of an aperitif, I might as well enjoy it myself. Pretty soon, I've parted my thighs to allow her to finger my actually quite horny clit and I'm kissing her back quite aggressively. As long as I can keep some degree of control ...

Within a few minutes, I know that I'm gonna have to take positive action if I'm not gonna get swamped. This girl has been here before, I realise. She knows a few moves, including a few interesting ones. My breath is already starting to come in short sharp pants. I push away from her and stare at her. 'Elaine, are you a dyke?' I ask. She shakes her head. 'So why are you doing this?' I persevere.

'Because you asked for me to,' is the reply.

God, she's annoying me again. So I slap her. She just looks at me, cooly, no hostility. 'I didn't ask you to,' I retort, feeling pretty sure of my ground. I'm getting pretty good at this business and I'm near-as-dammit certain I've never specifically asked this girl to fuck me. She shrugs and gets up from the couch. She switches on Cy's video and within seconds, a picture comes up on the screen. It's accompanied by an echoey soundtrack of muffled grunts and sighs. It takes me some time to sort the image out in my head. A blur of staccato movement resolves itself into bodies moving – bodies seen from above, I realise. A dirty blond-haired head lapping between some spread-eagled thighs while its brown skinned body rhythmically pumps into a mass of splayed dark hair below. And another, red-haired, pale-skinned body pushing a dark object into the blond's head, I think at first. Then, I realise, into the same body that is getting the blond's attention. With a shock, I realise that it is Bambi shafting my arse while Cy and me frantically suck each other off.

I turn and look at Elaine. She is sitting on the couch, almost demurely lubing the large, strap-on dildo round her groin. Then she looks up at me brightly with a ready-if-you-are expression over her face. Oh, shit, I think my bluff is being called here. Then a voice wafts down from above: 'It's what you asked for, Zita,' followed by a little chuckle. Well, at least I had been right about one thing. But where do I go from here? Am I getting a little out of my depth? Then a memory wafts back. This same room, one night maybe seven or eight weeks ago. Me, naked in front of some half a dozen strangers. Me, terrified but somehow calling the shots, walking away with a stunning victory. I realise now that all this is just Cy's attempt to revenge himself on me, my humiliation to counterbalance his. Fuck him, he's a fucking feral slacker, nothing more. I am me.

I lie back invitingly before Bambi, who is sprouting the biggest hard-on you've ever seen. Part of me, the part that is doing anatomical computations, is going hey, whoa there, just a minute. But I have my dander up, and that is in control. I part my pussy lips and lift my knees as Elaine kneels on the edge of the couch and rests the monster at my entrance. Then she works the head in slowly. She pushes my thighs up to maximise the curve of my arse and straighten the line of entry. It is stretching me almost unbearably but, eventually, Elaine penetrates me. I can take it only about halfway, it's so huge. She begins to slide it backwards and forwards inside me, only a matter of inches at first. She does it carefully, looking into my eyes all the time. I can see she is excited, too: there is a wild little hungry smile on her lips. She brushes my stretched, exposed clit with her thumb and I begin to respond myself. Soon, we are rocking together and I can feel my cunt being deliciously stretched. I'm being hard-fucked by another girl, a girl I don't even respect, let alone like. And, fuck, I'm beginning to enjoy it.

Then, I realise the material on the tape has changed. I can see the screen from where I'm lying and it now shows a swirl of night-time movement. Faces, bodies. It's familiar. I realise I'm looking at the outtakes form the *Outlaws* shoot. Me and Cy almost fucking. I stare at the screen, watching myself on the verge of orgasm as Elaine continues to push into me. She leans forward and croaks in my ear, 'He fucks me while we watch it. He shows it to everyone. I warned you.' I'm slipping away, I realise. I'm losing the plot. I even like the thought of their doing it. 'I wanna watch you,' I groan. 'I wanna see him fuck *you*.'

I can see Elaine wants this, too. Her eyes light up and she hollers for Cy to come down. Eventually, he appears, naked and fully prepared. She unstraps herself rapidly and throws herself down on the floor. 'Tell him, Zita,' she half shouts, almost exultantly.

'Fuck her, Cy,' I say. 'Fuck her really hard.'

Cy grins and mounts Elaine, who groans deeply as he enters her. I watch as his swollen cock forces her lips apart till they make a pure circle of plumped-out flesh, clinging round the base of his cock. Soon, he is deep inside her, pushing luxuriously into her, making her gasp with the depth of his penetration. Elaine's eyelids are open but her eyeballs are rolled ecstatically back. She groans with each of Cy's thrusts. His tight, downy arse is lifting and falling slowly in front of me. It is a fuckingly gorgeous arse, there is no possibility of denying it. A gorgeously fuckable arse. It takes me only a few seconds to strap the dildo on and relube it. I don't mess about but go straight for it. I am inside Cy before he has realised what has happened. He bucks a bit and struggles but that only serves to deepen my penetration. I am looking over his shoulder and I can see him wincing and his jaw go slack. But he's still fucking Elaine, who, sensing the commotion on top of her, has opened her eyes.

She looks up at me, puzzled at first, and then clicks what has happened. She stretches back and pouts in a big, losing-it grin. 'Fuck me, hard,' she moans, looking right at me. I force myself against Cy's muscular buttocks as Elaine simultaneously lifts her hips off the floor. Cy groans. We do it again. He groans louder. The groan segues into a distant rumble of thunder. Elaine begins humping back at Cy's groin as fast as she can. Cy's face is screwed in an agonised grimace as the rain starts in earnest. The harness of the strap-on is cutting into my fanny and a bulge is rubbing against my clit. It hurts, exquisitely. Then there is an intense white light and the whole stable block is shaken by an enormous roll of thunder. I get a momentary vision of the three of us, on video, grinding and pushing and flailing and rolling in some weird synch, like one of those old-fashioned threshing machines Cy has stored in the barn. Oh, I bet he is videoing this too, the bastard, but I can't stop now. I have no intention of stopping now. The harder I bang into Cy, the worse, or better, the strap-on harness rubs me. I am merciless. I enter him practically to the hilt. Elaine comes first, then I feel Cy buck and thrash between me and her. The bucking and thrashing starts me off. I roar. Three simultaneous orgasms at once. Is this a record?

24

The weather's gone all elemental on me. By the time I get the MGB's roof up, both the Roadster and me are soaked. My virginal white cotton dress is plastered to my body and Tanglebush looks like it's auditioning for the opening scene of *The Rocky Horror Picture Show*. C'mon, you get the picture. The thunder is more of your great-rending-*crrrack* type than your hearty rumble and the lightning rips through the inky black sky like a Silk Cut advert. When the hailstones start I jump into the car. No doubt the puddle I sit in will contribute another transparent patch to my dress and no doubt the puddle is connected with why the car won't start.

After five minutes of Paul's fucking museum piece making sad, wheezy noises I give up turning the key in the ignition. Fuck, even if it would start I'm not sure I'd want to drive anywhere in this storm. The windows have steamed up and the hail is rat-a-tat-tatting on the crappy vinyl roof. I'm starting to shiver and not just from the cold. Those modern myths about phantom hitchhikers that we frightened each other with at school are coming back to me in astounding detail. I hate the fucking country.

There's another almighty crash and something dragging and scraping across the Roadster's soft top. I scream. It's the headless-man-eating-serial-killer, I know it! I'm not going back in the stables. Fuck! Cy probably *is* the headless-man-eating-serial-killer, sick bastard that he is. Shit, I'm not waiting in the car for him to open it up like a corned-beef can. Nope, I'm legging it. I catapult out of the passenger seat (figuring that will confuse the serial killer) and run to the house. Incidentally, I don't do running, ever, so this is a mark of how freaked I am.

I slam the door behind me and stand dripping in the hall. I can hear the wind roaring away outside and every so often there are cracks and rendings and general scare-the-shit-out-of-the-city-girl noises. Inside, apart from assorted creakings and whining windy noises, it is quiet. No Nadine (again!). I guess she's shacked up somewhere in town. My stomach tightens when I think of Nadine. Or maybe it's 'cos of all that running. Yeah, it's the running. I push my dripping hair out of my eyes and start climbing the stairs. I like the way I leave damp little footprints in the dust like the little mermaid. Sorry, must curb this tendency to whimsy. The little mermaid was a loser, OK? She got legs and was crippled with pain so she could be with some dorky guy who dumps her in the end anyway. I don't like where this train of thought is going.

Luckily, I'm outside my old room so I don't have to think about it any more. I knock on the door. There is no response. I push the door and it swings open. Ivan is sitting in the turret watching the storm. I strike a suitably dramatic pose. 'Hi, Ivan!' He doesn't move. I decide to go straight into offensive mode, 'Ivan, why did you keep those outtakes of me and Cy at the shoot?' Ivan doesn't even twitch. Shit, why is everyone I know so fucking cool? I squelch my way across the room and tap him on the shoulder. He wheels around and knocks me to the floor (mattress, actually), flinging himself heavily on top of me. '*Owww*, Ivan, fuck off!'

Ivan takes his weight off me and takes the mini-speakers from his ears. 'Zita!' I test my limbs for any obvious breakages. Ivan sits back on his haunches and looks at me 'You are wet. You have wet my bed.'

'Yeah, right, and you are fat. You have broken my arm.'

Ivan squints at me and then does an explosive 'Hah!' before slapping the floor and throwing his big meaty paws around me. 'Zita, I have missed you. You make me laugh.' It's actually not unpleasant being wrapped in an Ivan. He's very warm. Obviously built for Russian winters. But he still hasn't answered my question. I reluctantly wriggle out of his grasp and immediately begin to shiver. 'C'mon, Ivan, why did you keep it?'

Ivan shakes his head. 'I did not keep it, Zita. I gave it to you. Come here.'

I automatically take a step towards him 'Yeah, and I must have left it here when I moved out and then you found it.'

Ivan turns me around and unzips my dress. 'You left nothing, Zita.' He tugs the sodden material away from my damp skin.

'So how come Cy has got it?' I lean on his shoulder and move my feet so Ivan can free my ankles of the sodden dress.

Ivan looks up at me. Even kneeling down he doesn't have far to look. 'Maybe you gave it him. Or maybe he took it from you. I don't know.'

My teeth are chattering so hard I bite my tongue (literally, this time). Ivan's telling the truth, I know. He doesn't do lying. Which means that if Cy has got it then he stole it from me. Fuck. What if Elaine was telling the truth? I am drenched in an acid flush of shame and anger, which leaves me shuddering even more violently. Ivan wraps me in his duvet and begins rubbing my arms and legs kind of vigorously like a sports coach. I wonder if this is his seduction technique and start giggling. Ivan sits me down on the mattress and rummages around in a large holdall. 'This will warm us up,' he yells over the storm.

Ivan and I sit close together, wrapped in the duvet, passing the bottle of Stolli between us. I'm beginning to steam. The turret feels even more like a ship than usual. The rain is still lashing down and the tree's branches are thrashing wildly. My owl won't be doing much wooing tonight. Ivan has gone into maudlin mode. He accuses me of avoiding him. I give up denying this. Apart from the fact that I'm fed up of lying, Ivan seems to want to make speeches tonight so I let him ramble on and on and on. In between 'We could have made a beautiful film together' and 'Zita, you were exactly what I needed,' it crosses my mind that he's been hiding away here all on his own. Jesus, no wonder he needs to talk. No wonder he's maudlin and, hang on, did he mean he needed me professionally, emotionally or sexually? Bollocks, he's going to go all little mermaid on me, I know it. Nope. It's worse than that. It's Eeyore. Ivan says he will soldier on, he still has Yolande. Yolande! Her heavy-hooded eyes flash into my head. I'd forgotten about Yolande. My hand reaches for my throat. It is bare. I feel uncomfortable, squirmy. It's like being reminded of a holiday romance in front of your boyfriend, or something. I take a swig of Stolli and slur, 'C'mon, Ivan, you can't be an honorary gal-pal if you gonna bring up embarrassing incidents. It's a rule.'

Ivan takes the Stolli from me and says, 'You must never live your life by rules, Zita. Because there is only one that matters.'

He takes a big swig of vodka and I'm left going, 'And . . . ?' He raises an eyebrow at me. I roll my eyes. 'And the only rule is . . . ?'

Ivan stretches. 'The only rule, Zita, is –' he takes another glug; I'm nodding furiously '– there are no rules.'

I start shaking again. Of course there are rules. Everyone knows there are rules. Everyone except Ivan, that is. I stare at his carved-in-rock profile. Shit. Look where not having rules got Alison. Or Ivan himself for that matter. Like, he's really going to finish *Red Angel*. I can't find the words to say this. Inexplicably, I start to cry. Ivan pulls me closer to him. He smells of cinnamon. I like being close to him. When he starts rubbing my feet again, I like that too. In fact I love having my feet rubbed. I fall backwards and close my eyes as Ivan presses his thumbs into the balls of my foot. I watch Ivan through my teary eyelashes. Blurry, I can see how he would have looked fifteen years ago. With those big, wounded, soulful eyes, he must have been to die for. This just makes me cry more. I know, at the moment, he's suffering inside. I know that *Red Angel* was a deeply personal dream for him and just telling me about it was an intimacy. I know the awful truth is that I killed the poor bastard's dream and instead of hating me he is stroking the most unattractive and (clit aside) sensitive part of my body with a kind of gentle intensity that is sending shock waves through my entire body. That's when I have my inspired insight. There's not much I can do to resurrect *Red Angel* but there is something I can do to make up for killing it.

'There are no rules, huh?' I ask. Ivan continues his foot therapy. Reluctantly, I pull my foot from his hands and reach up and put my arm round his neck. He smiles at me. A heartbreakingly sad, honest smile.

'No rules,' he repeats.

I pull him down to me and kiss him with my best erection-inducing, cheer-you-up-no-end smooch. I'm famous for it. It's infallible. Ivan braces his arms so he's doing a kind of push-up on top of me and looks into my eyes. He looks worried. Sweet!

'Zita, I . . .' he starts to say, but I shush him and snake up till I'm clinging limpet-like to his big bear's body. My hand reaches down to where he keeps that bear-sized cock but Ivan outmanoeuvres me. He kisses me back. Shit! And I thought the foot rub was good. Ivan slides his body along mine until his face is over my cunt. I freeze. How embarrassing is this! Ivan smells like cinnamon, and I've got a fucking herring factory between my legs. Ivan drops his head and kisses me. His stubble scratches against my skin and I remember that I have recently been shorn. Ivan kisses me some more and does some sniffing. 'You know what I like about you, Zita?' I am going to die of shame. I shake my head. 'You always smell of sex.' I don't have to respond because Ivan drops his head between my legs and begins nibbling at my cunt.

His stubble, my stubble. Why am I thinking of kitten's tongues? Nadine? Nadine! I don't want to think of her. I want this on my terms. I use my elbows to hook myself out of Ivan's tongue range. He looks up at me. His head framed between my thighs. Shit now everything's gone all gynaecological and why does that make me think of Paul? '*No!*'

Ivan's body jacknifes so he ends up kneeling in front of me. He looks confused. Fuck, I'm not surprised. I'm confused. He springs to his feet and throws his head back and lets out an almighty roar. Shit. Now what? He paces about a bit doing some more roaring and then says, 'I am sorry, Zita. I am so stupid. I thought . . .' I'm not listening. I'm looking at his body. I was being mean when I called him fat. Oh, by the way, did I say that Ivan has gone native and is thus unclothed? Anyway, he's broad and solid and, for a white guy, he has the most wonderfully rounded buttocks. But fat? Nah, the only fat thing is swinging between his thighs and, well, I wouldn't mind some.

'Ivan!' I say to catch his attention. He stops mid pace and stares at me. 'It's OK, Ivan, you thought right,' I add gently.

Now he looks even more confused. 'No Zita. I was wrong,' he growls, and he looks like he's going to do some more of his wounded-bear roaring again. Pre-emptive action is called for. I stand up too and, as he throws his great shaggy head back, I throw myself at him. On him, actually. Unlike with Paul, it's quite a stretch getting my thighs round his waist and, unlike with Paul, he doesn't stagger. I don't give him a chance to start with the roaring again. Instead I kiss him. Long and hard. I bite his lips and flick my tongue into his mouth and then while still holding his face in my hands I slide down his body. I keep kissing him, making him bend his head and shoulders forwards. I rub my belly against his cock. It feels warm and deliciously hard. I think I'm about to experience belly-button sex, which, though sounding delightful, definitely takes second place to good old-fashioned cunt sex.

I keep sliding downwards, pulling Ivan with me. Eventually I make him topple. We land in a great heap of arms and legs. Fortunately, Ivan has the foresight to roll himself under me or there would be a great big Zita-shaped hole in the mattress. I lie on top of him, my nipples pressing into his broad smooth chest, his cock still a reassuring bump. He raises his head to look at me, causing his stomach muscles to harden against my belly. We are both panting. He makes a sort of phwwf noise and says, 'You take your wrestling seriously, Zita.'

I nod. 'Mmmn, very seriously.' And I begin to rub

myself over Ivan's body. His skin is something else. Smooth and luxurious, almost like a woman's. Over the muscles, there is the thinnest layer of fat. And it's velvety, like he spends a fortune on body lotion. I begin slithering my way south, intent on introducing myself to Mr Porky, but Ivan clasps his hands around my waist. (Incidentally, if you haven't already done so, then invest in a guy with big hands. Having someone able to span your waist with their mitts is *so-o* cool.)

Anyway, hands round waist, I am *so-o* near the end of his cock that I'm not giving up now. I bend my head and take one of his small brown nipples in my mouth. 'Zita!' I'm not talking. Instead I nip him hard. As I planned, he loosens his grip on me and I slide further down until I'm sitting on top of his cock. Until his cock is inside me. Nearly my time to roar. Instead I gasp, but there is something not right going on. Either my cunt is so wet that I've dissolved his cock, or he's lost his erection.

Shit. I didn't bite him that hard. I look at Ivan for guidance. He won't look at me. 'Zita' he whispers, 'I have a problem.' *He* has a problem? I'm about to explode and *he* has a problem. 'Zita?' I look at him with a this-had-better-be-fucking-good look on my face. He meets my eyes. 'I am impotent.' As brush-offs go this one sucks.

'No you're not, Ivan!' I wail. 'You were hard before. You just don't fancy me.'

Ivan looks stunned, then he starts laughing and I know he's lying. The Big Bastard. I hit him and he laughs harder. I wrap the duvet round myself and turn away from him. He asks me if I'm angry and I snarl, 'Yeah,' and he asks me if I'm hurt and I snarl, 'Yeah,' and all the time he's laughing. 'What's so fucking funny, *Ivan*?' I scream.

He stops laughing and squats down in front of me. 'You are Zita. You are so wonderfully self-centred. I tell you my shameful secret and you think it can't be him, it must be *me*.'

I look into his face and I realise that he is telling the truth. Fuck, *that's* what Celia meant. His *condition*. Fuckfuckfuck. First, I kill his dream and then his pride. I jump to my feet and I throw my head back and ... Nothing happens.

'Shout, Zita!' Ivan roars. 'You are angry and you are hurt and you are frustrated, so *shout* it out.' There is an almighty clap of thunder and I scream and the storm is right over us and Ivan catches hold of me and buries his face in my cunt. My legs are shaking and I'm going to fall and I don't care. I want to go over. I come screaming and roaring. 'Like a Russian,' Ivan says.

I wake up alone on my old mattress-bed. Ivan has gone. Gone where? My own voice answers me, 'Down a drain, back to England, into the hereafter.' Into the hereafter? Shit! I sprint from the room. I know exactly where he is. The DON'T GO THERE door is ajar. I hurtle through it. I practically fall over my feet in my attempt to stop. I stand on the threshold looking in. It is a huge room, a ballroom. Was a ballroom. The floor has gone, there are only sporadic joists where pretty feet once waltzed. The room is massive. Vast. Echoing. Empty. Except for Ivan, sitting on the far side, beyond the balcony windows. He is sitting, naked, on the stone parapet. On the very edge of the fucking parapet, staring out into the rain.

The whoosh that drains my body leaves me trembling and stupid. Ohmygod, I have brought him to this. He is in despair. Considering the unnamable. I have to stop him. I grit my teeth and stare fixedly ahead of me. I begin tightrope-walking across the thickest joist I can see, forcing my jelly legs into each step, my eyes fixed on Ivan's back. I'm not even a quarter the way across when I realise it's no good. I'm going to be sick. I'm going to throw up. Ohmygod, I've frozen. My eyeballs slowly start to pivot downwards in their sockets. I can't help it. I'm going to have to look down. Down into the pit of eternity. Somehow, I force the word out. 'Ivan!' I wail.

He turns. He swings his legs back into the room. He lunges towards me bellowing, '*Zita! No!*'

For one second, our eyes meet. Then the beams underneath him dissolve in a foam of powdered, ancient, rotten wood and he plunges downwards from my view.

25

I've acquired a past. I am the girl that witnessed Ivan Punin's fall from grace. Everyone at work knows (something) about it. Oh, Ivan didn't die or anything as epic as that. No, he just acquired multiple fractures and a new nickname. No one calls him I-vos any more. He's the Red Bull now. Yup, you got it. 'Cos he's big, he's Russian and he thinks he's got wings.

I laughed when I heard it. Course I fucking did. I'm on the inside now and I know the rules. Ivan would understand. He'd probably laugh himself. I dunno if he's heard it or not. Since I last saw him in casualty, I haven't been able to bring myself to visit. I know I promised to be his friend and everything but, shit, does he really need a friend like me? I mean killing the *Red Angel* was bad enough but nearly killing him! As fuck-ups go, that's quite a biggie. Anyway, I hear through Celia via Clare that he's gonna be OK, so I figure that I'll leave them to sort out their own lives. I've got enough on my plate trying to get my own in order.

The couple of days I have left before Paul gets back have been filled with production meetings, the evenings with cleaning, and the nights with bad dreams. I'm trying to put things right but, no matter what I do, everything still feels somehow wrong. The only thing keeping me sane right now is the thought that Paul will be home soon. Paul and normality are what I crave. I dunno, I guess Paul was right all along. I can't believe I doubted him. I mean, he was right about Ivan being a joke. Shit, he's more than a joke: he's a fucking punch line. (What goes with vodka and thinks it can fly? Ivan Punin. Boom-boom.) The only rule is there are no rules? Yeah, right. I broke the rules and what did it get me? Cy, for fuck's sake! I can't believe I was conned by him. I can't believe I fell for a manipulative, posing loser like Cy when I had Paul. I just went a bit wild this summer, that's all. Too much sun. Too many intoxicants. Too much Nadine. Poor Paul. I don't even believe he's been shagging Saskia any more. More likely, he's been working nonstop in a humid mosquito trap of a country where you can't even get the phones to work while I've been spending my time screwing things up. Or just plain screwing.

Not any more, though. My dancing days are over. Paul's back tonight and I'm gonna make everything better. I run through my jobs list once more. The MGB's been valeted and is all tucked up in the garage. The flat is gleaming. The blinds are down and I've dusted and I've cleaned and I've scrubbed the floor and I've rubbed the sticky marks from the kitchen trolley with nail varnish remover. I've polished the fridge and I've even washed and ironed the (new) 100 per cent Egyptian cotton sheets. They look pristine. I can't wait to sully them.

So did you think when I said 'Not any more' that I meant I was giving up sex? C'mon, as if! I meant that I was giving up sex with anyone other than Paul, that's all. OK? So I've made a few mistakes this summer, starting with fucking Nadine. Yep, literally. And fucking Cy was a drastic mistake. And Elaine. Shit, she's one big huge mistake all of her own. The cowboys? Well, kind of a mistake. The *bembe*? We are not going to talk about that. Yolande? Mistake, if a nice one. And Ivan? I don't wanna go there, either. I'm not sure if what I did with Ivan counts as fucking, but a mistake it definitely was. Whatever. It's all gone. It's the past. I can't do anything about it but there is something I can do to make it up to Paul. You see, Clare says that the secret of success is learning from your mistakes and I reckon at least I can let Paul benefit from all the learning I've done this summer.

I wile away the last few hours getting myself ready. Paul will be *so* impressed with my time management. Between working and my marathon cleaning sesh, I've squeezed in a little specialist shopping. Hurrah for the Internet and special delivery, that's what I say. You see, I figured that as Paul and I had some unfinished business, and knowing how much he likes it when I'm Professional, I thought for his welcome home present I'd combine the two. Finish off our business in a professional manner, I mean.

Remember that Barbarella frock I wore to the dream BAFTA's? The one where I turned into Saskia? Well. There's no chance of that happening now because I've found the frock. A similar one, anyway. It doesn't have a zip but it is rubber and it is fanny skimming. I sprinkle the inside with talc and put it on like a waistcoat. A very tiny waistcoat. Now for the tricky bit. How to join the edges together. You see, although the dress doesn't have a zip running down its front, it does have a serious collection of straps and buckles. I decide to start in the middle, figuring that, once I bridge my belly, it will be easy-peasy from then on in.

Not so. However, once I have each strap fastened on its first hole, it is relatively simple to tighten it. This has an amazing effect. I discover that I can alter the shape of my body. By lying on the bed, breathing out (a lot) and yanking on my magic straps, I achieve a tiny waist. My tits are so high that my chin's practically resting on them, and every curve I do have is exaggerated by the constricting rubber. I need the talc to get into my boots, too. Like the frock, they're rubber. They do have a zip, which is just as well, 'cos I wouldn't have got into them otherwise. There's a gap of about six inches between the top of the boots and the bottom of the dress. To complete my ensemble I couldn't resist the wrist cuffs and my favourite thing of all. The Temptress wig.

I decide against checking out how I look until I am completely dressed, to get the full effect in one go. Then I'll know how I look to Paul. I totter into the bathroom where the full-length mirror is. I have to take very small, wobbly steps on the platform boots, partly because they are very high and partly because I have my eyes shut. When I open them I am confronted with a whore. Her mouth is a glossy red gash. Her hair a matching red asymmetric bob. Her eyes are lost in pools of black kohl. Her skin bulges obscenely between the tops of her thigh-high boots and her crotch-length dress. I don't recognise myself. Neither does Paul.

'What the fuck are *you* doing in *my* flat?'

I catch Paul's reflection floating behind mine in the bathroom mirror. He looks tanned and tired and a bit angry and very, very sexy. And he really doesn't recognise me. I adopt a husky voice. 'Waiting for you to come home, babes.'

'And who are you, waiting for me to come home?'

I turn around. Lit from behind, my face will be barely visible to Paul.

'I'm your welcome-home present.'

I think I see a glimmer of realisation but Paul doesn't let on. Instead he leers at me and takes hold of one of my buckles. He pulls me towards him. I go to kiss him but he catches hold of my face and turns it away. He must have been drinking on the plane. I catch the familiar sweet smell of rum on his breath as he whispers in my ear, 'I'm not going to kiss *you*. I don't know where you've been.'

A guilty flush washes over my body. Paul squeezes my arse hard. 'I know someone you can kiss, though.' Paul pushes me down, forcing me to drop to my knees in front of him. 'Take my cock out.' I undo his fly and his erect cock springs out. 'Now let's see how far along it you can spread that lipstick.'

Paul puts his hands behind my head and pulls me on to his cock. He rams into me, making me gag. I can feel his cock swelling in my mouth and a first telltale bleachy hint of sperm coats the back of my throat. I think he's going to come but he pulls out. My eyes are watering. I can feel gloopy puddles of kohl forming in the corners of my eyes and my glitter-tipped eyelashes are batting like a hummingbirds' wings. Enough of this.

Paul's cock is still impressively tense and at a very convenient height. I use it as a handhold to scrabble upright. Not very dignified, but, once I'm standing, I feel more in control. The ridiculous height of the platform boots does make me as tall as Paul. It's weird not having to look up to him. I like it. Paul is looking down at his cock, gripped between my (false) red nails. I tense my fingers, making my nails dig into the shaft. Paul makes a strangled 'Owww' as I squeeze his dick. I place a finger over his lips. He smirks at me like he's humouring me but doesn't say a word. I smirk back, then tug on his dick. His smirk wavers slightly. I dig my talons in further, not enough to hurt but enough to let him know that I could if I wanted. His dick twitches in my hand, then he takes a step towards me.

I'm not sure what I'm going to do but I don't want to lose my height advantage by getting horizontal and

I do know that I like leading Paul round by the cock. We do a lap of the living room, then I lead him to his desk and, placing my fingers on Paul's shoulders, push *him* to his knees. 'Wait!' I command. He's still wearing his I'm-only-humouring-you smile but he does as he's told.

I rummage round in the drawer and dump half of its contents on the desk before I find what I'm looking for. Gaffer tape. Paul's eyes flash but he stays put. I walk behind him and drop to a squatting position. Not easy but I'm getting the hang of these boots. I tape Paul's hands to his ankles. I walk in front of him and perch on the desk so that Paul is kneeling between my thighs. He's still wearing his not very impressed face, until he tries to move, that is. I lift my legs and place my heels on his shoulders, then, with my nails digging into his scalp, I force him on to my cunt. 'Lick my pussy out!' Paul makes a muffled 'mmgh' noise but I don't care if he's playing or not. I didn't realise how much I needed this but, once I start, I can't stop. My arse is resting on the edge of the desk; my smoothly shaven fanny is right in his face. I ride him, grinding my dripping cunt on to his mouth, his chin, his nose. I don't care if he participates or not, 'cos I am aching. I fuck his face fiercely and angrily, rocking like a mad-woman, my fingers grasping at Paul's hair. There's a wave building inside me. When it arrives, it slams into me, nearly bowling me over with its force. It makes me want to shout. So I do. Loudly.

The blood is thumping in my ears, more or less in time with the nagging thumps coming from City-Bitch-Girl upstairs. I need to set this girl straight. 'Go fuck yourself,' I yell at the top of my voice.

'Zita, for Chrissake!'

Paul looks horrified. He shimmies his shoulders from underneath my feet. It's quite funny watching him trying to move. He manages to shift from a kneeling to a sitting position. I hop down from my perch and bend my face to his. His is sodden with juice from my cunt. I take hold of his face in my hands and kiss him. When I let go his face is a jammy smear of lipstick and come.

'Who told you to speak?'

Paul is still struggling against the gaffer. 'Zita, this isn't funny.'

I rip off a square of gaffer tape and hold it over Paul's mouth. 'Now who the fuck is Zita? And are you going to shut up?' Paul eyes the square of gaffer in my hands and nods his head. 'Good.'

I drop down to my knees and investigate Paul's flies. His dick has shrunk somewhat and is now poking out rather sadly. I bend down and lightly kiss the end. It swells a little. I run the point of one of my nails the length of the thick blue vein. Paul's cock bulges. That's better. I take the cock between my teeth and gently nibble on the underside. Paul gasps. Good. I think, I've got his full attention now. I sit opposite Paul with my legs open and slowly circle my clit. Paul's unblinking eyes don't move as I slide my fingers one at a time into my cunt. I wank myself until I'm hungry for some real cock. I slide my sticky fingers out and place them in Paul's mouth. 'Your turn,' I whisper, 'but only if you behave yourself.' Paul nods furiously, still sucking on my fingers. I cut him free of the gaffer tape and tell him to strip. I turn my back so I don't have to watch him struggling to get his jeans over his big feet. So unsexy. When I turn back round, he is naked. 'Good boy. Lie down.' Paul squats in the middle of the discarded clothes strewn over the floor, looking at me expectantly. I smile and position him how I want. Staked out like a captured cowboy in a western.

I straddle Paul's cock and slowly lower myself

down. Teasingly, I slide my parted lips along the length of his cock while I watch his tanned body straining against the gaffer to meet mine. I rub my hard, hungry nipples in his face until he takes one in his mouth and suckles me greedily. Then I lift my hips till his tip is against my wet, juicy hole and I lower myself really gradually on to his bulging cock and, as it slips into me, I finger my clit and he's biting my nips and now I'm grinding down harder and harder as his hips struggle to rise up to meet mine till I can feel his cock welling up inside me and I fall forward on top of him as he surges and pumps away inside me and I'm yelling fucking obscenities again. Bitch Girl upstairs is banging her broom handle. She's so repressed.

I wake first. Paul is sprawled out untidily next to me, snoring loudly. There's lipstick and mascara smeared all over my freshly laundered pillow cases. I feel a twinge of annoyance. Hey, how domesticated is that? The old me wouldn't have noticed, let alone cared. I peel a glittery eyelash from Paul's cheek and shuffle my way out of the bed without waking him.

I'm still soaking in the bath when Paul appears. His face is crisscrossed with sleep lines and he looks grumpy. 'Hello?' I beam at him. He grunts something at me and heads for the toilet, where he pisses the longest, loudest piss in history, finishing with a rather dramatic fart. 'Wow that's *so-o* romantic,' I say in a not-too-sarcastic voice. Paul just scratches his belly and begins running water in the sink. At least he's gonna wash his hands. Paul starts splashing water on his face. 'Paul, hang on. I'm getting out now. Why don't you get in the bath?'

Paul gropes around for a towel and yawns. 'Haven't got time.'

I sit up. 'Come on, Paul, you can't be working today.'

He's started cleaning his teeth, so I have to wait for him to spit before I get the answer. 'Arranged to meet Sassy.'

I don't believe this. 'Paul. It's your first day back.'

He finishes rinsing his mouth and says, 'It's only a meeting, and besides shouldn't you be at work, too?' I step out of the bath, leaving the floor drowning under a pool of bubbles. Paul tuts.

'I took the day off, Paul, so we could spend some time together.'

Paul throws his hands up. 'Zita, you can't do things like that. It's so amateurish.'

I wrap myself in a towel. For some reason I don't want Paul to see me naked. I stomp past him back into the bedroom and start throwing clothes on. Paul follows me and stands in the doorway. 'Look, Zita. You've got to get grown up about this.' I continue trying to get my faded combats over my damp skin. 'You're not wearing those to work are you?'

That's it. 'Jesus, Paul. Nadine was right about you. You are a fucking control freak.'

Paul looks like I've slapped him. The row we have is a nasty, spiteful row. Paul can't slag me off about my career any more 'cos all of a sudden I've got one. Instead he lays into my friends. They're all losers and, if I want to get on, it's high time for me to dump them. He's even heard about Ivan and my part in his downfall. 'You've acquired quite a rep, you know, Zita. Know what they're calling you?' Oh, here we go. I give him a come-on-surprise-me look. He does. 'Hannibal.'

Hannibal? I must look as puzzled as I feel.

'Yeah, Zita. Hannibal, 'cos you're a man eater.'

I can't help it. I start laughing. Until Paul tells me who he heard it from. Sassy, of course. I'm furious and kinda guilty 'cos I don't know what else he might have heard. I'm clutching at straws, searching for something to hit back with, when I remember the passport photos. I storm past him, grab them from his desk and wave them in his face. 'Tell you when you were fucking each other, did she?' Of course, it all tumbles out. He's been fucking her since before he met me. 'You fucking hypocrite,' I snarl. 'What happened to never-fuck-the-people-you-work-with?'

Paul looks at me pointedly. 'Don't you mean the honesty-about-infidelity rule?' he snaps, then laughs and adds hollowly, 'Hannibal?' I slap him hard enough to bring tears to his eyes.

I'm crying too. I had so much wanted things to be normal. What went wrong? Neither of us goes to work. We have one of those hand-wringing, tear-stained, how-did-it-all-go-wrong? sessions. Paul's phone rings incessantly till I seize it and hurl it into the bathwater, where it makes a little phut sound before sinking to the bottom. Had to be Dahling Sassy. I know now why he was so anxious for me to get the Big World job. Once I got an income, he could get me out. And move Sassy Dahling in? My carefully considered strategy falls apart. I so much do not want to be an Alison, I insult, I cajole, I implore, I confess. So much for 'deny everything'. I tell him (some of) the things I've done. I'm shamed at my recalcitrant ways. It was all Nadine's fault. But the thought of losing him to Saskia makes me sick, literally. Paul softens and helps me clean myself up. Somehow, I win. We'll stay together. He will stop seeing Saskia, except for strictly professional reasons. I will focus on my career. We will be a successful meejah couple. I promise not to see Nadine ever again.

26

Now I've seen the light, I'm a fanatic. No, I'm not a born-again or anything, get real! I've discovered the joy of being organised. Planning. Imposing order where once was chaos. Being in control. When I was disorganised, I was an unfocused ditzy failure and now look at me: great job, great flat, great boyfriend. Everything I ever wanted.

I am *so-o* organised that my lists have lists. Paul and me have been so busy for the last couple of weeks we've hardly seen each other. So I've scheduled myself a day off. Unfortunately, Paul is working (well, his life is other people's schedules). That's scuppered Plan A: to be all couple-ee and go to Ikea or something. Plan B was shopping but the weather's miserable. So it's Plan C, then. C for clear out: throwing out the junk that was the old me. All the stupid knick-knacks I've kept 'cos of some misplaced sense of significance. Like the travelcard from when I went for the room in Shepherd's Bush, a bar menu from the Lido, the necklace I got in Cuba. Paul says that's tourist tat. I explained how it's an *ileke* and how I got it (heavily edited, natch) but he said they staged the *bembe* to chisel money from the tourist. 'No way,' I argued. 'It was the real thing and I only gave them twenty dollars.' Paul really took the piss then. Like, twenty dollars is six months' pay or something in Cuba. I felt an idiot and threw the necklace into my junk box. I got it into my head it was bad luck. Something to do with the madness that was this summer.

As I untangle the *ileke* and lift it out of the box, a shaft of sunlight breaks through. The beads sparkle prettily, amber alternating with coral. I fasten it round my neck. It might be tourist tat but ethnic is always in and, besides, it's cheerful. And the sunlight means it's stopped raining, so I can shop!

I want something more grown up, for work, y'know, but I can't get enthusiastic about any of the clothes I see. Maybe it's 'cos the sun's out but it looks *so-o* dreary. So un-me. I buy myself an ice cream instead and think about what to do. Although this is a legitimate day off, I feel guilty. Like there's something I should be doing. There *is* something I should be doing: Plan Q. Visit Ivan in hospital. Rumour has it that he's being discharged soon, to where I haven't a clue. This might be the last chance to see him without a visit to Celia's (too embarrassing) or Tanglebush (impossible). So, Plan Q it's gonna be.

I decide the only approach is the in-yer-face-one. I slam open the door to Ivan's room and bounce in brandishing the bouquet I bought from the hospital florist. Ivan is pleased to see me. We bitch the nurses and I eat all of his chocolates while Ivan toasts me from the bottle of Stolli he has secreted away. 'Come with me to Russia, Zita. We will have fun. I need you!'

I laugh. 'Sure, Ivan, I know the kinda help you need.' I'm assuming this is all an Ivan joke, till he fixes me with his eyes blazing.

Really, I go back to Russia. There is nothing here. *Red Angel* is finished. My marriage, too, Zita. Finished.'

I feel horrendously guilty and ask, 'Because of me?'

He shakes his head and explains how the problems with Celia go way back. It was always either fighting or fucking but, in the early days, that was fun. As Celia got more and more successful, and his career went the other way, funnily enough the fights stopped. But so did the fucking. He stayed with Celia 'cos he couldn't think what else to do. Till Nad and me shook everything up with the ridiculous idea he direct a promo and he remembered he was *supposed* to be a filmmaker.

'Zita, my friend. You saved my life. I will miss you.' This wipes me out. It dawns on me this might be the last time I see Ivan and I start to cry. I blubber like a baby and everything comes out all jumbled up: Cy and Tanglebush and Yolande and Santería and how I had just gone too wild this summer and become an Alison and Alison was my friend but I abandoned her like I abandoned Ivan and then she fell and she made too much noise and we had sex and then Ivan fell and me thinking 'cos I went a bit wild and I shouted, 'cos I broke some cosmic rule, I made Ivan fall too.

Ivan hugs me into his chest and I'm breathing cinnamon while he talks. 'Zita, Zita, baby. Believe me, making noise is good! Your friend, she didn't fall because of sex. No! She risked everything rather than lose something important and precious. But she lost.' Ivan kisses me on the forehead then says, 'You forgot already, huh?' I shake my head. Forgot what? 'I tell you the only rule, Zita: *there is no rule.*' I'm not convinced. I still believe that everything is my fault but Ivan interrupts, 'You saved my life.'

'I didn't save you, though, did I?' Ivan looks very seriously at me. Then he takes my hand and softly places it on the cellular blanket, lightly covering his groin. I feel a distinct ridge. Well, not so much a ridge as something on the scale of the Ural mountain range, actually. 'You bastard, you weren't impotent at all. You *lied* to me,' I squeak, and push him away.

'Zita, I do not joke about something so serious,' he says severely.

I almost believe him. Then I remember something. 'OK, Ivan. How come you got it up with Yolande?'

His face brightens. 'You like to watch, huh?'

I glare at him. 'Don't change the subject.'

Ivan shrugs and says, 'Yolande was a witch.'

Yeah, right. 'And that would make me a witch, too, huh?'

Ivan looks sly. 'Maybe, a little.'

There's not much more to say after this. Ivan holds me at arm's length and says softly, but with fire in his eyes, 'Come with me, Zita. You have a Russian soul.'

I turn away and explain the situation with Paul. Then we make noises about email addresses and I say, 'Goodbye, Ivan,' in a funny stilted voice. He nods at me and I leave before I start crying again. I'm pinching my nose as I leave the ward, so I don't see Nadine till I've walked into her. We do one of those silent step-to-the-right-step-to-the-left dances to get out of each other's way. I'm so shocked by the encounter, I sit down on a chair outside the ward to recover. I'm still there when she eventually comes out. Yeah, I know what I said to Paul but I've seen her now, so the promise is already broken. Besides, there's something that's gotta be said. Thing is, I don't know what.

She solves the problem. 'You still here?' she asks curtly.

I nod. 'Yup.'

She steps around me and starts walking briskly away. I have to jog to catch her up. She increases her pace, then I do, until the pair of us are running full pelt. Whitecoats clutching clipboards flatten themselves against the corridor walls as we steam through. It's so ridiculous that, by the time we burst through the sliding glass doors on to the street, we're both hysterical.

I throw my arms around her and hug her before she can escape again. I don't understand what happened between us but I do understand that I want her to be my friend again. She hugs me back. I guess she feels the same. When we've stopped panting and giggling there's a stilted silence. Nad breaks it by saying she's got to move her car before she gets a ticket and do I want a lift?

I fall into step with her and ask how things are at Tanglebush. 'Terminal,' says Nad. 'They've moved the demolition date forward. 'Cos of Ivan falling and everything.'

I'm shocked. 'Fuck, I won't be seeing Tanglebush ever again either.'

Nad looks at me shyly and says, 'I'm going there to pick up the last of my stuff. Wanna come for the ride? Say goodbye or something?'

We drive out of London in silence as the Capri glides along the wet road. The rain is back but it lifts again just as we swing into Tanglebush's drive. The trees glint in an uncertain sunlight. The wet leaves are noticeably a deeper green than before. Everything seems darker. First of all I think it's 'cos of the rain, then I realise why. The leaves are beginning to turn. Summer's nearly over. The house looks like it's decided to demolish itself before the bulldozers get going. For the first time, I notice how decrepit the building really is, like an old friend who is terminally ill. Bits have fallen off and there are UNSAFE: DO NOT ENTER signs everywhere. We lounge out back on the verandah, looking over the rank, overgrown hayfield that once was the lawn. It's better looking at this than back through the French windows into the house. Into the room where Nad expounded her wonderful everything-will-be-all-right-and-we-will-rule-the-world plan. The room where I lay on the parquet floor in the golden evening sun watching Nad's head burrow softly between my thighs. The room that Ivan fell into. Now the parquet is completely buried under a thick coating of rubble. Dreams are buried there, too. It's like everything has fallen apart, for everyone. I shudder.

'Let's go someplace else,' I say. Nadine shrugs and we wander back, past the kitchen. I notice a sack of Dali's chickpeas spilling on to the floor. 'The rats have been at that,' I say, mostly to myself.

Nad stops abruptly and says, 'Y'know he's gone off with Dali?'

At first I'm totally befuddled about what she's saying. Then it dawns. '*Cy* has gone off with *Dali*?'

Nad starts laughing. 'The rat's been at everything. Elaine. You. Me. Dali.' The thud is my jaw on the ground.

I feel sick. 'You? When I was ...'

Nadine stops laughing. 'No, before. Started about the time you met Paul. I never had the chance to tell you. Plan was to move here and be creative. It was all over by the time you got here. In theory.'

'But what about Elaine?' I ask, shocked.

Nad looks at me slyly. 'Cy's sister?' I'm confused. 'He's got a sister called Elaine as well?'

Nad raises an eyebrow, 'As well as what? Poor Zita. You really are naïve, you know.' This time, I'm too dumbfounded to argue. Nad continues, 'They came as a pair, part of the game. He likes games, Cy, as I guess you noticed. They shared me, initially. Then everything sorta shifted round. We were sharing him. I put my foot down but neither me nor Cy would move out. A pride thing, I suppose. And I loved this place.'

'Fuck, Nad, how did you handle it?' I ask. 'I mean, weren't you jealous?'

Nadine chews on a piece of grass for a long time

before answering. 'I wasn't jealous of Elaine but I was jealous of you.' She looks me dead in the eyes. 'Shit, I'd only just temporarily prised you away from Paul.' I blush but Nad carries on. 'I tried to explain, but ... it came out all wrong. In the edit suite?' She grins ruefully at me. 'All a bit of a fuck-up, wasn't it? I expect you've got a rule to cover it.'

A silence falls between us while I ponder what an idiot I've been. I thought the game was between me and Cy. I thought I had the rules sussed. Except, everyone else just happened to be playing a different game...

I link arms with Nadine. 'Ivan says the only rule is there is no rule.'

Nad's lip curls in a cynical smile. 'The more rules you have, the more crimes there are to commit, innit? I'm the worst. I gave you a hard time over Cy, Zeet, but I had no right. You were searching for something. Something that wasn't there with Paul.' I open my mouth to protest but Nad keeps on going. 'Danger, whatever. Don't feel bad about it. I was searching too. Fucking hell. We said we were *outlaws*, living here.'

I smile at her. 'But you and Cy were so cool. I was really impressed by how you lived.'

Nad shakes her head wearily. 'Cool, huh? Me and Cy? Ms Ting, the hip-hop-garage-queen, and Mr Cool, the shag-happy trustafarian? Sorry, artist. Some outlaws. Cool? More cool fools.' Nad winces. I've never really seen Nad down like this before. She's so rigorously upbeat about everything. She just looks incredibly sad. But the sadness seems to become her. I realise just how beautiful she is. Another person I really fucked things for.

She punches my shoulder. 'Don't know why you look so miserable. You're happy, right? You've got Paul.'

Her eyes search my face but I can't look at her. There's a little thing that's eating me. If being with Paul is the only right and sensible thing to do, how come it's so, well, predictable? But when I tried getting more feral, look what happened. Me shagging Cy fucked up Tanglebush just as surely as Alison shagging Damien upset everything in Shepherd's Bush. It's all my fault and I gotta do something about it.

I grab Nad by the hand and start running, pulling her along with me. 'What are you doing, Zeet?' she calls irritably.

'Taking you.' I grin.

'Where?' Nad snorts derisively, but allows herself to be led.

'To exorcise some demons,' I shout.

The stable block smells musty and damp and derelict now it is Cy-less. I hear Nad's voice close to my ear in the dark 'OK, Zeet, now what?'

I don't know. I peer up at the hayloft, Cy's lair, and freeze. Someone is watching us. Judging by the way Nad's gripping my arm, I think she's seen them too. A ghostly white form hangs in the shadows, tottering on the edge of a beam. My heart is pounding.

'They're gonna fall,' I croak.

Nad squeezes me tight and whimpers, 'Duppies don't fall.' And then we both scream. There's no sickening thud on the floor. Nope, just a woo-oogh and the waft of feathers over our head as the barn owl flaps silently through the open doors out into the dusk.

'Fuck!' Nad eyes me curiously as I sink to the ground. 'Are you all right, Zeet?'

I shake my head and try to explain the height thing to her, the whole rushy-whooshy-head-spinning terror, but it's no use. It's my own problem and I've gotta do something about it. Nad watches me anxiously while I clamber up the rope ladder Cy used to get up into the rafters. Once I'm up on the joists, I hesitate. I wonder if this is such a good idea but I steady the tremor radiating from my groin. Nad's voice floats up to me: 'Zeet what are you doing?'

'Exorcising demons,' I yell down, and begin tentatively walking a joist, tightrope style. The rush I'm getting as I edge out across the nine-inch-wide timber is incredible. It builds and builds till I think my insides are going to fall out and my head explode. But, though it seems to take hours, I manage to get across, arms held out like a trapeze artiste, bare feet carefully feeling for the beam. When I reach the far end, I slowly make a wobbly turn. Oh, shit, I've still got to get back to the safety of the loft. I control the violent tremors in my legs and set off again. Halfway back, the whirligig in my belly is so outta hand I have to stop. I'm probably twenty feet above the brick floor. Very slowly, I look down. I can see a weirdly truncated Nad peering anxiously up at me, mouth agape. I vaguely hear her worried, 'Zeet I'm coming up!' I don't know if I can move to save my life. My right thigh is quivering like a double bass string; my breathing has degenerated into shallow, panic-struck pants. My knees are going to give way and I think I'm gonna fall. Nadine is up in the hayloft now. 'Zeet,' she pleads quietly. 'Come to me. Please.' I lift my terror-struck gaze to meet her own. I know I'm gonna succumb. The urge to jump is too strong.

I'm fighting to bring my heaving lungs under control but my treacherous eyes fall away, down to the floor. It moves and ripples, like the surface of a swimming pool. 'Relax,' it murmurs. 'Relax and jump right in.' I look deep into Nadine's eyes one last time. I know it's gonna have to be. She knows it, I know it.

For a split second, I hear Yolande's voice, 'Jump and Osún will catch you.' Here I go.

I cannot explain what happens next. Somehow, I am in Nadine's embrace, clinging to her living, comforting body. We collapse together in a heap on the hayloft floor, while Nadine strokes my brow and kisses me fervently and says, 'I thought I'd lost you there.'

I'm weeping, I'm laughing, I'm shouting exultantly, 'Done it, I've fucking done it.'

Nadine is laughing, too. 'That was wild. Zeet, you are mental.'

I feel high. There must be half a ton of adrenaline pumping round my body. There's a wild pulsing in my groin and fuck, I feel so *horny*.

Cy's old mattress is still in the corner. I grab Nadine and half drag her towards it excitedly, growling, 'Get undressed.'

She looks back at me, confused, and laughs again. 'Pardon?'

'You owe me a rematch. C'mon,' I snarl, ripping my clothes off.

Nadine is looking at me, perplexed, but, I can see, excited as well. I remember something. I reach behind my neck and carefully unhook the *ileke* and hang it, thankfully, on the handy old nail. Other memories come back too. 'Nad,' I ask, 'did you fuck Cy here, too?'

'Who didn't?' she replies, a frown obscuring her smile.

'So?' I ask.

'So-o?' she replies cautiously.

'So,' I tease, 'are we gonna exorcise these ghosts, or what?'

Nadine's still frowning. 'Zita, are you telling me you wanna wrestle me 'cos of Cy?' she asks uncertainly.

'Nadine, I wanna wrestle ya 'cos I love ya. Now, you

gonna get naked and have a good time, or what?' I growl leerily.

Nadine's face lights in a huge, dippy grin. 'I *knew* it turned you on!' she giggles, wriggling out of her clothes. 'I love you too,' she whispers as we throw ourselves at each other, kissing hard as our bodies interlock. I quickly have her wrassled on to her back and pinned to the mattress. Somehow, I feel that Nadine would prefer to do something else rather than fight. I guess it's payback time.

I've never been down on a girl before, as you know. It feels mysteriously dangerous as I lower my head between Nad's smooth, skinny thighs to the vast dark bush between them. I gently part her lips and place my tongue on the bud. Nadine responds within seconds, her pelvis rolling up against me with short, anxious, circular motions. There's a tugging on my legs as they're pulled astride Nadine's face and she clamps on tight. I feel a grateful shudder as my hungry clit gets the attention I'd temporarily forgotten it needed while Nad's fingers begin unashamedly exploring me. I'm stroking the hard, gorgeously smooth ballooning curve of her arse as the tip of my tongue vibrates the burgeoning flesh of her clit. As Nad is contentedly revolving her hips and purring beneath me, I realise something. Nadine is a truly, wonderfully, beautiful friend and I just wanna make her happy and have this endless velvety sex with her. No rules about it, I just do.

We stay, locked together, bathed in waves of pleasure till we're lost in one tight, sexy bundle of girl love and there's a warmth spilling through my whole body, radiating from my cunt to the very tips of my fingers and toes. Suddenly, Nadine bucks and struggles in my grasp and her purring becomes a roar. I hold on tight, feeling my sexy friend's body strain violently against mine as she enjoys a huge, fierce tiger roar. It breaks and rolls round the cavernous space around us, echoing away into the night. Then, I open my thighs wide and Nadine's teeth gently grasp my clit, sucking and tugging, enticing me on to the point of no return, till I do my tiger roar too.

Nad looks into my grinning face and asks, 'Why so pleased with yourself?'

I feel light-headed and incredibly happy. I scrabble around for an old blanket to cover us with and say, ''Cos I've realised something.'

Nad smirks. 'Bit late, isn't it? I could have told you you're bi all along.'

'Well, maybe. But not that. No, I've seen the light. I know what I've gotta do, but I'm gonna need your help.'

We cuddle up and plan for hours before we finally drift off to sleep, entwined together. There'll be more questions to be answered tomorrow, I know. But they can wait.

27

Slo-Mo Films International, Soho, London. Office of Celia Draycott, MD.

'Didn't take you long to ditch the Punin, did it?' Celia looks up. She's had her hair done. The ash-blonde bob is now a platinum crop. Dealings with the clitterati, no doubt. She smiles (a Botoxed mouth-only smile). 'Nadine. I do wish you'd make appointments. And ... Zheetah, isn't it? Do sit down. Tea?'

I hate the way she does this but I have to admit she is fucking good. Everything is normality with Celia. Nothing surprises her. (Maybe it's the Botox.) I watch her as she buzzes through a refreshment order to some minion. Superficially, her attention is on us (well, Nadine, who is doing the talking) but I clock Celia checking her schedule/checking the time/allocating us an unplanned what? five? ten? minutes. She doesn't even respond to Nadine's Punin crack. The woman is an android.

Tea arrives and I think a detect a flicker of impatience on Celia's expressionless face. Our ten minutes is nearly up. She stops Nad mid-flow with one manicured finger. 'Your video is doing very well. Lots of interest.' Hang on, what video? And what exactly did she mean by 'I do wish you'd make appointments'? Celia checks my stricken expression (unlike her, I still have facial muscles that work). 'Don't worry, Zita. It reflects very well on you and, of course, being Ivan Punin's last work is a fabulous USP!' My dangerously expressive face gives me away again. 'Crossover potential, Zita. It's being discussed on art review shows. It's not just MTV!'

I don't let her know that I've only half a clue what's going on. (I can do kabuki mask, too.) Instead, I wrinkle my nose. 'I'm not being funny, Celia, but is that what Ivan is to you now? "Crossover potential"?'

Celia goes all Tony Blair sincere on me. 'No, it's not funny is it, Zita?' (Shakes head, anguished smile.) 'If he doesn't get a grip on himself, he'll self-destruct.' (Head nods, concerned smile.)

I try some nodding back. 'Mmmn . . .' (Raise eyebrows, look innocent.) 'Maybe you could help him?'

Genteel tinkly laugh from Celia. 'To self-destruct?'

Rising-inflexion Hahhahhah from me. 'You've already done that.'

Ooh, direct hit. Celia's impassive face looks, well, slightly less impassive, then the big smile returns. 'How amusing. Clare warned me about your sense of humour.' (That's the I'm-mates-with-your-boss threat, incidentally.) I smile back my best do-I-give-a-shit? grin. I distinctly hear Nadine yawn. Both Celia and I look at her. She stretches, flashing her out-y belly button lasciviously at Celia. I wince. Appropriate negotiating stance? I don't think so. Celia's expression shifts slightly again, but she is fucking difficult to read. Is that a serious smile? 'Now, Zita.' (Nope, business smile, gotta be.) 'Are you suggesting, in your insouciant way, that Slo-Mo should finance Ivan's project?'

I steal a glance at Nad, who is still giving her the I-wanna-do-dirty-things-with-you smoulder. Shit, Nadine, just 'cos Celia's had her hair cut doesn't make her a Patsy Cline fan. Then Celia speaks, quickly, like she's embarrassed, while glancing repeatedly at Nad. 'It's a sweet idea, Zita, and shows charming loyalty to poor old Ivan, but this is business. Frankly, *Red Angel*, whatever it's called, is just too old-fashioned.' She wants rid of us. 'It's not our kind of project, there's no market.' Yup. We are about to be shown the door.

Then Nad cuts in. 'Celia?' Both Celia and I look at her. 'Let's trade.'

What?

'You listen to Zita's pitch, then we discuss where my dress is currently hanging. Y'know, the one you borrowed that night you threw up?'

My eyes dart between them. Nad grinning saucily, Celia flushed a very unattractive cherry red. Something like Nad's shagging dress in fact. Fuck, I get it. This is newspaper-headline negotiation! The rejected-husband's-death-dive-after-telly-boss-wife's-torrid-lesbian-romps version, I do believe. It's hypocritical and morally wrong. But hey, it's showbiz!

And it works. I get to pitch. The pitch I tried out on Nad last night, the full-on *Gone Wild* pitch. The *Red Angel* storyline has evolved somewhat, into a heady mix of girly sexual discovery, exotic locations and a lot of very fit young men. It involves Cuba. It involves hip multicultural connectivity. It involves the sultry diva Yolande Siboney, the established star with the mysterious voodoo background. And feisty Ragga chick Nadine, who will provide an authentic wall-to-wall soundtrack. I finish with a cool, 'You realise, of course, the *Outlaws* vid is fantastic prepublicity?'

Celia stares at me. 'You propose to produce?' I nod. 'What about *Massive*? You can't do both.'

I stare right back. 'You're right. I can't do both.' A definite twitch starts in either corner of Celia's mouth. I wait till the twitches have nearly merged into a gotcha smirk before I finish, 'So I quit Big World this morning.'

Celia sits back in her chair and studies me. Then Nadine. I'm self-consciously twiddling with my *ileke* for something to do. After what seems an age, Celia takes a deep breath. 'OK. We'll allocate three point five to start with, provided that's matched elsewhere and there's presales interest in the States. Maybe Slo-Mo should handle that for you. I suppose you'll need something up front? I could release fifty K as development money. And we'll forget that little matter of the six thou Ivan liberated from our joint account to finance your little, erm, research trip to Cuba. OK?' I'm staring hard at Celia's mouth. Did I hear her right? Celia raps her fingernails impatiently. 'All right, make that sixty for development, but no more till I see Ivan's script. Yes?' I swallow and nod. 'Good. Now, I've really got to move on.'

I'm already floating to the door when Celia clears her throat. 'Oh, and Zita?' Oh, shit. Here it comes. I knew it was all too good to be true. I feel sick as I turn to face her. She's smiling. Not a tiger smile but a sad, faraway smile, from a nearly forgotten past. 'Good luck. With Comrade Punin . . .'

I manage to keep the lid on till we reach the Slo-Mo foyer. Then I scream. 'Three and half million! *Aaarrgh!*' I grab hold of Nadine and wrestle her down on to the obligatory black leather couch, slobbering her with kisses. Nadine makes congratulatory noises while I jabber like an idiot about telling Ivan and everything else I'm gonna have to do. After ten minutes of this, I calm down and prepare for the git-go. Then, shit, I realise how selfish I'm being. Nad, who's 50 per cent responsible for my success, is homeless. I throw my arms round her. 'Oh God, where are you gonna live?'

Nad starts laughing 'You are amazingly naïve, Zeet.' Slowly, cogs whirr into place. 'But all that dress stuff? You said . . .' I stammer.

'I said I wanna sort out where I'm gonna hang my clothes,' she says, making eyes as big as saucers. 'For the winter. I told you I planned to move back some-where central. I hear Clerkenwell's very central.' I am naïve. Nad holds me at arm's length. 'Get on with making your movie, Zeet. Go on, fuck off. Get on with it. I'll be around when you need me.'

She pulls me towards her and kisses me. A long, lingering, sexy, sensual kiss. A kiss that tells me not to worry about anything, 'cos Nad is the one constant in my life who will always be there for me. I'm so lost in a warm, sentimental soup of emotion about her that it's Nad who has to stop the kissing. When we finally pull apart, she nods at the security camera over the doorway. 'Keep her on her toes, eh?' Nad propels me out on to the street, shouting, 'Go wild, Zeet.' Then, with a final 'Gotta sort my wardrobe, babes,' she pats my arse and buzzes herself back inside. What a gal!

Right, but first I've a few things to do. I make a list. It takes the rest of the day, running round the West End, to sort Numero Uno. By early evening, I have time for Numero Dos: Paul. Conveniently enough, when I return to his flat, I get to do Numero Tres (Saskia) at the same time. They look like they've been expecting me. My stuff's neatly stacked in cases and boxes in the hall. Not exactly difficult to arrange, as I never did get round to unpacking. Saskia looks thor-oughly pleased with herself. Paul just looks shifty. 'Paul,' I say. He kinda winces. 'Paul, I'm sorry but it's over.'

Gratifyingly, his mouth drops open. Saskia snorts, 'Took you long enough to notice, darling.'

Paul digs her and they both look at me like they expect me to do something weird. I do.

I take them both by the hand and say, 'You two really are well suited, y'know?' They exchange a look. I'm mind-blowingly sincere. They really are. Saskia's just another boring career woman with an act and

Paul's so far up his own arse that I'm surprised he can walk. Poor Paul. He was so wrong for me. My wrong guy. Like Damien was poor old Alison's wrong guy. I smirk graciously at him. 'Hope you live happily ever after, Paul, I really do.'

Paul clears his throat. 'I meant it when I said you can stay as long as you need to, Zita.' Sweet. Paul's a gent. Or maybe a dirty boy who wants to have his cake and eat it. I'm seriously tempted to accept, just to piss Saskia off, but remembering Alison has made me think of a better way.

'No. It wouldn't be fair,' I say thoughtfully to Paul. Then, I turn my sweetest smile on Saskia. 'Dahling, see, I really *do* come like a shithouse door!' Back to Paul, who's turned an interesting puce colour. 'I mean, how could you get it on with Sassy, with *me* in the next room? Put you right off your stride, eh?' I grin lasciviously at him. 'Perhaps you could just store my stuff for the time being?' (C'mon, I gotta do something to screw his newly de-Zita'd domestic arrangements.) 'And maybe I could take a bath, too?'

I spot Ivan at check-in. This time, I sorted the arrangements, so it's Club Class all the way. The check-in guy and gal are falling over each other trying to be of assistance to him. I don't blame them: with all that enforced clean living in hospital, he's lost a few pounds and the combination of lightweight tropical suit and walking stick makes him look distinctively rakish. He's looking . . . well, louche men in suits really do it for me, I gotta be honest.

'Zita, baby,' he roars.

The check-in fan club rubberneck as he limps over. I get a one-armed bear hug that envelopes me in cinnamon. He is definitely slimmer, and the muscles in that big body have got some definition. Something else, too. I can sense his energy. Like the big ol' bear's been hibernating and now he's woken up, leaner, meaner and just raring to go. Speaking of which . . . I squeeze him tight and say, 'Is that your walking stick or are you pleased to see me?'

He laughs his '*Hah!*' laugh and, nodding towards the disapproving airport staff, stage-whispers, 'Zita, baby. Restrain yourself. What will the staff *think* of us?'

I whisper back, 'I don't do restraint any more, Ivan, and I don't give a fuck what people *think* of me. The only rule . . .?'

See, I've finally understood. That there are no rules to life. People do what they do for all sorts of reasons: 'cos they're scared of being alone like Alison, or fancy a bit of strange like Paul, or believe in their talent like Nad, or just plain fucked up like Cy and Elaine. Me, I was so terrified of doing the wrong thing that I held back from doing anything. Unless, of course, someone told me to do it. I've also realised something else. 'Ivan, y'know?' He cocks an eyebrow. 'You've never, ever told me what to do.'

He shrugs. 'Why should I? We must do what we want to do and just let it be.' He looks pleased with himself then adds, 'Like the song, huh?' I look blank. Then, an Ivan moment. He takes a breath and lets rip at the top of his voice. 'Let It Be' by the Beatles, every single verse. He is *so-o* fucking Russian.

La Habana, Cuba. A sky-blue, bulbous-nosed, chrome-striped, leather-seated fifties dream machine. One cool chick, in diagonal-striped glittery top and embroidered cut-offs. Yolande, a study in seventies Harlem, resting her butt on the car door, her long chocolate-brown legs stretched out in front. Her baseball cap is pulled low over her eyes and her face is wreathed in cigar smoke, but I know she's watching us. As we get closer, her face cracks into a grin and her gold tooth flashes in the sunlight. Ivan breaks into a limping, skipping trot and throws himself on her, yelling, 'Baby, surprise huh? We are back!' Ivan's smothering her saves me from having to say anything myself. It's stupid but I feel kinda nervous.

Yolande slides out from under him, laughing. She scratches her neck lightly, her long fingernails slipping under the beads of her *ileke*. Maybe I'm spacey from the flight, maybe it's exhaustion, but I experience a warm tingle of *déjà vu*. Yolande fixes me with her pitch-black gaze. 'No. You would come back, I knew.'

We pile on to the Buick's front bench seat together. Although it's only nine in the morning, Havana is heating up. Yolande drives one-handed with Ivan on the passenger side, me in between. Ivan hasn't stopped ranting. 'Two months ago, I come to Cuba. With nothing. No money, half an idea, an unknown producer. No one has time to meet me. I am a has-been. But now?' He doesn't wait for an answer. He is yelling exuberantly at the street. 'I have six million dollars. *Six million dollars!*' he roars at a passing bicyclist and turns to us. 'I think they will all have time for me now, huh?' Yolande's long fingernails scratch the back of my neck and we smile at each other. Oh, they will, he can rely on Osún for that.

Balconies, marble foyers, torpidly rotating ceiling fans. The ochre-painted Hotel Inglaterra has them all. Naturally, Yolande accompanies Ivan and me to our suite (OK, I know 60K don't last for ever, but I'm giving shabby-chic a rest for a little while). I walk over to the minibar. 'It's only early, guys,' I say. 'But I fancy a cocktail. Howzabout a daiquiri?' I locate the Havana

Club Gold, the grenadine and, yes, the fresh limes (this *is* a classy hotel: they've provided *exactly* what I specified).

I bend over, slicing the limes on the cool marble floor, fully aware that my short skirt will have ridden up to expose the curve of my arse. I waggle it unnecessarily provocatively while I squeeze juice into the shaker, to make sure I have their attention. I'm aware of Yolande slinking down beside me. Her nails scratch at the nape my neck again. 'Mmmn. We will need a little ice. For this cocktail, No?' she says.

'Yes, I'm very hot,' I reply as Yolande carefully places my unhooked *ileke* with her own on top of the fridge. Then she rummages in the little ice box till she finds the ice, slips a slim brown hand round the back of my head again and pulls me towards her. Holding an ice cube between her teeth, she circles it round and over my lips till meltwater is running down my neck and between my breasts. My mouth is almost numb but my cunt feels like it's on fire. Yolande tuts and begins removing my wet cotton voile top. Still gripping the cube, she circles my nips, which respond enthusiastically with their finest sombrero impressions.

Stripping me of my teeny, wrap-round mini, so I'm naked but for my sandals, she lays me back on the cool marble floor, Then she slides half-melted ice round my bellybutton and down till it is poised at the top of my freshly shaven cunt. (Paul will kill me: I've ruined another razor.) I gasp as freezing water runs into the naked crevasse of my pussy. I twist and look to the couch, arms stretched behind me, hips wriggling, as Yolande teases the tip of my clit with the remains of the ice. Ivan is watching, eyes on stalks. 'Aren't you hot, too, Ivan?' I ask as casually as I can. I take the gruff, grumbling rumble from his throat to mean he is. Very hot indeed. 'Well, why don'tcha cool off?' I ask.

Yolande stops the ice business (the cube's melted now) and removes her glitter top, then wriggles her cut-offs over her hips and down to the floor. Both Ivan and I stare at her in awe. Star quality, huh? I'd forgotten how entrancing she is. The thick mass of curls sprouting from below a gently curved belly, the texture of her skin, her breasts high and full and round. She stretches herself, playfully running her hands around her curvy torso, enjoying the attention, before fixing Ivan with a mock-serious stare. 'Comrade, undress, please. In my country, a revolutionary does not remain clothed in the presence of naked *compañeras*!'

With as much gravitas as he can manage, Ivan removes his suit and all the rest till he is naked, too. I do believe I have mentioned that Ivan's structural adequacy in the cock department has been obscured by poor performance. Well, as suggested by the hospital-bed incident, it appears that problems are being overcome here. The cock is extremely taut and rigid.

'So, the Zita treatment worked? That is good,' says Yolande, raising an eyebrow. 'You have much to do.'

With that, she walks to the couch and kneels on it before him, flexing her arse so her cunt is presented perfectly at cock height. 'Take me first, *compañero*, I have waited longest.'

Ivan steadies himself on one perfect buttock and enters her, his tip parting her already moist lips. Soon, they have attained the lazy, syncopated rhythm of a rumba. I watch Ivan's new, slimline body sway as he enters and re-enters her. I watch as Yolande undulates back against his thrusts while I drink my daiquiri. It takes a few minutes, but I realise something is missing. This cocktail appears to have omitted one vital ingredient. *Me*.

I sashay over and locate Ivan's cock. I find it, slippy with Yolande's juice, and close my hand on it firmly. Ivan gasps. Then, without further ceremony, I yank it away. Yolande's turn to gasp. I push her down hard on to the couch and take her position. I open up as Ivan slides deep inside me. Without a break, he continues to rumba, with me in place of Yolande, while I am faced with her cunt, dark and primitive and slick with juice. I look up at her. She stares back at me, eyes ablaze, teeth bared in arousal. Angrily, she slips off the couch. I hear her stomp away while Ivan continues to plough my sodden groove.

The fridge door clicks. Within seconds, Yolande slithers snakelike beneath me, her cunt presented to my face. She lithely hooks one ankle behind my head and pushes me down so I am buried in her thatch. Her musky sex aromas remind me of Nadine. My tongue seeks and finds her groove, then runs along it till it reaches her clit. It blossoms immediately under my attentions. Yolande shudders and her long legs stretch open till they make a perfect V. My tongue finds her hole. While Ivan continues to take me from behind, I greedily lap at her sopping cunt. She stretches her legs wider and wider apart, allowing me to penetrate her deeper. Her salty juices drench my face till I am drowning in Yolande's come. Her fingers investigate, then penetrate, my own cunt. Hot and cold together. A burn, as an ice cube, then another, is forced into my sodden hole. My cunt contracts even tighter round Ivan's erection. His cock is unspeakably swollen, stretching me almost beyond endurance. Yolande continues choreographing, holding ice cubes against Ivan's balls, prolonging his erection to make me suffer.

We continue for what seems like hours. I have escaped from captivity to voluntarily enter a world where I am chained to others by golden threads of desire. It's a gift. Osún released it in me. I don't know how I will survive so much pleasure.

I only wish Nadine were here, too. I miss her already. All these entanglements. Not that I'm a two-timer. I'm a three-timer, or is it four? Oh, fuck, I really can't be bothered to count. I need to concentrate. Yolande is inflicting unbearably pleasurable agonies on my sensitised, hairless cunt. I love her for it. Ivan is frantically bucking into me with his enraged cock. If he doesn't come soon, he'll have a heart attack. I love him for it. The ache in my clit is excruciating. I take Yolande's swollen, purple bud between my teeth and bite it hungrily, doing to her what I want done to myself. She responds like she's telepathic. Ivan groans. Yolande moans. I'm gonna come now too. With my *compañeros*. My gorgeous, sexy, horny, brilliant, witty, wild, up-for-anything *compañeros*. I love them all, I really do.

So I said this wasn't a love story? Yeah, OK. So I lied.

Hey, I'm a producer, aren't I?

Visit the Black Lace website at
www.blacklace-books.co.uk

FIND OUT THE LATEST INFORMATION AND TAKE ADVANTAGE OF OUR FANTASTIC FREE BOOK OFFER! ALSO VISIT THE SITE FOR . . .

- All Black Lace titles currently available and how to order online
- Great new offers
- Writers' guidelines
- Author interviews
- An erotica newsletter
- Features
- Cool links

BLACK LACE — THE LEADING IMPRINT OF WOMEN'S SEXY FICTION

TAKING YOUR EROTIC READING PLEASURE TO NEW HORIZONS

LOOK OUT FOR THE ALL-NEW BLACK LACE BOOKS – AVAILABLE NOW!

All books priced £7.99 in the UK. Please note publication dates apply to the UK only. For other territories, please contact your retailer.

PAGAN HEAT
Monica Belle
ISBN 0 352 33974 8

For Sophie Page, the job of warden at Elmcote Hall is a dream come true. The beauty of the ruined house and the overgrown grounds speaks to her love of nature. As a venue for weddings, films and exotic parties the Hall draws curious and interesting people, including the handsome Richard Fox and his friends – who are equally alluring and more puzzling still. Her aim is to be with Richard, but it quickly becomes plain that he wants rather more than she had expected to give. She suspects he may have something to do with the sexually charged and sinister events taking place by night in the woods around the Hall. Sophie wants to give in to her desires, but the consequences of doing that threaten to take her down a road she hardly dare consider.

CONFESSIONAL
Judith Roycroft
ISBN 0 352 33421 5

Faren Lonsdale is an ambitious young reporter, always searching for the scoop that will rocket her to journalistic fame. In search of a story she infiltrates St Peter's, a seminary for young men who are about to sacrifice earthly pleasures for a life of devotion and abstinence. What she unveils are nocturnal shenanigans in a cloistered world that is anything but chaste. But will she reveal the secrets of St Peter's to the outside world, or will she be complicit in keeping quiet about the activities of the gentlemen priests?

Coming in November

MAKE YOU A MAN
Anna Clare
ISBN 0 352 34006 1

Claire Sawyer is a PR queen with 'the breasts of the Venus di Milo and the social conscience of Attila the Hun'. At the sharp end of the celebrity food chain, she is amoral and pragmatic in equal measure. When the opportunity arises to make a star out of James – a down-at-heel sociology student and guest on a reality TV show – Claire and her friend Santosh waste no time in giving the young man the make-over of his life. They are determined to make him magazine material, tailoring everthing from his opinion in clothes to his sexual preferences. Determined to transform him into the beau of the Lndon celebrity circuit, the girls need to educate their provincial charge in the sexual mores of modern women. What they don't bank on, is their new living doll having a mind of his own!

TONGUE IN CHEEK
Tabitha Flyte
ISBN O 352 33484 3

Sally's in a pickle. Her conservative bosses won't let her do anything she wants at work and her long-term boyfriend Will has given her the push. Then she meets the beautiful young Marcus outside a local college. Only problem is he's a little too young. She's thirty-something and he's a teenager. But Sally's a spirited young woman and is determined to shake things up. When Mr Finnegan – her lecherous old-fashioned boss – discovers Sally's sexual peccadillo's, he's determined to get some action of his own and it isn't too long before everyone's enjoying naughty – and very bizarre – shenanigans.

Black Lace Booklist

Information is correct at time of printing. To avoid disappointment check availability before ordering. Go to www.blacklace-books.co.uk. All books are priced £6.99 unless another price is given.

BLACK LACE BOOKS WITH A CONTEMPORARY SETTING

BLACK LACE BOOKS WITH AN HISTORICAL SETTING

To find out the latest information about Black Lace titles, check out the website: www.blacklace-books.co.uk or send for a booklist with complete synopses by writing to:

Black Lace Booklist, Virgin Books Ltd
Thames Wharf Studios
Rainville Road
London W6 9HA

Please include an SAE of decent size. Please note only British stamps are valid.

Our privacy policy
We will not disclose information you supply us to any other parties.
We will not disclose any information which identifies you personally to any person without your express consent.

From time to time we may send out information about Black Lace books and special offers. Please tick here if you do <u>not</u> wish to receive Black Lace information. ❏